THE GOSPEL STORY IN ART

THE MACMILLAN COMPANY
NEW YORK · BOSTON · CHICAGO · DALLAS
ATLANTA · SAN FRANCISCO

MACMILLAN & CO., Limited
LONDON · BOMBAY · CALCUTTA
MELBOURNE

THE MACMILLAN CO. OF CANADA, Ltd.
TORONTO

PILATE WASHING HIS HANDS. (REMBRANDT)

THE GOSPEL STORY
IN ART

BY

JOHN LA FARGE

WITH EIGHTY FULL PAGE PLATES

New York

THE MACMILLAN COMPANY
1926

PRINTED IN THE UNITED STATES OF AMERICA

Norwood Press
J. S. Cushing Co. — Berwick & Smith Co.
Norwood, Mass., U.S.A.

9182

PREFACE

For many years before the present volume was actually begun John LaFarge had cherished the wish to write a book on the representation of the Christian story in art, a work for which few men were so well fitted. Born and educated in the older faith of Christendom, he brought to his task not only the reverence of a believer, but also full knowledge of the widely different forms through which the life of Christ has been expressed by artists. He was familiar with the classic writings of the Western and the older Eastern world, and with the legends and traditions told from father to son by the firesides of Europe, or among the islands of the South Sea.

Through early study he so trained his eye and mind that after fifty years he could recall the composition and colouring of a picture. He did not, however, trust to his memory wholly, and in almost every instance the painting or sculpture mentioned in the following pages was described with an engraving or photograph beside him. The originals could not all be reproduced, but those omitted are brought before us by his comprehensive words.

Much of this, his last work, was dictated, with frequent intervals due to pain or weariness, and the end came before he could give it the searching and minute revision he would have wished to bestow upon it. No other hand could supply this lack, and the work

v

remains substantially as its author left it. A friendship of many years has led the present writer to do what was necessary to prepare the manuscript for printing; some errors due to the copyist have been removed (though it can scarcely be hoped that all of these have been detected), a few references have been supplied, an occasional repetition excised, and finally the material has been rearranged in accordance with a plan outlined by the author.

To this brief note of introduction may fittingly be added the last words of an intended preface which was not completed : "The lesson to ourselves in these pages, which contain the record of impressions, at times contradictory, by men even more various than their work, is that we cannot know all the notes in the great song of the human soul. Nor can we now know whose were the hands that first worked; perhaps, as the poets tell us, we shall know them through some discovery, or at least in another world. Art was called by the Greeks a virtue; we may imagine, then, that the impressions of the bodily vision and of the earthly execution have passed away, and only the thought and intention remains."

MARY CADWALADER JONES.

September, 1913.

THE demand for a new edition of this book is an evidence that the great truths which it opens to the world do not die. Though often incomplete in form the conception of the Gospel story which John La Farge reveals in his subtle and elusive manner is of truly mystical beauty.

Few if any could speak today with equal authority — an authority born not only from a profound knowledge but also from a deep conviction of the significance of Christian art.

Every great man's accomplishments are the result of some conviction — John La Farge's was based upon an absolute belief in the great tradition in religious art. That conviction is expressed in these pages as it was expressed in his religious paintings. He tells us that only a scant half-dozen religious paintings have been created since Rembrandt. To this number may be added the one religious painting of our time — his own "Ascension" — a masterpiece, which though essentially modern in its tendencies is yet strangely removed from our matter-of-fact day and surroundings. This painting repeats again in the artist's own notes the "Great Song" and is a vital page to add to the Gospel Story in Art.

BANCEL LA FARGE

MOUNT CARMEL, CONNECTICUT,
    January 25, 1926.

CONTENTS

CONTENTS

CHAPTER VIII

CHAPTER IX

CHAPTER X

CHAPTER XI

CHAPTER XII

CHAPTER XIII

CHAPTER XIV

CHAPTER XV

CONTENTS

CHAPTER XVI

ILLUSTRATIONS

INTRODUCTION

As a boy at college I was reading the Greek Testament, and was suddenly taken aback by the difficulty of bringing two associations — the one Jewish and the other Greek — together and then separating them again. The New Testament writer in Greek was obliged to use pagan words for his Jewish and Christian ideas. He had no choice. So, when the Jewish preacher talked in Greek on matters of spiritual connection between the visible world and another, almost all his words had meanings which were not really his own, and which did not represent the Jewish descent of thought. If it were so with the words he used, how much more so it must have been with any attempt on his part to make pictures or statues representing or symbolizing his ideas. And so, when he first began to make pictures of religious subjects, Christian ones, he used pagan symbols, that is to say, those belonging to people around him, and his way of drawing and painting is exactly like that of the most abominable idolatries and immoral representations. The same painters who have left us the frescoes of the catacombs, where they buried their friends in Christian peace, must in the light of day have worked on the walls of their non-Christian friends upon the paintings which we see in the palaces, or in the ruins of Pompeii and Heraculaneum.

There is another difficulty introduced; the artist may not express himself easily and completely; his art is not an adequate means. He may be a saint, he may be Paul himself, or even John, and not be a good painter. These considerations should make us hesitate about any too close and narrow views as to the exact limits between what our vagueness of words calls "Christian Art" and "Pagan Art." Perhaps it may be well again to re-member that race has much to do with the apprecia-tion of works which, in the art of painting or writing, are meant to carry a religious sentiment. For instance, the Spaniards have painted wonderful religious paintings, or carved wonderful statues, and to some of us, as to the Spaniard, they carry an extraordinary amount of religious feeling. Tradition tells us that these artists were deeply religious in their lives and thought, and yet, to some types, such as certain English people, or some accurate and casuistic Frenchmen, their love of humanity, their splendour of sympathy, would not be sufficiently proper and prudish for men and women brought up in nar-rower ways, and also (and it is worth noting) in a more worldly manner, for the mark of the Spaniard is un-worldliness.

So we may turn with safety to the earliest pictorial representations and feel that their paganism is merely the necessity of the painter of that date. His symbolism was all ready, for what we call "mythological representa-tion" represents an idea by symbols. There are a num-ber of these symbolic renderings, among them being the famous one of the Shepherd carrying the Lamb, and also another in one of the sacramental chapels of the Cata-comb of Calixtus, in which Christ consecrates the fish and bread, symbols of the Eucharist, clad in the pallium of the philosopher, with bare arm, than which we cannot imagine a more "pagan" representation. It is not an attempt at reality, which was not in the air of the period, but a symbolism, and we must not in any way be disturbed by the suggestion of something apparently opposed to Christian influence.

One of the earliest paintings is known as "The Breaking of Bread." It is upon a wall in the Capella Græca, in the Catacomb of Priscilla, and belongs to the first decades of the second century. The elder men who looked at it might certainly have known others who knew the Apostles, or Saint John in his traditional old age. We are apparently in realism; and centuries will pass before anything so simple and straightforward will be put again on the walls of a church or within the frame of a great canvas. The representation of the Story of the Gospels, or even of ceremonial, will have something of artificial solemnity, of ecclesiasticism, which is not here, at least to our accustomed eye. Seven persons are seated at a table, on which are two plates, with five loaves and two fishes. We see apparently the record of the Lord's Supper as celebrated in this very crypt. There is one woman among the communicants. We see the chalice with two handles, as used in the catacombs. One of the figures, in profile with a beard, wears the pallium or cloak, which belongs to the personage of rank, especially ecclesiastical rank. He may be a bishop or a priest. It is he who breaks the large loaf of bread, and the picture is well named from the New Testament phrase. The feet of the bishop, or clergyman, rest upon the same level as the chalice, and that is explained by the learned as indicating that below, both in the picture and in reality, were the tomb and relics of some martyr saint.

My intention is to bring together a certain number of paintings in which the Gospel story is told. I have begun with this entrance into our life of the Church which has changed everything in our arts. We may even believe, as some do, that in the human countenance, certain expressions pictured since Christianity has remodelled human sentiments had no previous existence because these feelings had not until then permeated humanity. This is a view not insisted on by me, but worth recording and considering. In point of fact the portraits of the early Christians, such as are recorded for us in the Egyptian remains, belong to the pagan world, very much as do the faces of the average persons of to-day.

The greater part of painting for centuries has been more or less connected with stories of religion, and out of thousands we have to take a small handful. Nor is it easy to know where to begin, as in the pictures in the catacombs we might go as far back as Noah, or even Adam, who with Eve becomes again at certain moments of late art the excuse for wonderful successes and splendours of execution, usually in some vague recurrence of a wish to rival the arts that belonged to purely pagan times. Indeed it is a mere action of the will to decide and divide the Old and the New. Thus we have the history of the Jews, the sacred race, explained in the work of Rembrandt, and it might be a pious and meritorious work to take what the great painter left of his enormous creation and tell the story of the Bible from beginning to end. Rembrandt's story is a real one. He has absorbed the Jew; and his Old and his New Testament is the story of the Jew in his splendour and in his disgrace. Heine has told us what happened to a certain Prince:

"He was called Israel;
  Him the curse of witches turned into a hound,
  A hound with houndish thoughts.
  The whole week he roots through the dirt of Life,
  But every Friday evening
  At the hour of twilight
  Suddenly fades the charm.
  The hound takes up again the life of man,
  A man with the thoughts of men;
  Cleanly clothed he steps into his Father's Hall."

The Jew whom Heine sang was painted by Rembrandt as he had not been painted before, nor has he been so painted since. It seems incredible that nobody should have used the type of the sacred race in the representation of the Sacred Story before Rembrandt's hand carried out the stories of the Bible in the characters of the people whose story the Bible is. Nor has anyone dared go on, and with the works of Rembrandt the representations of the life of the Bible are almost closed, although a few Spaniards will lengthen out the list.

The eighteenth century is not to be taken seriously. Pictures may fill churches and go on in Venice until almost the end; in the nineteenth, Goya in Spain may make us feel his own regret at having missed his chance; Delacroix will paint five or six times something from the Bible Story, — even Corot may breathe a prayer, — but authoritatively there is nothing.

THE GOSPEL STORY IN ART

CHAPTER I

HELIODORUS

BEFORE we return with Rembrandt to the reality which we touch for a moment in the painting of the catacombs, we shall find in more arbitrary and unreal works of art the mark of the time which produced or countenanced them, for the artist has only the choice of the language he has learned and which he has modified to some extent. That language may be more or less stilted, heroic, idyllic, epic, or commonplace; he can only ride the horse that is brought to him by Fate.

Let us take two great conventional pictures, the subject of which precedes the story of the New Testament and represents an unreality sufficiently modified to suit our present sense of proportion. They are the Heliodorus of Raphael and the Heliodorus of Delacroix. Usually we do not know the story very well, because it is in the Apocrypha, which we are not often taught. It made a beautiful and decorative subject for a picture, and with Raphael its meaning is an expression of the views of the great Pope Julius regarding the behaviour of wicked intruders upon the rights of the Church of God.

The English text is so expressive that we quote it:[1]

[1] II. Maccabees, iii.

6

"Now when the holy city was inhabited with all peace, and the laws were kept very well, because of the godliness of Onias the high priest, and his hatred of wickedness;

It came to pass that even the Kings themselves did honour the place, and magnify the temple with their best gifts;

Insomuch that Seleucus king of Asia of his own revenues bare all the costs belonging to the service of the sacrifices.

But one Simon of the tribe of Benjamin, who was made governor of the temple, fell out with the high priest about disorder in the city.

And when he could not overcome Onias, he gat him to Apollonius the son of Thraseas, who then was governor of Celosyria and Phenice.

And told him that the treasury in Jerusalem was full of infinite sums of money, so that the multitude of their riches, which did not pertain to the account of the sacrifices, was innumerable, and that it was possible to bring all into the king's hand.

Now when Apollonius came to the king, and had shewed him of the money whereof he was told, the king chose out Heliodorus his treasurer, and sent him with a commandment to bring him the aforesaid money.

So forthwith Heliodorus took his journey, under a colour of visiting the cities of Celosyria and Phenice, but indeed to fulfil the king's purpose.

And when he was come to Jerusalem, and had been courteously received of the high priest of the city, he told him what intelligence was given of the money, and declared wherefore he came, and asked if these things were so indeed.

Then the high priest told him that there was such money laid up for the relief of widows and fatherless children:

And that some of it belonged to Hircanus son of Tobias, a man of great dignity, and not as that wicked Simon had misinformed: The sum whereof in all was four hundred talents of silver, and two hundred of gold:

And that it was altogether impossible that such wrongs should be done unto them that had committed it to the holiness of the place, and to the majesty and inviolable sanctity of the temple, honoured over all the world.

But Heliodorus, because of the king's commandment given him, said, That in any wise it must be brought into the king's treasury.

So at the day which he appointed he entered in to order this matter; wherefore there was no small agony throughout the whole city.

But the priests, prostrating themselves before the altar in their priests' vestments, called unto heaven upon him that made a law concerning things given to be kept, that they should safely be preserved for such as had committed them to be kept.

Then whoso had looked the high priest in the face, it would have wounded his heart; for his countenance and the changing of his colour declared the inward agony of his mind.

For the man was so compassed with fear and horror of the body, that it was manifest to them that looked upon him, what sorrow he had now in his heart.

Others ran flocking out of their houses to the general supplication, because the place was like to come into contempt.

And the women, girt with sackcloth under their breasts, abounded in the streets, and the virgins that were kept in ran, some to the gates, and some to the walls, and others looked out of the windows.

And all, holding their hands toward heaven, made supplication.

Then it would have pitied a man to see the falling down of the multitude of all sorts, and the fear of the high priests, being in such an agony.

They then called upon the Almighty Lord to keep the things committed of trust safe and sure for those that had committed them.

Nevertheless Heliodorus executed that which was decreed.

Now as he was there present himself with his guard about the treasury, the Lord of spirits, and the Prince of all power, caused a great apparition, so that all that presumed to come in with him were astonished at the power of God, and fainted, and were sore afraid.

For there appeared unto them an horse with a terrible rider upon him, and adorned with a very fair covering, and he ran fiercely, and smote at Heliodorus with his forefeet, and it seemed that he that sat upon the horse had complete harness of gold.

Moreover two other young men appeared before him, notable in strength, excellent in beauty, and comely in apparel, who stood by him on either side, and scourged him continually, and gave him many sore stripes.

And Heliodorus fell suddenly unto the ground, and was compassed with great darkness; but they that were with him took him up, and put him into a litter.

Thus him, that lately came with a great train and with all his guard into the said treasury, they carried out, being unable to help himself with his weapons; and manifestly they acknowledged the power of God.

For he by the hand of God was cast down, and lay speechless without all hope of life.

But they praised the Lord, that had miraculously honoured his own place; for the temple, which a little afore was full of fear and trouble, when the Almighty Lord appeared, was filled with joy and gladness.

Then straightways certain of Heliodorus' friends prayed Onias, that he would call upon the Most High to grant him his life, who lay ready to give up the ghost.

So the high priest, suspecting lest the king should misconceive that some treachery had been done to Heliodorus by the Jews, offered a sacrifice for the health of the man.

Now as the high priest was making an atonement, the same young men in the same clothing appeared and stood beside Heliodorus, saying, Give Onias the high priest great thanks, inasmuch as for his sake the Lord hath granted thee life:

And seeing that thou hast been scourged from heaven, declare unto all men the mighty power of God. And when they had spoken these words, they appeared no more.

So Heliodorus, after he had offered sacrifice unto the Lord, and made great vows unto him that had saved his life, and saluted Onias, returned with his host to the king.

Then testified he to all men the works of the great God, which he had seen with his eyes.

And when the king asked Heliodorus who might be a fit man to be sent yet once again to Jerusalem, he said,

If thou hast any enemy or traitor, send him thither, and thou shalt receive him well scourged, if he escape with his life; for in that place, no doubt, there is an especial power of God."

In Raphael's great and rightly famous painting[1] we have the following points :

1. The artist has to place his subject within an architectural space of a certain shape, which requires the continuous preoccupation on his part which we call sub-consciousness.

2. Then he must fit these many figures to the scale of his room, and next tell the story, which itself is divided into three parts : the triumph of the Jewish Church, its deliverance from its enemies, the punishment of its persecutors.

In the picture the scene is witnessed by Pope Julius II, who ordered it for its meaning. He was at that moment triumphant in having established the power of the papacy — incidentally of the Church. There could not be a more beautiful choice of a subject ; one freeing the mind from any small allusion and bringing up the perpetuity of the Church and its meaning from the past : and, to bring it more directly home, Pope Julius is carried into this remote time, some two thousand years back, in his usual manner, with his usual attendance, and he gazes with the proper interest of an official spectator. The picture almost explains itself without any text, although several incidents have been put together at the same moment ; the answered prayer of the high priest who kneels far back ; the anxiety, and also the relief of mind of the Jewish crowd ; in contrast, the steadiness and certainty of the few priests, and then on the right-hand side the miracle : the angels who drop down upon the intruder Heliodorus, and the other angel, the warrior who rides a horse that tramples

[1] In the Stanze of the Vatican.

HELIODORUS. (Raphael)

upon the fallen tyrant. On the edge of the picture the plunderers are dropping their booty. All the details of the great picture are famous, perhaps none more so than the flight of the two avenging angels across the open space of the temple. In a moment their whips will be down upon the tyrant, and not only shall Judæa be avenged, but the Pope will remember his last triumph over Venice, and the lashing of Heliodorus may recall to him the official blows with scourges given to the ambassadors of Venice and other excommunicated enemies in the ceremony of their repentance.

"Va fuori d'Italia, va fuori o stranieri !"

In his great painting of the same subject,[1] Delacroix gives himself the pleasure of rivalling Raphael, innocently and easily, with that special good-nature that belonged to him. He has not chosen the arrangement of Raphael, a remarkable one that leaves the centre of the painting open and the interest on the sides. This was a form of composition of which Delacroix was fond, but which here he has not followed. Heliodorus is stretched out before us on the wide steps ; the plunder is all about him ; his men are interrupted as they carry out the golden vases, and down upon him come the avengers. No one, either Raphael or any other Italian, has ever done anything more splendid than the fall from heaven of the angel in the centre. Above him the rider on the white horse guides the beast to strike, with a certain accuracy not belonging to Raphael. The rider and animal have something strange and supernatural which is in the meaning of the story and is carried as far as possible. The temple

---

[1] In the Church of Saint Sulpice at Paris.

is open above as in Raphael's picture, but with a novelty; the great curtain that hangs between the columns is flapping in the wind which always comes with the things that happen from afar off.   There the great painter has introduced for the first time something that never has been taken up since : the story told by inanimate things. The mere outline of those curtains and of the pillar do not, we feel, belong to something of every day and yet they might be photographed from nature.   It is the same wonder that we see with Michael Angelo : the transmutation of ordinary clay into gold.   There is also the inclination, common to both Raphael and Delacroix, to suggest the story beyond the limits of the canvas.   The crowd is there outside the picture; we are only given the fringe of it, but it tells its tale while it leaves us to all the poetry of the main expression.   Of course we should have known beforehand that the representation would be carried out by the great dramatic painter — the only dramatic painter of the last two hundred years — so as to suit the surface of his neighbouring walls.   The painting has not as much as usual of the colour of which he was a master, but colour with him was simply a form of rendering what Taine has called "the living passion of things." He saw further than the outside of beautiful objects; he saw men themselves with their anxieties and their delights, and to each one of his perceptions he gave a form of colour and shape, as Mozart or Beethoven give us their meaning in arrangements of sound, of which they know the secret.   As Taine goes on to say, he is the revealer of a possible new world; and of the only thing which we really need, "*la seule chose dont nous ayons besoin.*"

The Angel is traditionally represented to us even in

HELIODORUS. (Delacroix)

non-artistic Jewry. We have the Ninevite and Egyptian, and coming down the ages we find the Sun and Moon Angels of Buddhism and also of the Byzantine Mosaic in Saint Sophia, where Christ stands flanked by these testimonies of the power of the Creator, each one of which praises his Maker in song as he follows his appointed path. Each of these images is derived, yet each is independent. Our Byzantine Angel, as he stands in conventional form, has already passed into ecclesiasticism and is a symbol of doctrine and of a new order of the world, as well as a reference to the older one connected with it. He is arbitrary — his life is not as free as that of his Buddhist congener, who belongs to some of the most adequate spiritual expression devised or inherited by man. Kwannon and the Deva bring up the curious problems of the spiritual expression which we miss or do not see in Greek or Roman art, or in any until the East had poured its light upon the world: "Ex oriente lux."

In the dreams of my youth I used to wonder what we should have found in the statues of the Three Graces which that immortal sculptor Socrates made and which Pausanias saw. Did he contrive to put into those images a meaning, a spiritual expression, such as his words have given us? But the statues have disappeared and we never think of Socrates as a sculptor. Perhaps that one case might have changed the notion of what the Greek would have done. We have the actual expression of a martyr in the agony of death. Who will remember — I do not recall his name — the Christian captive martyrized in Morocco by being buried alive in plaster? We have his actual image, and some fifty years ago Charles Dickens

c

wrote about it. I forget how adequate the illustration was, and it happened before photographs were common. That is the one authentic case. We see expression as felt by artists — perhaps the love of Christ in fellow-man — but such an expression on such a face as Saint Francis's is most difficult of representation. There is, however, a new and distinct feeling which is wanting in the great spiritual teachings of the ancient world; love has been introduced into the necessities of the soul. That is the difference historically, and gradually, all through the art influenced by Christ, this distinct spirituality of love has marked, almost without intention, the turn of the artist's mind, and more and more his hand. Even yet we feel it in some few pieces of modern art, but it has entirely disappeared from religious painting.

CHAPTER II

THE PROPHETS AND SIBYLS

IN ancient history there was a time when the prophecies of the Sibyls represented for the pagan world what the Jewish prophets did for the Hebrew story, and Michael Angelo, by his work in the Sistine Chapel, gives us the power of realizing this, as it did for the people of his day. His Prophets and Sibyls surround the great ceiling and form an accompaniment to the story of the Old Testament with which he covered it. The whole is a masterpiece, and besides being a masterpiece, it is the invention of a new form of decoration, and we know that it is splendid and wonderful, and a lesson, or rather a collection of innumerable lessons, for all painters and sculptors since its date. But although we acknowledge its power, we do not always absorb the story told by the painter. He has given us the histories which are the very foundation of the Christian faith, which from the beginning of time have made it necessary — all the chapters taken from the Bible telling of the creation of the world and the course of human wickedness. Man is by himself incapable of escaping sin : hence the necessity of Redemption, and it is the Redeemer who is desired and predicted by the row of Prophets and Sibyls.

To-day the part played by the Sibyls in the early life of Christianity is further away than things really more remote, the explanation perhaps being that the necessity for prophetic confirmation is less practical to us of the last centuries, and the poetry, the charm, the intense importance of the meaning has faded with the fading of the meaning of Rome. So that when we take up the representation of Michael Angelo's Sibyls we may be puzzled to get back to the influences under which he worked. How much more were the Sibyls to him than they are to us? The "Dies Iræ"—with its "Teste David cum Sibylla"—had been written before him, and when we hear it sung to-day it carries nothing but a poetic association with it. And yet the great man did justice to David as to the Sibyls, and the latter surround the Sistine Chapel together with the Prophets, a base to the Christian story as well as to the decorative scheme of the ceiling.

In these great creations, the last reverberation of the awful meaning attached to their names brings us to accept them as they are, without explanation. No student who looks at their photographs quietly need ask what they really mean. They are sufficient and prophetic — surcharged with significance — and types indeed of Michael Angelo himself, whose meaning runs along, in and out of what he has done; so that we can imagine — or, rather, we *know* — that a complicated, hidden sentiment fills the visible representation, over and above the comprehension and rendering of the subject as a fact. Dreams and contemplation must have filled the shapes which the lover of Plato drew out of the heavenly storehouse.

Perhaps — and most probably — he read or was read to from the Sibylline verses. Surrounded by so much learning he might not escape the accumulation, especially as the moment was just that when the original tongue, if one may speak inaccurately, was beginning to be the object of discovery and study. I am speaking of the fierce Sibylline predictions, not of the sweet recollections which the pagan Virgil brought to us — that memory of his own prophecy which fits him later to walk with Dante in the imaginary other world as "leader and master."

Who were the Sibyls and what were their names are questions confused and tossed about. Of some we know, and as soon as we know they melt into others. Greek and Roman prophecy was limited to their speech, remembered or written. Varro has told us that the Greek word means the "counsel of God." Another tells us that the Sibyl is native of Babylon; Greek writers have referred to several. Varro has ten; Pausanias gives us four: Hierophile (a Libyan), She of Marpessus or Erythræa (said to have prophesied in Asia and at Delphi), Demo of Cumæ (the Chief Sibyl of Roman history), and the Hebrew Sibyl Saba (old — the Sabbe of the Psalmist), who is also known as She of Babylon and Egypt. In the books of the Sibyls, which are beautifully unauthentic, this last one went as far back as the Deluge. Even the Queen of Sheba was supposed to be one of them.

In thinking of their names, so interchangeable and uncertain, one is reminded that the names of the priestesses of the Eleusinian mysteries were abolished by throwing their written titles into the sea, with danger of death for those who should reveal them.

The Sibylline prophecies and songs were poems wherein the Hellenistic Greek speech was used to attack the old

Greek creed, and were Jewish in greater part, because they chiefly owe their origin to the forced colonization of Egypt by the Semites under the prosperity and wealth of the Ptolemies. The captivity of Babylon had scattered the Jews, who succeeded in Egypt, learned the language of Plato, and tried to imitate him, but they remained Jews at heart, and kept the hope alive of a final reversal.

Some of them asked themselves if the times foretold so often by the Prophets had not come at last, if God should not now at length appear and establish upon the world the rule of his people. They believed in such an event, and addressed the Greeks, exhorting them to give up their idols and be converted. Nor did they hesitate to invent ancient prophecies. Had they talked to Jews, they would have made Daniel or Isaiah speak; for the Greeks they chose prophetesses who had credit with them.

The Sibyls had been popular once; hence false Sibylline oracles were created, and in these oracles for five centuries the desire, the wrath, the hope, of the disinherited was expressed. They charged the Sibyl to preach the unity of God, chastity, charity, the advent of the Messiah, and the glory coming to Israel in another world. "Isis, O unfortunate goddess, alone thou shalt remain on the dried shores of Acheron, and on the earth there shall be no more memory of thee. And thou, Serapis, thou shalt groan seated in the ruins of thy temple, and one of thy priests, still dressed in his linen robe, shall cry, 'Come, let us build an altar to the true God; let us leave the beliefs of our fathers who sacrificed to gods of stone and clay.'"

Still further, in dreams of the future (which we call

THE LIBYAN SIBYL. (Michael Angelo)

now Socialism), they invented a time when all should be in common. "The earth then shall be divided among all. It shall not be separated by limits; it shall not be shut up by walls, there shall be no more beggar or rich man, no master or slave, no little and no great, no kings, no chiefs; all shall belong to all." Then as to the rich: "To extend their domains and to make servants, they plunder the poor. If the earth were not seated and fixed so far from the sky, they would arrange that the light should not be equally divided among all. The sun would be bought for gold and would shine only for the rich, and God would have to make another world for the poor."

These songs are full of violent invective against the Roman rule. They carry the hatred felt in many nations against the great empire known to us by its glory. Divided by origins, for they come of different races, they united in hating Rome. "Ill luck to thee, ill luck, O Fury; friend of vipers, thou shalt sit widowed of thy people on the shore. O wicked city where songs are sung, thou shalt be silent. In thy temples the maidens shall no longer keep up the eternal fire; thou shalt bend thy head, O proud Rome; fire shall devour thee whole, thy wealth shall perish, wolves and foxes shall live in thy ruins, thou shalt be as if thou hadst never been. . . . When shall I have the pleasure to see this day, terrible for thee and for all that Latin race?"

All this came from Syrians and Egyptians, but also from Jews and semi-Christians who wished to avenge their faiths. Nothing occurred, and the empire stood firm, but the Sibyls went on predicting. They seem very near to us in one instance, when the great eruption

s which destroyed Pompeii brings this out:
he entrails of Italy shall be torn, when flame shall
into the vast heaven, killing men and filling the
nse air with a cloud of dark ashes, when drops shall
from above, red as blood, acknowledge the wrath
a God who wishes to avenge the death of his just."

The end of the world is predicted in the usual way:
"Ill luck to the women who shall see that day. A dark
cloud shall cover the world on the side of the rising and
the setting sun, on the south and on the north. A river
of fire shall pour from heaven and devour the earth.
The heavenly torches shall run one against the other;
the stars shall fall into the sea, and the world shall be
empty. The race of man shall grind its teeth when the
earth shall catch fire under its feet; all shall go into dust;
no bird shall cross space; no fish shall part the sea; the
sound of trees tossing in the wind shall no more be heard;
all creatures shall come to burn in the divine furnace,
devoured by thirst and grief; they shall call death to their
help, but death shall not come; there is no more death
for them, no more night, no more rest."

We feel the trace even to-day of all these threats,
but they do not come to us through the Sibylline verses.

How much of what we have just been reading was
actually in the memory of the painter and his contemporary admirers, or visitors, or teachers? For it was the
moment of the learned man, the prodigy of absorption,
the devourer of books, of all that gigantic power of accumulation which we see in some great cases of that
time. In that moment also the world was attacked by
the invention of printing and the putting of great quantities
of documents into final shape. We shall attempt to

follow these possible sources of influence as we now take up the figures of the vault.

The pose of each Sibyl is not only the attitude of the person, but also the attitude which will best fit with the adjoining Prophets. They form part of a rhythmic whole, however they may look as though struck out at a blow. We have, for example, in the Libyan another meaning through a sketch which Michael made. The attitude is the same in so far as she sits edgewise and turns and half lifts herself, as Vasari remarks, but in the sketch she has taken up a child, not the book, which so wonderfully fills up to our mind her meaning as the reader or teacher of a great lesson.

Michael hesitated. Did he mean something special? — Is there a text for *a* child — beside *The* Child? If he thought of the last, he could not place so important, so all-important an image — the one to which all else has to point a meaning — in the side issue of the Sibyl border. I have not found a text as yet — and still I am loath to let the matter rest.

Descriptions have been overworked, but Vasari's words may give at least a contemporaneous word of admiration.

"As much (in praise of beauty) may be said for the Libyan Sibyl who, having completed the writing of a large book taken from other volumes, is on the point of rising with a movement of feminine grace which at the same time shows the intent of lifting and putting aside the book — a thing so difficult that it would certainly have proved impossible to any other than the master of this work."

Vasari is professional, and admires at once the solving of an enormous difficulty. This solution is so complete that we do not notice it any more than we do in nature.

THE GOSPEL STORY IN ART

...tions — if I may use words of that date — the
...ns of this very great man are such that we praise
...sily for the obvious; we praise him for the difficult;
...orget to praise him for his relation to the ordinary —
...e thing that one sees all the time — in which this exceptional creature connects with his Italian ancestry of
sculpture and painting as well as with the future reality
of Dutchman and Spaniard, and even perhaps with the
last success of the arts of record, the instantaneous
photograph. Let us take the marvellous Raphael, or
any best Frenchman of the past; when they come to a
very noble effort we feel that the accidental vision of
nature has not been theirs. They have composed or
perpetrated something wonderful and beautiful, but
there has not come down to them from heaven a revelation of ordinary life.

Whether these are new remarks or not I do not know;
but as I sat day after day looking at the ceiling with a
companion — a Spanish peasant pilgrim — we talked
of the nature of these things. The figures are as humble,
as good-natured, as any sketch that you may come across
in a newspaper. The attitude of Jeremiah, one of the
very great creations of art, is one that we have seen every
day or so in every railroad station, perhaps in the very
car in which we have travelled, and yet here it is, elected
out of all other possibilities, and suddenly we say: This
is the most marvellous ideal reached by man.

What really makes the astounding superiority of this
colossal human being is that in certain ways his humility
is as great as his pride; he, one of the proudest of all
men, to see the very great and the very noble has only
to open his eyes on the appearances of every day.

THE PROPHET JEREMIAH. (Michael Angelo)

With that in our mind we may pass to what Vasari says next of the Prophet Jeremiah :

"The prophet is seated with the lower limbs crossed, and holding his beard with one hand, the elbow of that arm being supported by the knee, while the other hand is laid on his lap; the head is bent down in a manner which indicates the grief, the cares, the conflicting thoughts, and the bitter regrets which assailed the Prophet, as he reflected on the condition of his people. There is evidence of similar power in the two boys behind him; and in the first Sibyl, that nearest to the door, in whom the artist has proposed to exhibit advanced age, and not content with enveloping her form in draperies, has furthermore placed the book which she is reading very close to her eyes, by the way of intimating that her power of sight is weakened by the same cause."

She is the Persian Sibyl (Persica), and again the painter's accuracy and honesty of vision and appreciation of every-day life comes in.

In a more ironic time than Vasari's, we may enjoy Michael's half-amused rendering of the tremendous old lady who finds it difficult to read her own handwriting, perhaps written many years before. Of course she is wrapped up, as Vasari says. Those folds, now trans-lated into lines of grandeur and heroic memory, may be the recollection of any old crone in Rome, sitting on out-side steps, or at home in the housekeeper's room poring over accounts, and we recognize the manner of attitude that belongs to one's own work, to what we are personally interested in, and not to the reading of an official book.

In ample contradiction to the ancient and somewhat prosaic lady who is marked as the Persian, the Delphic Sibyl recalls the Greek beauty of line and "ample pinion," spreading out in a great sweep, and ending in the mystic scroll. One could almost imagine that Michael had seen

Greek work, so harmonious is the balance and proportion and curve and direction of each part of the dress and drapery. She has also a freshness of expression, a look of finding the world beautiful, which sets her apart among the various women her companions. Why she should ever have ceased delivering her oracles in verse has been, as we know, debated, and Michael's painting of her does not explain it, whatever Plutarch might have thought (or rather, perhaps, his friend Cleo) in his speech on the Temple steps at Delphi. As the reader will remember, Cleo says that "the use of speech seems to be like the exchange of money; there was once a time when the stamp and coin of language was approved and passed current in verses, songs, and sonnets; for then all histories, all learning, all functions and subjects that required grave discussion were written in poetry and fitted for musical composition, and what now but a few will scarce vouchsafe to hear, then all men listened to. All delighted in songs and verses. When they had to teach, they did it in songs fitted for the harp; their praises of the gods and songs after victory were all in verse; afterward, the conversation of man altered with his change of fortune; changed also were golden topknots and silken vestments loosely flowing in careless folds; long locks were clipped, and men taught to glory in sobriety and frugality. Then it was that history alighted from versifying, as it were from riding in chariots, and on foot distinguished truth from fable; and philosophy began to dispute after truth in common and vulgar terms. And then it was that Apollo caused the Pythian priestess to surcease calling her fellow-citizens by strange names (even the rivers being called mountain-drainers), and, discarding verses of uncouth words and obscurity, taught the oracle to speak plain. Ever since belief and perspicacity thus associated, it came to pass that men were desirous to understand clearly and easily, without flower of circumlocution, and they began to find fault with oracles enveloped in poetry, overshadowing the sentence, and they also suspected the very truth of the prophecy itself, muffled up in so much metaphor. The ancients stood in need of double meaning and obscurity. The deity, when he makes use of mortal prophets, does not go about to express the truth, but only eclipses the manifestation of it, rendering it by the means of poetic umbrage less severe and ungrateful, for it is not convenient that princes or their enemies should at once know what is by Fate decreed to their disadvantage. But the Pythian priestess is naturally, when busy with the deity, in more need of truth than of minding the praise or dispraise of men, and her language is what the mathematician defines a straight line to be, that is to say, the shortest that may be drawn between two points; and she has been obnoxious to strict examination, nor could ever any person to this very day convict her of falsehood; but on the other side she has filled the temple with gifts and offerings. There were others who blamed the ambiguity and obscurity of the oracle, as others to-day find fault with its plainness, and they are both alike foolish in their passion, like children better pleased with the sight of rainbows that circle the sun and moon than to see the sun and moon themselves. They are taken with riddles and figurative speeches which are but the reflections of oracular divination to the apprehension of our mortal understanding."

D

So far the wise man justified the ways of the gods. The later Judeo-Christian verses say that, three thousand years before, the first Sibyl had come from Helicon, where she was bred by the Muses, though others affirm that she was a daughter of Lamia, whose father was Neptune. There at Delphi she sat upon the famous cleft rock, while in Michael's painting she sits upon an artificial rest made by human hands. (This is probably a privilege of composition.) Our same informant, Cleo, tells us that "she had extolled herself as one that would never cease to prophesy, even after death, but after her decease should make her abode in the orbit of the moon, being metamorphosed into the face of that planet; that her voice should be always heard in the air, intermingled with the winds, and by them wafted from place to place; and that from her body should spring plants, herbs, fruits, whereby man would be able to foretell all manner of events to come."

"That orbèd maiden with white fire laden,
    Whom mortals call the moon,"

might then be our Delphic Sibyl talking to us from high heaven; and though it may not be that Michael saw Cleo's text, the name of "orbèd maiden" suits well her wonderful curve.[1]

Plutarch's reference to the Delphic Sibyl and description of her conduct is matched by Lombroso's description of the behaviour of certain mediums of to-day. The trance beginning with a change of voice and tears and tremors and the jerking of hands and feet, paleness and nodding of the head; then the state of ecstasy

---

[1] This special impression of circular movement has been noticed by many admirers.

THE DELPHIC SIBYL. (Michael Angelo)

(whatever that may mean) with hysterical gestures; then conversation and moans and shrieks, and deep sleep. And then from this being blows a vapour, sometimes warm, sometimes cold and sensible to the touch. (This refers to the famous Eusapia.) This curious wind blows also from her left leg, stiffening out her skirt. For Mr. Lombroso, this is the "creatic" (*sic*) frenzy of genius, which otherwise is a psycho-epileptic paroxysm, as in Shakespeare. Plutarch does not quite give us the same view, rather the contrary, but the analogies, as the wind blowing and the vapour, seem apparent connections with the various points made by the ancient describer of the Sibyls, who were under "spirit control" like our mediums. It is quite natural that some of the ancient heroes should have spoken through them, just as to-day, according to Lombroso, the dead are endowed with power sufficient to impart ideas to the medium.

Here comes in beautifully what Phædo was told by Socrates:

"All prophecy is a madness, and the prophetess at Delphi, when out of her senses, conferred great benefits upon Hellas both in public and private life, but when in her senses, few or none. And I might tell you how the Sibyl, and others, who have had the gift, have told the future aright, but that is obvious; where plagues and mighty wars have been bred, owing to ancient wrath, where madness, lifting up her voice and resorting to prayers and rites, has come to the rescue of those who are in need."

The Cumæan Sibyl — Demo is her name — has never been properly described in words; Vasari is inaccurate, and Zola is like himself. The picture is there for us to see, and we need only notice the mighty arm, which marks for many critics the beginning of Michael Angelo's

tendency to the expression of extreme muscular power.
But the old lady is massive enough to warrant the great
arm.   She seeks some passage in the heavy book propped
on the edge of her seat; other big books are brought
by the attendant boys.   Her frown indicates naturally
enough the difficulty of picking out the special prophecy
which perhaps she had confided, as we know, to the leaves
which blew out from her cavern.[1]   Æneas tried to beg of
the Cumæan that she would not confide her songs to
leaves, lest they should fly before the winds in turbulent
mockery.   We all remember the wonderful passage
wherein, weeping over Palinurus, Æneas is carried to the
Eubœan shore of Cumæ, where stands a great temple of
Apollo with sculptures or paintings that tell the stories
of the gods.   They sacrifice, and the priestess calls them
to where, out of the rock, is cut an enormous cavern
with a hundred openings, whence reach as many voices,
the answers of the Sibyl.   Then suddenly she appears,
flushed and breathing hard, with dishevelled hair, and her
breast heaving, the cords of her throat swollen with
frenzy; and she seems greater than a mortal.   Her
first words freeze the bones of Æneas, who begs for the
prophecy of his future, in the hope of a rest for Troy,
and he promises in the future great temples for both
Phœbus and herself.   Then she rages to free herself
from the god, but all the more does he fatigue her wild
mouth, and from the hundred doors of the great cavern
pour out the answers of the oracle.   The hero, taking
hold of the altar, asks that he may enter Avernus, where
he wishes to see his father, who has called to him, and she
tells him how easy is the descent of Avernus, how difficult

[1] Hence the expression "Sibylline leaves."

THE CUMÆAN SIBYL. (Michael Angelo)

the return. But there is in a dark wood a tree with a branch of gold sacred to infernal Juno; that he is to pluck, for when the first is torn away another golden one is not wanting. But how shall the Golden Bough show itself in the night of the immense forest? And he appeals to his mother Venus. At his prayer twin doves come down and alight, and guide him to the tree from which he breaks the reluctant branch and brings it to the Sibyl. Then the enormous rock gapes, the hero calls on Achates and sacrifices, while under his feet the earth groans, the summits of the trees move, and the dogs howl in the shadow as the Sibyl comes.

And so on until hell itself is entered, as Dante will enter it again. Occasionally the Sibyl admonishes Æneas, and at last the priestess of Phœbus hurries him to the gate, and bids him place the Golden Bough on the threshold as they leave. Then later we have the glorious prophecies of the future fate of Rome (which even to-day are continued), and the famous prediction of the boy Marcellus who is to be, and then two gates of Sleep are before them: the one of Horn and the other of Ivory, and the Sibyl and Æneas leave by the Ivory Gate.

Much must have happened after that before tradition brings the Sibyl (for whom apparently no great temples were built by Æneas) to offer to sell Tarquin her books, one of which she consults in the painting. First, nine she offered, and then she destroyed three, and offered six at the same price, and again destroyed three more and offered the remaining three, still at the same price. Thereupon Tarquin, as we remember, bought them and they were entrusted to a college of Fifteen, known under that name, which preserved them,

and consulted them on occasions of exceptional danger —
not exactly to discover extraordinary future events, but to
ascertain and carry out observances, to avert calamities,
and to expiate (according to habit), prodigies.   They
were written in hexameter verse in Greek (hence the two
Greek interpreters), and were burned with the temple of
Jupiter on the Capitol in 83 B.C.

Michael must have read the great, joyous, luminous
prophecy also quoted by Virgil, wherein we are told how
the last age has come of the Cumæan song, and a great
order is born, and the Virgin appears, and

"'From high Heaven a new progeny comes down.'"

One is tempted to quote anything out of the wonderful
poem, so fully worthy of the subject, and equal, in the
most civilized shape, to any prophecy of any time.   No
wonder that later the Virgilian lines were appealed to
and the Cumæan Sibyl justified; — Saint Justin even
goes so far as to mention Saint Paul's reference to the Sibyl.
If this could be true, how beautiful the reach of the
Cumæan verse !   Cannot we delight in the thought of
Paul listening to the prophecies — and indeed he must
have heard them, for they were known throughout the
entire world, wherever the Jew mingled with the Greek.

The Emperor Constantine used that wonderful Fourth
Eclogue as a basis of argument in a famous oration.   He
took up the proof of the divinity of our Lord from weighty
authorities.   Then he quoted from the Sibyl, bringing
up also that Cicero knew the prophecies, and especially
that one which is contained in an acrostic made up of
thirty-four verses with headings that give us: Jesus-
Christ, the Son of God, the Saviour, and dwelling on the

THE ERYTHRÆAN SIBYL. (Michael Angelo)

fact referred to by Cicero that the verses of the prophecies are arranged for acrostics. Hence Cicero is supposed to have seen or known that famous acrostic wherein the judgment of the world is predicted, and that Rome is coming to an end.

So said Constantine, who must have derived his opinion from the Book of Divination written by Cicero. But Cicero — if I remember rightly — speaks ill of these verses of the Sibyl, which he says fell from her in a fury, "that fury which is called divination, but which is such that a person distracted seeth what a wise man sees not, and that he who has lost human abilities has acquired divine ones"; he also properly says that "the Sibyl should be kept secret and sequestered from us; that, as it hath been ordered by our ancestors, the books be not read without permission of the Senate. They should draw nothing out of them rather than a king, which neither gods nor men will ever hereafter suffer in Rome." This he speaks in relation to the design of Cotta, his colleague, to have Cæsar proclaimed king, and Cicero, referring to the use of an acrostic, shows that the artifice was common to the Sibylline poems, and remarks that this thing shows circumspection and not fury. It is argued that Virgil could not have read the Sibylline verses, since they were hidden, and as to that a charming romance has been brought up of Virgil on his visit to Rome having met Herod of Judæa.

The Emperor Constantine, calling again upon Virgil's testimony, invokes the verses as to the Virgin's coming, and says: "Who then shall be the returning Virgin but she who conceived by the Divine Spirit?" Justin Martyr complained to the Emperor, "that through the working of

evil spirits it is forbidden upon pain of death to read the
books of the Sibyl, for fear that those who should read
them might be diverted from taking cognizance of good
things : but we not only read them, but also recommend
them to your inspection, knowing they would be accept-
able to you all."

Commenting on Plato (who described ecstacy as being
inspired of God), Justin says "he clearly and manifestly
sought into the oracles of the Sibyl, for she had not, as
the poets have, the power to correct her poems after she
had written them, and to polish them, as to what concerns
the exact observation of measures ; she accomplished what
was of her prophecy, and the inspiration failing she no
longer remembered the things she had said ; hence comes
it that all the verses of the Sibylline poems were not
preserved." Again Justin, being at the City of Cumæ,
tells of those who "led him up and down and showed him
the place where she spoke her oracles, and a certain urn
of brass where they said her relics were conserved."
And further : "Submit to the most ancient of all the
Sibyls, whose books, it has so happened, are preserved
all the world over, and who, by oracles proceeding from a
certain powerful inspiration, hath taught you concerning those who are called Gods that they are not such."

Petronius refers to her as endowed with the coveted
and burdensome gift of immortality, bestowed by
Apollo on his mistaken favourites, and tells us that
groups of merry children, tired of playing in the sunny
streets, sought the shade of the temple, and amused themselves by gathering under the familiar jar and calling
out "Sibyl, what do you wish ?" A hollow voice like
an echo used to answer from the urn : "I wish to die."

THE PROPHET EZEKIEL. (Michael Angelo)

We pass from the Cumæan to the Erythræan Sibyl at the other end of the line. The Erythræan — the Red Sibyl — is sometimes made out to be the proper claimant of the Delphic seat. In the Sibylline verses she places herself, as is natural, in the sixth generation after the Flood. Is she the Hebrew Sibyl, or are we to call the Persian one (known also as the Babylonian or Egyptian) by the name of "Saba," old? In the third Sibylline verses the Sibyl explains that she is not an Erythræan, nor a daughter of Circe, but a native of Babylon, and a daughter of Noah, and tells some awful stories about herself which go beyond the very possibilities of outrage and wrong. Pausanias, who should know, tells us in his list of four, that the Erythræan prophesied at Delphi. We know that most of the ancients made the Erythræan Sibyl the daughter of Jupiter or of Apollo and Lamia or of the shepherd Theodorus and the nymph Idea; nor is it clear how they could have made her born at Erythræa, a city of Asia, if they thought her the daughter of Circe, dwelling near Rome upon the mountain called to this day Monte Circello.

When the books of the Cumæan in the temple of Jupiter on the Capitol were burnt with the temple, the senate sent ambassadors to Erythræa to collect the oracles afresh. They brought back one thousand verses. The older collection of Sibylline oracles seems to have been made in the time of Solon, at Gergis on Mount Ida in the Troad, and attributed to the Sibyl of Marpessus. At Gergis they were preserved in the temple of Apollo; thence they passed to Erythræa; in some manner the collection found its way to Cumæ and from there to Rome. They then were revised under

E

Augustus and placed at length in the base of the statue of Apollo Patrous. They were there in the year 363 A.D., forever connected with the fate of the Roman Empire, and hence they were burnt by Stilicho a few years later, in 400. These strictly pagan ones might disappear, but of a mass of them the Church could not get rid, and for centuries the supposed prophecies and the real ones, the Sibylline verses, ran up and down the discussions of the Church, and I remember reading heavy books of battles between Protestants and Catholics concerning their value, written as late as 1671. Now we can hardly realize how important they once were, for their record is only carried out in the images of the painters; from being beautiful, they became commonplace, then tedious, and at last merely names for the tag on the frame of a picture, until now we do not even know what is meant by a Sibyl. She of Erythræa might have foretold this as she turns on her seat and looks up the passages, marking one with her forefinger. The deputation from Rome has just come in; it is growing dark, and the boy is lighting the lamp. Before turning to the ambassadors, the Sibyl repeats to herself what she has marked, and we can see her lips move. Her right arm hangs, of course thoughtlessly, in the great folds which are always our admiration, and her strange costume is perhaps nothing more than a modification of some lady's dress or peasant's garb. But it is with universal consent one of the beautiful arrangements of drapery. In another moment the folds will fall as she uncrosses her leg, and she will get out her prophecies and send them to Rome.

The Prophets are the most monumental figures known to painting, whose poetic intensity is superior even to

THE PROPHET ISAIAH. (Michael Angelo)

the other creations of the greatest poet who ever painted.
To follow their pictures would be fully sufficient, but one
may hope to note some point which may bring us nearer
to the author and give us a little more the reasons of the
actual appearance before us.

For each one there are, as with the Sibyls, two attendant figures, probably with no meaning other than that
of contrast and composition, but occasionally so impres-
sively placed and with such curious details that many
have thought them meant as sources of inspiration —
beautiful servants of the Most High as well as of the
Prophet — perhaps indeed invisible to him. As we take
Ezekiel, for instance, at first the feminine child pointing
up and looking far away seems to mean something. It
may be nothing more than the arm repeating the fold of
the Prophet's cloak, but one might wish some explanation of this most curious type, something also which
would explain the frightened look of the other beautiful
attendant. As to the Prophet, he is easier to read; a
narrow turban is tightened on his head — the head of
an evident enthusiast. He speaks, announcing to the
Jews the end of their captivity, the restoring of the
Temple. His cloak rises about him in the wind of prophecy, as if he had suddenly been called; we feel the
argument, the reason he is giving: it is not merely a
declaration, it is a formal proof, and as with all else of
Michael's, the fusion of the greatest solemnity and the
most accurate observation is complete.

Isaiah has left one hand on the book to mark the
passage he was reading. We feel that he has been thinking it over. His other hand has been uplifted — perhaps
he was leaning his head upon it — and is still raised me-

chanically.   The angel speaks to him; the Prophet's lips
begin an answer; he turns slowly to the accustomed
call which disturbs him.   Again it is a scene of ordinary
life transmuted into the "tremendous majesty" of the
hymn.   He, like the other Prophets, is accustomed to
talk with Jehovah.

Joel has come to the end of the long roll of prophecies;
with one hand he holds it; the other stops the dropping
of the parchment.   He finds some hard passage; he
frowns and his lips are pursed in the effort of discovery.
One of the boys behind him points to the other, directing
him in some way.

Zachariah we see in profile turning over slowly the
leaves.   His two attendants wait.   He himself has
dropped a foot from his stool and perhaps may rise when
he has found his place.

Daniel is still young and powerful.   A great book is
spread upon his knees and partially held up by his muscular left arm.   His one imaginary attendant stands
beneath the big volume, gripping it hard, and holding
it as if he were a pulpit.   The young Daniel, meanwhile,
absorbed in his task, turns to the right.   He makes a
note on another volume or scroll as if comparing the
two.   He is as violently anxious and interested as the
other Prophets so far have been certain.   The wind
of prophecy blows his mantle in many folds about him
and over the background of his chosen place.

Jonah is almost naked in the triumph of drawing
admired by the Italians of the time, as Condivi has
noted, and turns far over, counting on his fingers the
forty days which remain for Nineveh.   Beside him is
the sea-monster from whom he has escaped, and behind

THE PROPHET JONAH. (Michael Angelo)

him his attendant angel looks at whatever is happening, with a frightened face, while the leaves of the gourd with which God rebukes the over-anxious personality of the Prophet blow in the wind of prophecy. Here, again, we feel that same frequentation with the Most High Jehovah. Nothing could better express the feeling of remonstrance and disappointment in argument than the entire figure of the anxious Prophet.

Jonah concludes the series of the Prophets. He is above the altar, and perhaps Michael may have thought then of the painting which he put upon the wall below years after, where, for the first time, appears the Saviour whose coming is specially predicted by the figure of Jonah.

When in the Sistine on Good Friday the "Miserere" is sung, and each light goes out in sequence, the mighty figures, as they disappear, seem to pass into the terrible story of the Old Testament which Michael has once more resumed on the end wall in the "Last Judgment."

The immense importance of the work of Michael Angelo should not lead us to be careless of many representations which preceded it, because these made up the obscure processes by which we gather into ourselves what our predecessors have done, partly by actual sight, partly by that mysterious tendency, half physical, to repeat the actions of our makers, whose very signature or movement of the hand we reproduce for generations. A wonderful series of sculptors led up to Michael, and each one in his way represented these very characters or others near them. Jacopo della Quercia Michael must have known in Bologna in early days, and many have

noticed the similar movement of the lips. Then there
are Ghiberti and Brunelleschi and Michelozzo, and Donatello — Magister Donatellus de Florentia, Taglia Pietra,
as he signed when he promised to do as well as any man
ever did. Donatello was very near and yet very far;
the others seem almost ready to speak the language of
Michael Angelo. Far back, John the Pisan gives us
Prophets and even Sibyls (alongside of Plato and Daniel)
and in his pulpit at Pistoia has almost indicated the idea
of the Prophet accompanied by his inspirers.

One recognizes a possible, indeed a necessary, memory
of the old man's work by the younger, and we ask ourselves whether Michael Angelo at that date had seen
Pistoia and John the Pisan's work. There the Sibyls
sit or stand with an importance of intention which makes
them, as it were, the ancestresses of Michael's. One
is erect, arms crossed, absorbed in thought; an angel
flutters past her; the Prophets almost scream on either
side. In the same way another one is tortured by the
insistence of the angel; another again by the insistence of
the Prophets who urge and appeal. Another resents,
as it were, the spirit that is taking hold of her, the news
and knowledge which are sure to oppress her and tear
her to pieces in a moment. For hers is no pleasant task:
it is a surrender of body and soul to something obscure
and controlling. One more elderly and well balanced
prophetess tells us what she knows. A little angel whis-
pers softly, and two prophets have ceased to trouble her.
Yet another is all disturbed, but gently, by what the
angel tells her. Only her hand and the movement of her
head tell us that this is no easy message that she gets,
for we must remember that the word "angel" means a

THE VIRGIN CROWNED BY ANGELS. (Botticelli)

messenger of the Most High, and is not only so in the Greek form which we inherit, but in the older forms of the biblical story.

We have already spoken of the well-known painting which represents the story of the Sibyl who predicted to the Emperor Augustus the coming of the Child-Saviour. In memory of that event the Tiburtine Sibyl is painted with Augustus on either side of the arch above the high altar of the Church of Ara Cœli, built upon the spot where Augustus was said to have raised an altar to the Son of God (Ara Primogeniti Dei). We cannot do more than refer to the many renderings of Sibyls and Prophets made throughout Northern Europe until, as we remarked before, the memory of these subjects, in the Sibyls of late Italian painting, merely gives a name for some handsome figure filling the purpose of a picture inside of a frame.

These beautiful beings look upward in some recognized religious expression (that is to say, the religious expression of the end of the great period) and one is reminded of the joke of one of their creators, a very illustrious painter, who said that he knew at least one hundred ways of making the eyes look up to heaven. And a greater than he has painted a charming series which we all go to see in Santa Maria della Pace in Rome. They are four in number; their names are Cumana, Phrygia, Persica, and Tiburtina — three at least beautiful and young, and above them lovely angels float with scrolls on which are written quotations. These are "The Resurrection of the Dead" for the Cumæan; for the Persican, "He will have the lot of Death"; for the Phrygian, "The Heavens surround the Sphere of the Earth"; and the Tiburtine,

"I will open and arise." Then one angel holds the scroll
with the seventh line of Virgil's Eclogue: "Already a
new birth," etc. When the very great Raphael did these
very beautiful things, he marked a distance between
himself and Michael, who had given him the impulse
which we feel regretfully. But the accidents of failure
in such a gigantic career, the failure which belongs to the
fatigued mind even of a genius, we have to excuse. We
excuse it also because of the beauty pictured, and even
as a sort of tribute to Michael, without whom these things
could not have existed. One realizes how just were
Raphael's thanks to Heaven that he had been permitted
to live in the time of Michael Angelo.

CHAPTER III

THE ANGELS

As Michael Angelo must stand for us as the great exponent of the Sibyls, so Botticelli will rise naturally to our minds when we think of angels, and there are few painters of whom that can be said, however successful their representations may be.

We have seen the angel in Michael's formidable expression, or Raphael's elegance and sweetness, and have even come down to Delacroix. But those angels, messengers or creatures of the other world, have a meaning because of their errand, and the action of which they form part. The angels of Botticelli would be lovely always, and it is a part of their life, of the ideal that they represent, that they are sufficient for themselves, and come together on certain great occasions ; they are capable of extreme sadness, but that is because they are so sweet.

We shall see them in triumphant circles in the "Assumption of the Virgin," in the National Gallery in London. There are concentric circles, in the order of Dante's description, and in three ranks are patriarchs, prophets, apostles, and all the holy host. Round about them, and through them, angels sit or kneel or pray, and high above, around the Footstool, they collect as little children, along with the worshipping Madonna. Exultant joy, no vestige of anything but happiness, fills all, repeated every moment by these notes of sweet beings who carry out the great theme. Below, as we know, the tomb is filled with flowers, and the Apostles look in, while far off stretches a landscape which may be sad, as Leonardo thought,[1] but which has all the far-away vision of a dream. The donors of the picture kneel on either side, the poet Matteo Palmieri and his wife. The painting gives us a view of angels in which we find it difficult to recognize the suggestion of anything contrary to Dante's orthodoxy, but which brought down the wrath of the clergy in the general fear of heresy. Vasari tells us how Botticelli made this picture for Matteo Palmieri "with celestial zones wherein are represented patriarchs, prophets," etc. All form a project traced out by Matteo, who was a lettered man and a man of merit, but certain malevolent people said that Matteo and Sandro had gravely sinned in heresy. The good Vasari goes on to say that it is not for him to judge; it is enough that the figures of Sandro should be worthy of all praise, and like us, he recognizes the care with which he represented the circles of heaven and intermingled the holy figures with angels. So for two centuries the painting was veiled; it was even supposed that it had been burned, as well as the heretical poem that had inspired it. Matteo Palmieri, a student of all things and of theology, occupied various positions of embassy and magistracy, and was buried in a holy chapel of the Church, but on some visit to the Italian borders where are the cavern of the Sibyl and Lake Avernus, the Pit of Hell and those fields where floats the vapour of an infernal world, he wrote a poem not to be opened until after his death. Its theology was based

[1] Leonardo said of this and other landscapes of Sandro: "These landscapes are sad."

THE ASSUMPTION OF THE VIRGIN. (BOTTICELLI)

on the negation of eternal hell, following the doctrine of Origen, which was proscribed by the Church.

Origen had arranged a view of angelic birth and life and hierarchy from which through sin some had fallen — how, we do not know exactly, — but there was a great battle, and Michael led the host that won. Many, however, took neither the part of God nor of the future Satan, so they were thrown out of heaven along with the wicked angels, and fell into the bodies of men and animals and fish and succubi, or demons; some even fell into the movement of the stars which they guide. Each of us then contains a bad angel, struggling against our gift of a good guardian angel. After migration from star to star, at the Last Judgment, in the end of everything, all these souls, these fallen angels, demons or men or what not in any shape, shall see open to them the gates of the heavenly Jerusalem. If I mistake not, this has something also to do with the Albigensian heresy. Palmieri was told this by the revelation of a friend of his who apparently spoke to him from the planet Mercury.

The painting to my mind is a very wonderful thing, even if not all by Botticelli's hand, and I do not feel the opposition which some persons have to its being by him or its being good. I still take refuge with Vasari in the belief that it is a very wonderful creation. And in knowledge such as I have of the number of hands which must have worked on these multitudinous paintings throughout the Italian land, it is of no consequence except as a success or otherwise, whether it be all by the hand of Botticelli or partly by Botticini.

Botticelli has come once within the ancient Jewish tradition in the "Coronation of the Virgin," where his

angels are a blazing fire; those above are the Seraphim, but all below and around comes that special
delight of his, suggested perhaps by his gala days in
Florence, when girls danced even into churches, — the
delight of dancing angels. Never again can that be
taken up; never again shall we have a mind attuned
to both childish and æsthetic and over-delicate and over-
spiritual raptures. Other artists, not so far removed
from our painter in time, Gozzoli and Angelico, have
invented and painted wonderful creatures who blow
through golden trumpets or play on harps. I have in
mind such a picture of heaven as the gold-grounded
panel belonging to Mrs. Gardner in Boston, where the
Virgin has left her tomb into which gaze the Apostles,
and, happy and absorbed, is surrounded by joyous angels
who dance about her and show the happiness that she
has in another way. But they are not the whirling,
twirling angels of Botticelli. As we said before, he must
have seen the dance of girls, when they danced in religious
joy around the confiscated works of Satan burnt by the
partisans of Savonarola. And then he would have
thought of their song of:

"O youth with beautiful hair, let it fall and do not tie it; let
it fall on thy shoulders. It seems like threads of gold and silk.

"Beautiful is the hair, and beautiful he who wears it.

"O youth, how beautiful dost thou pass! where thou passest
the tree flowers. For thee the tree flowers as the roses in April.

"When I see thee I think I see the sun and the moon, and I have
hold of Paradise.

"O youth, born in Paradise, why dost thou look for flowers when
such beauties flower upon thy white face? They are red and they are
white, and they are of every colour, for thy face is such as a garden
of roses.

THE NATIVITY. (Botticelli)

"O youth with the curly hair, O youth with the golden hair that parts around thy face, thou dost appear an angel seen from heaven, an angel of the Church, an angel of Paradise . . . ."

As we know, at the end of his life, after the great horror of the ecclesiastical murder of Savonarola, whom he had followed, he painted a wonderful picture of the Nativity which is in the National Gallery, London. It is almost all beauty; a little queerness only in the strange cavern which serves as a stable for the ass and the ox, outside of which is the leaning shelter under which the sweet Mother looks down upon her sweet Child, while Joseph, tired with the journey, is folded up in fatigue and sleep. An angel stretches out behind him a hand holding a branch and waving an inscription. There are three strangers of different ages there, and the Wise Men, and they balance two other beings who are more evidently shepherds and working people, from one of whom another angel unwraps a hood as if to take away even external blindness. He and all are crowned with the olive of peace. Everywhere the flower or the plant sprouts. Among roots and the clefts of the rock the devils crouch and disappear; one almost hears the hiss and spit of the reptiles whose size and whose appearance are hardly noticed in the peace and the joy and the sweetness of this marvellous religious song.

In the foreground is the memory of tragedy. Three angels embrace the Dominican monks; they kiss and hug them in the joy of their escape from the awful world which has destroyed their earthly figures in the fire. They are there : Savonarola and Buonvicini and Maruffi. Their faces are no longer those which we know in that solemn portrait of the great reformer. They belong

to the Sun; they are young and sweet and beautiful
and gay. Of course it is to them that the call of the
angels has been addressed; they are the men "of good-
will."

Then above, in obscure Greek, on the edge of the
canvas, are words which Sir Sidney Colvin reads thus:

"This painting was painted at the end of the year 1500 during the
troubles of Italy, by me, Alessandro, about the middle of that period
at the beginning of which was verified the eleventh chapter of Saint
John the Evangelist, and the second woe of the Apocalypse, when
Satan was let loose on earth for three years and a half. Passed that
delay, the demon shall be chained up, and we shall see him crushed
under foot as in this painting."

The joy of the angels, as we see, is not the joy of this
world, and we have another example of what we all know
but so rarely realize, — the division of our minds and
souls so that we are capable of grief and joy at the same
moment. Indeed if Plato is not out, they are but forms
of one feeling. How much our good friend Botticelli
may have known of Plato, we do not directly know, but
Plato was in the air, as the French say, as, for instance,
when Marsilio Ficino, who was Cardinal of Fiesole,
preached the Timæus at Florence at the Church of the
Angels saying: "In the centre of this church, we wish
to expose the religious philosophy of our Plato; we wish
to contemplate divine truth in the abode of angels. Let
us enter, my very dear brothers, with a very candid
soul."

Three more angels upon the roof kneel and sing the
"Gloria in Excelsis," already written in a book. Above
them whirls a gay round of delighted beings carrying
olive boughs as all the others do, and joining hands and

THE SACRIFICE OF MANOAH. (Rembrandt)

branches in such an ecstasy as no words can describe. No human being ever has done more than give the type of such motion of transport, and herein our painter is, as far as we know, the painter of angels.

In the Sistine Chapel, above the spaces of the Sibyls and Prophets, angelic figures float within the cloak of the God of Israel in Michael Angelo's paintings. Their being wingless is in the proper Jewish tradition; the wing does not come until very late, and in Rembrandt's great painting, "The Sacrifice of Manoah," the angel disappears without wings. He disappears; we see him fade in the smoke of the flames of the sacrifice, and we recognize the tradition of the angel vanishing in such manner. We remember that he had no distinctive name; he appeared as other men, and in Rembrandt's painting he is dressed in a gown, with long hair and crowned head, while husband and wife kneel and fear and believe and doubt before the smoking embers. This is no sweetly angelic figure; this is the story of the Bible. One realizes how that floating form could have been taken for any one (in a conversation with the good woman of the house who had gone into the field), and the doubts of husband and wife as to who this accidental stranger may be. The plainness of the Bible story, which carries its own authenticity in its words, is there in Rembrandt's painting, as it might have happened had he been there. For let us notice that things *happen* with him; he does not invent them.

We are not unnaturally brought back to the question of the angelic continuation by the reference to expression in Christian art. If we think for a moment we shall find the expression of an angel rarely more than that of a messenger delivering himself of his duty, a witness of joy or sorrow. Only very rarely does he come to the actual help of the saint or testify through his face his joy and feeling. He weeps desolately at the great drama of the Passion, but even there it is a suggestion of an elementary power weeping and suffering, like nature itself torn by the agony of its Maker.

The question of what the angels really are is perhaps worth bringing up in this connection. They are not far from the Dæmons of the Greek thought who flit in and out of Greek story, who tell Socrates, for instance, what he is to do, and bid him suffer death rather than go back on his duty. That is the protective good angel of the Jewish teaching, perhaps a freed soul coming back to take part in human actions. The rabbinical traditions are not quite averse to some meaning of that kind.

Rembrandt has elsewhere made them as they may have appeared to Abraham, when they sit and discuss under different shapes, and when Sarah listens to these conversations ; those angels must have had a form different from that needed for the solemn necessities of a short message.

Quite earthly they are in one sense, and Rembrandt has not added wings, which were often tacked on like those of birds. All is real, like the food of the Patriarch and the knife with which he is about to cut the most earthly bit of meat. But certainly the three angels are interested in their talk. They have become absolutely human, and we can see in each face the reflection of the receiving of their news by Abraham. They are as it were persuading him, while his face expresses the proper degree of doubt. Even the "bird of God" in the foreground, quite a little boy, tells you by the merest profile how anxiously he follows the belief of the Patriarch.

Rembrandt's angels are few, notwithstanding the many chances he had of using them. But the few all have that same look of extreme interest in their earthly work. The angel in Daniel's vision makes him see, whether he wills it or not, the animal that represents the coming Kingdom, and in the angel wrestling with Jacob there is also the expression of having thoroughly entered into human form and meaning, but with infinite superiority of control.

CHAPTER IV

JOACHIM AND ANNA. PRESENTATION OF THE VIRGIN. THE MARRIAGE OF THE VIRGIN

SAINT John Damascene says, "From the tree of Jesse stretches the branch on which blooms the divine flower; from Anna comes the vine which has given us the fruit." He was speaking of the solemn festival of the birth of Mary. In his time the apocryphal gospel of James was becoming popular. Therein we are told that Joachim, a very rich man, offered great gifts to the Lord; but this legend went on to say that at one of the great religious festivals where he with the other sons of Israel brought offerings to the Temple, Reuben refused those of Joachim, telling him, "Thou shouldst not offer gifts to the Lord; thou hast no descent in Israel." Joachim's grief was great, for he knew that all the Jews of his tribe had left successors, and so, abstaining from appearing at his home, he went into the desert, and there he remained forty days and forty nights, fasting. Meanwhile, his wife, Anna, wept over having no children. As she remarked upon the felicity of virgin beasts who (as it was then thought) were not cut off from bearing young, the angel of the Lord appeared and told her that she should become a mother. She was told in the same way that Joachim was returning to her, he also having received celestial announcement. At the house door Anna met him and threw her arms around his neck in joy. Next day Joa-

78

chim made his offerings, which were no longer refused, and returned home in happiness, and so was born Mary, according to the Gospel of James.

In some gnostic story, Joachim is urged by an angel to offer a holocaust to the Lord, which he does, and the angel returns to heaven in the smoke of the sacrifice. Whereupon Joachim falls upon his face and remains from the sixth hour up to the ninth. Servants in fright lift him up, and learning of the vision, they exhort him to return to his wife. At the Golden Gate of Jerusalem, the end of a long journey, he meets Anna. Thus it is in the apocryphal gospels; and the story is so told by Giotto.

The sentiment of pagan antiquity appears in one of the earlier images, a Greek manuscript of 1025, wherein Anna lies in bed and three women bring her food or gifts from outside, — a record of the three Parcæ, Clotho, Lachesis, and Atropos, who were present when a child opened its eyes to life.

This legend begins to be lifted into the height of beauty and importance when Giotto takes hold of it. The frescoes in Padua begin with the enclosure, a priestly place within which stands the priest with a mitre upon his head, who absolves a kneeling worshipper. Outside of this chancel, if it may be so named, lies an empty pulpit, and behind the priest is a form of ciborium, supported by columns, all of which in some way records the Temple. Outside of the little enclosure stands Reuben, also mitred, with long white beard and curled hair falling upon his shoulders, frowning in indignation. Joachim, a dignified and beautiful figure, not at all a broken-down ancient man, turns away, grasping in his hand the offering refused.

In the next painting we see him walking; he has turned the corner of some rocks, and is coming to his own sheepfold; he looks down absorbed in thought, not noticing the delight of the dog welcoming him. Two of the shepherds, on seeing their master approaching in meditation, look at each other, questioning, as if to ask what has happened. Meanwhile the door of the sheepfold is open and the sheep scatter out.

In another picture an angel speaks to Anna in her imaginary little house. He comes through the window suddenly like a bird, and she gazes in surprise, kneeling, but already her folded hands accept the grace of the Lord. Outside, her servant is spinning long threads from her distaff.

Again, in another painting Joachim kneels crouching before an altar upon which he has offered the holocaust of a lamb, according to the divine word told by an angel who stands at some distance from him, giving the order with his hand — a beautiful and most classical figure. At the angel Joachim gazes with most intent eye. Flame and smoke pour up from the altar; another angel disappears, passing into the cloud from which the hand of God is extended as in the early Christian works. A shepherd stands gazing into the sky behind his master. Around them play the sheep.

We have, also, the Presentation of Mary. In explaining certain great works of art for which we rightly care, the imaginary, the poetic comment, has its place as well as the facts of the real truth. And in thinking of the Gospel story we must remember that in the far-away beginning there was the settlement of the Church and of the

THE SACRIFICE OF JOACHIM. (Giotto)

State, the fusion of various nationalities, many gospels, and many accounts of the Gospel story, some having no particular bias, others charged with heretical meaning. All these were a manner of spiritual help and also of relative record, making up for the paucity of what the Church had decided to be the correct one. The question of heresy — the question of a version being in the direction of such and such a deviation from the law of Church and councils — was settled afterward. Meanwhile, the necessity for something more than mere record was filled by the apocryphal gospels. And so we shall take up the apocryphal gospel of the Nativity, wherein Anna goes to the Temple with Joachim to make the usual offering. She left Mary to be trained with other maidens who were devoted to the worship and praise of the Lord. The simple story, that becomes so important in certain paintings, tells us how, when the child came to the Temple, she ran up the many stairs without looking to right or left, and all were astonished, for she appeared no longer a little child, and her figure was white as of snow, and all she said was full of grace. In Eastern art, this procession of the child going to the Temple shows her of quite a marriageable age, as if fit for a bridal ceremony. In the West, we come at once to Giotto, telling us the story as if it were a reality. The little girl has already got up the fantastic steps, types of the real ones, and stands with joined hands, waiting, while her mother, holding her carefully, presents her with some shade of anxiety. The old man Zachariah, bearded and grave, reaches his two hands to the child, while the crowd of other young creatures, some much older and wearing semi-monastic clothing, gather in a curious group together.

Joachim, at the foot of the stairs, looks at the scene, but keeps an eye on the servant bearing gifts for the Temple. Round about, various priests and Levites look and comment. With Giotto, a temple of Israel becomes an Italian cloister. Continuously, after him, the cloister was distinguished from the church, according to what some one wrote in the twelfth century as to the dwelling of the Virgin being "near the outside portals and the nearest to the altar." In one of these early pictures one sees the steps, fifteen according to Byzantine tradition (because just so many were the psalms), and inside of the portico the momentarily cloistered virgins can be seen with musical instruments, singing the canticles of David. And so they are shown in the Italian representations, as with Gaddi and John of Milan. Zachariah and his assistants, at the entrance of the church, clad in sacramental garments, wait to receive the little maiden. From various places outside and within the columns of the interior, men and women look at the ceremony. Mary's father and mother stand at the foot of the steps; and children gather about surprised and amused, while others are climbing the stairs. All this has become more and more of a grand scene, as of a well-understood celebration. Occasionally Mary turns round to her parents, as if to let them see that she understands her part. There is a very noble sculpture by Orcagna in Florence. In the tabernacle in Or San Michele, which is an octagon, and where he was obliged to follow symmetry rigorously in all the bas-reliefs, Mary turns her back to us and climbs the little steps of the Temple. There, attended by two Levites, the high priest waits for the child, as he stands at the door. Some

THE PRESENTATION OF THE VIRGIN. (Sodoma)

of the maidens of the Temple can be seen; one of them
holds a psalterion.   Mary has the Book of Divine Doctrine in one hand, and turns slightly to her parents, pointing at the Temple where she is to enter, without intention
of return.   Further down (which fact is told by difference of size), the father and mother kneel, patiently
waiting for their child.   In this case the Virgin cares
little.   There are cases when, on the contrary, she shows
her sorrow at leaving her father and mother.   Instead
of the young girl in some of these works (which have a
sort of symbolism) we see in a lovely painting by that
delightful artist, the Sodoma, a little child of a few years
old taken hold of by the high priest, who grasps her arm.
She turns sweetly, smiling at her mother, who kneels
on the steps;   no longer fifteen as by old tradition.
The portico opens into air; columns stand about, and so
do fair women and majestic figures of men.   Thus a
charming domestic anecdote was placed within the arbitrary composition.

Not long afterward Venice had begun the final representations.   Cima da Conegliano places at the foot of
the stair that same old woman whom we shall find in the
great painting of Titian.   Up the long steps, which we
see on edge, a little girl mounts slowly and with care,
for the steps are very high.   Above, the Levites and a
Temple virgin stand waiting for the child.   Below are
father and mother and relatives, clad in correct oriental
dress according to the day of the painter.   A beautiful
landscape, perhaps a reminiscence, opens far back.
Some little children linger to see what will happen.
Far away, people of Eastern costume and manner wander
through porticos, and in front two stand so near to us

that we can see they are portraits. This is at Dresden, a beautiful painting in itself, even if we did not understand its subject. In Milan, at the Brera, there is a Carpaccio which gives us the story on a much smaller scale. On some little steps again we see our small maiden holding her votive candle, her long hair down her back, kneeling before she rises to be welcomed by the high priest. Inside the cloister, venerable Levites stand. At the foot of the stairs, her mother and father watch, with others of the family. A boy looks up, in conversation with one of the good-natured Levites, who is probably ordering him away, for the child has brought a tame deer with him, and is too near for the proper respect of the Church.

Then Tintoretto uses this subject for one of his great triumphs of composition, an ideal subject, for more than ever the story is disguised. Up circular steps one looks, and sees above grave figures of sacerdotal import. Up those steps a tall woman moves with her baby. Below, another noble Venetian woman shows to her little girl a faraway little maiden detached against the sky at the top of that long flight of stairs. Along these many steps, not very well seen, people are seated. One stands and looks around; perhaps the father. An indifferent woman sits on the lower step playing with her child. We feel that, with Tintoretto, the thing happened so and he could not help it; he had to use all his marvellous powers of painting, of drawing, of composition. Then, at length, comes the final representation, famous throughout the world — the great Titian at present in the Gallery of the Academy at Venice, there entirely out of place, and deprived thereby of half its majesty. It represents a

THE PRESENTATION OF THE VIRGIN. (Carpaccio)

ceremony wherein senators and important noblemen of
the Republic appear, in the open space before a building
with Corinthian capitals and columns and pilasters;
a palace out of which look down the gentry, curiously
watching. In the distance are the beautiful mountains
of his native place, and this adds still more to the certainty that we are within the marble limits of a spacious
outer court in an ideal Venice. Meanwhile, the pretty
little Mary, dressed in blue, her long hair tied in a tress,
lifts her skirt as she ascends the staircase, at the head of
which the high priest is ready to receive her. Two
important figures, like those of cardinals, stand near
the high priest. One of them comes down from an inside
stairs, a lame man with a cane, leaning heavily on the
little balustrade. Mother Anna seems to rejoice in the
middle of the multitude below, but one of her relatives
or friends points to the child in a sort of admiration or
fear. Meanwhile, near us, a little boy plays with a dog,
a senator gives alms to a poor woman holding a naked
baby in her arms; and in front of the steps sits an old
woman, who stops counting her money for a moment and
looks with astonishment at the procession of people coming up to the Temple. Thus Titian placed, more decid-
edly than was given to any one else, the Sacred Story in
a Venice of joy and senatorial importance; his own
Venice, of which he was the great exponent.

Were we to stand before the painting of Giotto in
Padua, we should find it difficult to realize, in our present
habit of passing over legends, how important these legends
once were, how they came from early times, how they
were the gospel truth until the Church decided to leave

them out. The proto-evangel of Saint John, which tells of the birth of the Virgin and of her sojourn in the Temple, comes at length to her espousals. By order of an angel, Zachariah called out the unmarried men and ordered them to bring each one a staff ; and also announced that the Lord would tell him by means of some sign on whom the choice should fall. Joseph joined the number ; the high priest Abiathar received these staves and prayed within the Temple. No sign appeared of the divine choice until at length Joseph came up with his staff, and at once on his head a dove alighted. Zachariah said to him : "God hath elected thee to take this virgin," but he refused, saying : "I have children, and I am an old man, and she is young, very young ; I should disgrace myself in the eyes of the sons of Israel." Then the high priest threatened him, reminding him of the punishment of the disobedient. So Joseph took the Virgin and said to her : "I shall bring thee to my house, but I shall have also to go to my work," for he was a carpenter. Now it happened that the priests wished a veil for the Temple, so that virgins of the tribe of Israel were called, and among them also Mary, because she, too, was of the tribe of David. The choice of colours was made by lot ; gold and yellow and scarlet and purple, which last Mary took away to weave.

This detail of the legend, "The Weaving of the Cloth," is an echo of the Roman world. It was a tradition and habit that when brides left their families for the home of the husband, the women present should call out, as we remember in Latin verses, "tallassio," the name of a basket for wool, which cry was to recall to the bride her home duties as the

THE PRESENTATION OF THE VIRGIN. (TITIAN)

spinner of wool; and with that they beat their hands in measure.

We need not describe the Byzantine or Latin drawings, for we shall come as usual to Giotto. We see the unmarried men of the tribe of David all reaching out their staves to the high priest, who is seated behind a desk. They come in gently, with some doubt: Joseph also, with white hair, and alone. The next picture is the contest of these pretenders to the hand of the Virgin. On the altar, all fastened together in a bunch, are the staves; the supplicants, kneeling anxiously, look forward in many different attitudes of expectation, awaiting the celestial choice. The high priest has left his seat behind the altar and kneels with two Levites. Then we see that the miracle has taken place and Joseph, whose staff now has bloomed, while a dove lights upon it, receives the hand of the Virgin to place upon it the ring handed to him by the high priest. The son of the high priest steps up with the intention of striking his rival Joseph. Passing outside of the picture, the men who have lost show their despite in various ways; one of them breaks or bends his staff, a ceremony repeated many times in other paintings. Then, in yet another picture Mary, followed by her companions, as a queen with her ladies, walks alone, a delightfully majestic and yet timid figure, toward her home, while young men crowned with flowers play on violins and other musical instruments. From the house above them a branch of palm spreads out — a type of peace. Later, in the fifteenth century, the pictures remain the same in their general meaning, but they vary with the chance of describing something more picturesque than the usual orderly disposition. But before

them the followers of Giotto will have told us this story
in many ways, and in one or two there appears the sign
of a future of greater development, as in the painting of
John of Milan in Santa Croce, Florence. There the
women of the Temple and their companions are grouped
closely around the high priest, so that there is just
room for the bride and bridegroom to join hands. Orcagna gives us a type of marriage in the famous set of bas-
reliefs of the Baptistery. Two noble figures, Mary and
Joseph, stand beside one another. Joseph still bears his
flowering staff; his right hand passes a ring over the
finger of Mary, and the high priest carefully lifts the
bride's arm. On the side are seen two angry suitors,
beautifully grouped to finish the composition. We
are in 1300, but the next century, and indeed the entire
future of possible sculpture, is marked in such simple work
as that on which the great Orcagna has put his hand. Then
Angelico spreads out the scene in a semi-ecclesiastical way,
so that we know it has some hidden meaning. It is outside
of the Temple. The Virgin stretches her arm towards
Joseph, the women are grouped apart, and the men show
that they are angry in the usual way. Even the Blessed
Monk brings in some special point of the tradition not
known to us, for one of the men raises a fist to strike poor
Joseph at the altar. Ghirlandajo in Florence again gives
us the crowd and Joseph struck by one of the unmarried.

Luini at Saronno tells a story in his own manner, the
beautiful manner personal to himself, but derived from
Northern antecedents. The bride and bridegroom are
somewhat separated; the grouping of the young men is
what we might expect from one of those lovers of young
men that circle around Leonardo; the disappointed

THE MARRIAGE OF THE VIRGIN. (Giotto)

suitors show no anger; nothing but a gentle sweetness and melancholy. In Milan, the Venetian Carpaccio paints the preparation or the beginning of the ceremony. Joseph goes up the steps. Mary at a distance folds her hands, accepting the declared facts. The high priest speaks. His clergy listen respectfully. Far off, in a Renaissance Church with Jewish details of religious importance, the unsuccessful candidates break their staves and hold up hands, etc. Then comes Raphael, closing the cycle for us at least, for we have all been taught to notice the result of his entrance into Italian fame. The painting is almost too well known to describe. It has, far at the back, the creation of a special building, foreshadowing the future of the architectural development which is to come, and the picture is filled with the grace and almost the indifference of the great man. The stupid or barbarous beginning, developed out of strange semi-Judaic inventions and traditions, comes here at length to a perfection which is classical, but for which there is no more future. The religious story is really over. The youthful Raphael may have felt the breath of Siena, and also the more fantastic traditions were fading before the want of interest or the slight frown of the Church. Moreover, there comes now a period of devotion to special saints, representations of the givers of particular graces. In following their traditions, in grouping them about the Holy Family, the painter could entrust his talent to his feelings, sure to be safe from ecclesiastical criticism, which could not reach works of art not intended to be doctrinal.

We may return to a special case connected with our story — to a representation of Saint Anna. In Northern

Europe, she was almost always the patroness of societies of a maternal character, where girls were educated and taken care of, for Saint Anna, mother of the Virgin, must have formed the most perfect of the daughters of man, and it was shown how she herself taught her child to read, that Mary might learn the words of the Lord and meditate upon them.   One of the most modern of all artists, Delacroix, has painted that subject, perhaps decisively. It is well known that there was a battle over it in 1845, and it was refused at the Salon.   It belonged to George Sand, and there is a story about it which is worth quoting. Delacroix, returning from some little walk at Nohant, said to her, he being her guest: "I saw in the park there a subject which touched me deeply.   It would be the motive of a superb painting.   It was your farmer's wife with her young daughter.   I was able to gaze at them for plenty of time, from behind a bush where they could not see me.   They were both seated on the trunk of a tree.   The older woman had her hand placed on the further shoulder of the child, who was taking with great care a lesson in reading.   If I only had a canvas, I should paint that subject at once."   "It is a pity," answered George Sand; "I have no canvas."   On which Delacroix, seeing a package in a corner of the hall, found within some heavy linen meant for use as kitchen aprons, and at once began the work, which shows the want of preparation of the canvas for the use to which it was put, as some parts have disappeared more than others. The Virgin is partly leaning and partly seated, and follows in the big book which Saint Anna spreads out on her knees before her.   It is an idyll of peace and simplicity, far away from the turmoil and cruelty of the fight for life in the world.

THE MARRIAGE OF THE VIRGIN. (LUINI)

CHAPTER V

ON the vaulting of the fourth chamber in the Catacomb of Priscilla appears the figure of a woman seated, to whom a youth stretches a right hand lifted as if in announcement. Upon that blackened and ruined plaster is the first form of a representation which was soon swept into the movement of the world, which we can follow in its development and variations, and in which we see the change of ideas or sentiment, as art brought together tradition and piety and was in all cases influenced by national character. Devotion to the Madonna, as the Italians called her (which has remained for us as the name for the image of Mary in painting), increased, as we know, through the ages, and although it has waned, there is still, to many souls, a religious necessity for worshipping the Christ as intimately united with the Mother who bore Him.

So the humble handmaiden of the catacombs becomes the glorified Queen, the Byzantine Priestess, and finally the Lady of Maternal Joy. The figure who speaks to her shall sometimes take the look of the glorious antique images of Victory, winged and splendid, or in sweetness of love and adoration shall kneel smiling, crowned perhaps with flowers before his return to heaven. But from an early moment in the Middle Ages the look of the scene remains the same. The

Church and tradition keep for this beautiful opportunity of art a respectful habit of representation.

In the catacomb, where the painting is of the third
century, Gabriel speaks to the Mother of Christ seated,
without wings, without the staff of travel or the sceptre,
and quite as a human being. The early Christian artist
may have remembered the pictures of Telemachus and
Penelope, or Paris and Helen, as some acute eyes have
been tempted to notice in the Pompeian pictures. But
whether from incapacity or innocence of meaning, there
is nothing in this first painting which does not belong
to the moment; the humble following in danger and in
darkness of a faith not made splendid by art or by any
form of external power. The noble figure of Mary in
the future, even too grand at times for our reading of
the story, is far from the modest Mary guardedly moving
a hand while the angel tells her that she has found grace
before the Lord. The interpretation of the Gospel of
Saint Luke in that modest form of the Annunciation in
the catacomb has passed into the ages.

In the East the Gospel of Saint James (also in the
third century) tells us of Mary going for water while a
voice calls to her. She looks right and left, and, frightened, enters her house and begins again to weave the
purple tissue which it was her duty and privilege to make
for the Temple. She placed aside the water vase; then
the angel appeared and said to her, "Do not fear, Mary,"
and the other words of the Gospel.

The basilica of Santa Maria Maggiore was erected
in the fifth century, as a sign of victories over the Nes-
torians. In its great mosaic she appears as sovereign
of the inhabitants of heaven. A crown of jewels binds

her head; she wears rich clothing with embroideries, is seated on an ornamental chair, and angels surround the throne. She is at work, but has stopped while the messenger from on high salutes her with veneration. The angels have the splendour of the pagan glories, and, indeed, another of the apocryphal gospels tells us that Gabriel filled Mary's rooms with light, and that she was accustomed to the illumination.

Some marks of all this we find in the well-known sarcophagus which is near the tomb of Dante, and which carries out the reminiscence of antique art. Mary is spinning, with a basket full of threads beside her, and more are hanging from the loom. A noble angel, an imitation of some antique, bends slightly toward her and lifts a hand in salutation. Mary, seated like an Egyptian figure, is immovable.

On the contrary, in an old ivory at Ravenna, which belongs to the time of Justinian, there is a distinct rising of the Virgin, who abandons her spinning, lifts her hand in astonishment, and seems to withdraw somewhat from the look of the angel, who has still the antique tunic and pallium, and points with his right hand. He has great wings, and for the first time shows the nimbus, the ancient symbol of glory and empire. There is an attempt at retaining the antique, but it is a mere commonplace, only valuable because so little art of that age remains to us.

An ivory in Milan (of the Trivulzio collection) has a special charm of meaning and expression. The Virgin turns around in astonishment; she wraps herself within herself, and this graceful idea, however naïvely expressed here, will be the type of the future figures of the Madonna.

In the East, of course, the tendency has been to a petrifaction of types and stories and meanings, under the constant supervision and direction of the clergy, as is the case, even at the present day, in the laid-down laws of the Greek Church. The charming example of the Greek monk James in the Vatican library brings in an oriental efflorescence of delight in mere beauty; he has attempted to render with colours the different moments of antique legends and apocryphal texts. The Virgin touches the water jar and moves her head to listen to the voice of the angel who speaks from heaven. Then she goes back into her house and sits upon a seat covered with white and red and blue ornaments, spinning the purple veil, while an angel bends the knee before her.

In the baptismal font of Saint John at Verona there is a dramatic account quite different from anything before or after, and exceptional beyond measure. A mere account of it will show how an imaginative artist can disturb the current and indicate strange possibilities.

The drama expresses the perturbation of the Virgin. The angel advances toward her with a strong step, the movement accentuated by his draperies and by his stretched-out wings. She rises to her feet suddenly, taking hold of the spindle with one hand and pushing it behind her, and raises the left hand almost as if in self-defence, even drawing back a foot as though afraid of the contact of the messenger. In the background two female figures lift curtains; perhaps their figures may be the beginning of the future lifting of curtains by angels, expecially the angel of the tomb. Here they look like attendants or friends of the family, or perhaps the two

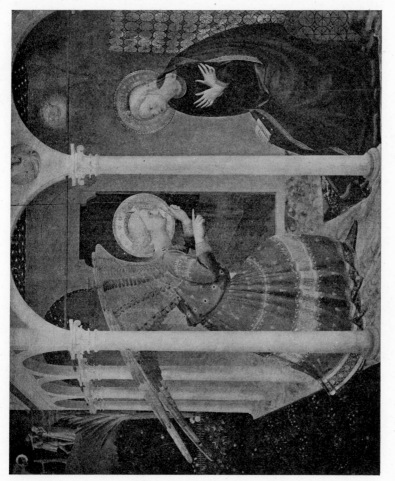

THE ANNUNCIATION. (Fra Angelico) At Cortona

women associated with the Virgin's story; and we may
connect with their movement, or with their expression
and their manner, an idea of curiosity which is distinctly
given in one representation, a fresco in the Church of
Saint Urban.

Dante gives to the archangel a palm, and the palm
begins to be an accepted attribute; in other paintings
the branch of olive appears, and then in the fourteenth
century we find flowering lilies — at first perhaps derived
from the imperial sceptre — also the lily of the valley,
among the opening blossoms of a garden. The whole
poetry of Christian art offers its flowers to the image of
Mary. Later they cover the very space of the scene
with gardens of suggested beauty. No longer does
Mary work, but she holds a roll, or often a book. In the
stories of apocryphal gospels the life of Mary is told,
and how she gave to prayer her early hours, and to work
so long, and then to prayer again, and then she meditated
on the laws of God and sang the canticles of David.

Then we find the arrangement of gold in which appears
the dove of the Holy Ghost. The image of the ray of
light, natural as we feel it, had to begin, and Tertullian
is quoted as saying that "the Word came from God
like a ray of light," but the poems of the Church give
us in many forms of verse the images which we have
accepted. Perhaps some antique tradition may have
suggested, through the forms of Jove commanding the
clouds, the image of the Eternal God who appears in the
later paintings.

Giotto in the chapel at Padua represents the Virgin
receiving the divine message serenely. With Taddeo
Bartolo she is pensive. She withdraws in fear in some

of the bas-reliefs of Orvieto; in the painting of Memmi
in the gallery of the Uffizi she seems the noble image of
purity, and at the words of the archangel turns to the
left, while she lifts a mantle as if to give herself protection.   Occasionally she sits on some antique chair with
cushions, her clothing adorned with gold, or in Gothic
edifices decorated with stars; again, through the door of
the chamber one sees, inside, the bed of the Virgin;
sometimes the chamber has a regal appearance with old-
time marbles and splendid tiling, coverings of oriental
carpets, and curtains embroidered with gold, while she
herself has a crown of gems on her blond hair, and gold
illuminating her mantle.   In such a way in the fourteenth
century was the Virgin honoured.

The extended hand, the oratorical gesture, was used
when the antique form of the archangel's attitude was
preserved.   Sometimes Gabriel crosses his arms over
his breast as he kneels before Mary, while she in humility
also bends the knee.

In the work of the Beato Angelico, the Virgin kneels
in a convent cell of San Marco, visible to the eyes of the
other pious monks, probably to Savonarola, who must have
seen it when he was at home; her slender figure kneels
on the high bench, the angel, with arms crossed gently,
speaks as if giving her a lesson; obedience, humility,
attention to what she is told appear in every line of the
figure of Our Lady; the fame of the painting is world-
wide.   The great Annunciation of Cortona is less known.
There Gabriel comes in with an impetuosity very much
in the feeling of the dear monk, who has used the same
movement several times, and the Angel's wings pass between the little columns of the chamber.   His hands

THE ANNUNCIATION. (Fra Angelico) At Florence

demonstrate and teach; one points to the Virgin and
the other above, as if to say: "This is what shall happen
to thee, so mind how thou receivest it." He is a real
angel, a messenger under orders, a being whose very
existence is that of the message, the carrying out of some
duty.

In other cases of Fra Angelico's treatment of the
subject we see how the real meaning of the story has
filled him. The plan upon which he works is different
from that of the mere artist, even if pious, or touched with
sympathy. It is like an exposition of doctrine. And
yet we know how his technical work advances the entire
trend of Italian art, and we can admire the accuracy
of gesture or motion and certain special points of form
or adornment. The Annunciation has with him something peculiarly virginal and simple; later the Madonna
enthroned, or lying in momentary death, is made more
stately, and so again when she triumphs in her Assumption
or in the crowning of her by her Son. Others have had
the same meaning; Lorenzo Monaco gives us a kneeling
Gabriel with one hand also explaining a lesson, while
the Virgin puts her hand to her throat as if her breath
stopped short, as one does at hearing some sudden
news.

In another Angelico, against a golden background,
Gabriel rushes in as before, and the Madonna bends
with a sweet expression of curiosity.

At Perugia the angel kneels at ease, carefully explaining, while Mary follows his tremendous message.

Or again in another convent room in San Marco
(on the door opening into a little cell) the Virgin sits
upon a wooden bench, and all is told as if kept within

I

the habits of ecclesiastical life. What exactly the good
monk would have given us later, had he followed this
subject all his life, one cannot quite guess, but his intention fits most beautifully the fact that so many of these
renderings of his beloved protectress belong to his youth.
Indeed, this youthfulness passes occasionally into the
bearer of the message, and gives him the look of some
young novice of the convent.

We must go back and contribute some homage of
admiration to other men less capable, sometimes even
awkward. In the painting by Simone di Martino a
kneeling angel bends toward the Madonna with arguing
hands and an olive branch, but she withdraws into herself,
full, as it were, of the presentiment of that life which
she explained to Saint Bridget in a vision; a life
equally divided between joy and sorrow. The gawky
gesture is sufficient to render the feeling, and it is a lesson
to us all who follow so closely our own admiration of the
technical beauties of art. We realize that in some cases
the intention is everything, and that to the poor and the
humble is given what the stronger cannot attain to.

In a fresco in Florence, whose author I do not know,
the angel kneels outside the little imaginary building.

Memmi passes a kneeling angel through columns
(evidently a trick of artists) and he smiles to himself
with pleasure at his message. On the other side, also,
within pillars and amid signs of household life the Virgin
sits, but with bended knee. Meanwhile the actual
Holy Ghost in the form of a dove comes lighting upon
her right hand, and illuminates her bosom. In contrast
to the spiritual significance, in a far corner behind the
stairs a cat looks up at the possible joys of food placed

THE ANNUNCIATION. (Donatello)

in a niche above her — a cat so badly drawn that it might be a devil or a wicked creature.

We ought to add a Spinelli, where the Madonna sits thoughtful within a little edifice, much ornamented in the Gothic way, which represents her room and her house. Her hands are crossed; she is by herself, all the more so that the angel is far outside and comes floating in a cloud through flowering bushes, with fluttering wings, but almost no motion. The same master gives us the Madonna again seated in some compartment; she has been reading and she listens to the story of the angel with attention, while he, very much intent, bends one knee, with crossed arms, and yet manages to lift two fingers in explanation.

One of the greater men, Orcagna, gives us, with the severity of his mood, a Madonna not too young, who, seated, looks down on the kneeling angel with the gravity of the more important person.

Piero della Francesca has a severe matronly lady within a columned receptacle, whose gesture means attention — it is not very interesting, but the angel's outline, with curved finger, is another variation worth noting.

Donatello carries us into the full meaning of future art. Not even to-day can we go beyond his power of expression, his skilful acceptance of all the difficulties of his task. In Santa Croce, in a vision of reality except for the ornamental background and surrounding, he has given to the Virgin a certain high noble beauty; she withdraws a little, almost out of the frame of the relief, so that she faces us, but turns her head to listen as if comprehending the full meaning of the message. Gabriel, deeply moved, with half-closed eyes and a dreamy bend of face and neck and body, half kneels in homage. He scarcely makes any gesture at all; his entire person tells the story and his lips barely whisper the message. That manner will be what Botticelli and others will keep to later, and so will Ghirlandajo.

CHAPTER VI

THE NATIVITY.   THE ADORATION OF THE MAGI

In one of the dark galleries which surround the Basilica of Saint Sebastian on the Appian Way, the Child, facing us with two animal companions, the ox and the ass, is painted on a bit of wood — a work of the fourth century.

We know little of the origin of this or that form of art, and we can never be absolutely sure. We may say that the evolution of the meaning becomes so entangled with the development of the technique that nothing appears individual, and yet any detail may be valuable, as indicating the spiritual training or influences of the artists who have left examples in the long trail of the world's history.

The moment of our story begins with the Gospels of Saint Luke and Saint Matthew, from which come the first descriptions of what is called, technically, "The Nativity," — the birth of Christ, — the entrance into the world of the entire Christian meaning. In those Gospels mention is made of Jesus, born in Bethlehem of Judæa while Herod reigned, and of Magi who, having seen a star in the East, followed it to render homage.

Saint Luke tells us what we usually see rendered: how Mary wrapped the child in swaddling clothes and laid him in a manger because the inn had no room for these good people driven to Bethlehem to be taxed by decree of Cæsar Augustus. Shepherds were keeping their flocks by night when an angel, wrapped in the glory of the Lord, came upon them announcing the good news, and with him a multitude of the heavenly host praising God, and the shepherds went to see what had come to pass.

The Gospel of Saint Luke does not speak of the Magi, but the two other Gospels melted together in the minds of the faithful. At first they hesitated at rendering the facts, especially those which brought in the actual human being, as the helpless child, or, later in the story, the sufferer dying on the cross. Abstract ideas are natural to the beginning of all art, and also prophecy and historical allusions. The prophet had announced that "The ox knoweth his owner, and the ass his master's crib: but Israel doth not know, my people doth not consider." Hence the images of the two beasts at the birth of a Redeemer. Saint Ambrose recognized in the ass the image of the Gentile, and Saint Gregory in the ox the Jew tied up by the harness of the law; he saw also in the ass the soul that carried a useless body of idolatry.

The more mystical the allusions of the Fathers of the Church were, the more the reality was impressed on the minds of the faithful, so that even to-day we refer to these images as if they were of events that we know. The pseudo-Matthew described the divine Child adored in the manger by the ox and the ass; the pseudo-Matthew was condemned by Pope Gelasius, but the ox and the ass remained forever attached to the meaning of the Nativity.

With the triumph of the Church through Constantine, we naturally have the tradition and practice of Rome, and the magnificence of marble and gold and mosaic to show the glory of the birth of Christ and the establishment of a great empire beginning with that happy day, then determined as being the 25th of December. The forms, the intellectual habits of him whom we call the pagan, must be used with a new belief; no longer in a compromise, with mere allusion, but with distinct affirmation, the affirmation of government both human and divine.

The pastorals of antique art came in to help the new artists. Already the early Christians had marked out in the darkness of the catacombs the figure of the Good Shepherd, so it was only necessary to take away the lamb from his shoulders and join him to the others at the stable where the Saviour lay in a manger. The first shepherds wear tunics, like those in the paintings of Greece and Rome. The Virgin brings back the type of the goddesses, perhaps a recollection of Juno, for the workman can only use the tools he has, and his habit of representing woman at a certain date must be that of the usual representation of women.

As far back as the third century we find stories like this: "There was in Persia a temple of Juno, built by Cyrus, and adorned by statues of the gods in gold and silver. By the conversation of these images the priest of the temple learned that Juno had not died, but had taken the name of Mary and had espoused a workman, and from this marriage was born the Prince of Work, who with infinite wisdom built the throne of heaven. Cyrus listened to the story of the priest. The roof of the Temple was open, and a brilliant star passing through the sky stopped at a column to the East, announcing the birth of a child who should be both the Beginning and the End, Salvation and the Ender of Death.

The wise men of Persia (the Magi) said to the king,
"'Go to Jerusalem and there you shall find the son of
the All-Powerful God under human shape in the arms
of a woman.' The star remained unmoved until the
Magi left and then went with them."

The Christian sculptors, like the poets, and the Fathers
of the Church, were obliged to keep to the style of the
pagans in explaining the new faith, and winged Victories,
leaving the triumphal arches of Roman rule, spoke to
the shepherds joyfully.

The first Magi, in Mythriac costumes, brought cornu-
copias and baskets of fruit instead of gold and myrrh,
hence some writers thought they represented the closing
of the older line and the beginning of a new dispensation.

As a continuation of symbolism, the star guiding the
Magi is often figured by a monogram written in a circle,
indicating to the faithful that the star was Christ, a
guide for men lost in the dark; and the Magi or kings,
according to the Fathers of the Church, called attention
to the contrast of Gentiles illuminated through truth, with
Jews persisting in the darkness of error. Mary herself
represented the humanity of Christ.

Long before Giotto (or perhaps merging into him)
the little stable had a roof and something to hold it up,
instead of the deep cavern rocks of Palestine. As we
have said before, the apocryphal gospels, not recognized
later, mingled their tales and their teachings with the
records of the memories of the faithful. Certain women
attended the Virgin, and Saint Joseph finds his place in
the story. The mystical representations no longer satis-
fied, and some splendour of divine illumination was sought
for.

In some of the earliest images we see the representation of a curious fragment in the pseudo-gospels, the healing of the arm of one of the supposed attendants of the Virgin, named Salome. She holds out her arm, which is cured by the Virgin. In another old ivory the Virgin listens to the complaint of Salome while Saint Joseph meditates or sleeps; this remained in the memory of the faithful, and far into the Renaissance Crivelli and Correggio continue the traditions so beautifully granted to the early painters.

After a long space of time we slip into Italy; what occurs there in art seems sudden, and yet we know that it was all prepared by the ancient knowledge of the South, and Nicholas of Pisa gives us, in an Annunciation, a classical goddess-like figure of the Virgin who kneels grandly and respectfully, and also that of an angel draped in the antique way, while near them (on the pulpit of the Baptistery at Pisa) Our Lady lies majestic, as grand, as antique, and as splendid as any later classical pupil of the Renaissance can hope for. The sheep and the shepherds gather around, while the Babe sleeps in a cradle shaped like an antique sarcophagus.

At Siena the story is touched by divine grace or by the Sienese air (for Siena was dedicated to the Virgin), and every figure becomes a little tender, however beautiful the draperies and the solemnity of the composition. Elizabeth in the distance is quite modern, and the Virgin smiles at her like any young girl.

The classical persists in Fra Guglielmo of Pistoia and John the Pisan (for sculpture keeps easily to the classical tradition from mere mechanism), and we find Orcagna giving us full curving draperies, which allow Joseph to sleep and the Madonna to dispose of the Babe (now full grown) in a long bed, guarded by ox and ass. Behind them is the wonderful suggestion of painting and of landscape which belongs to the great sculptor: a shepherd stands, a vulgar creature, in what might be called moonlight, if one dared to say that of sculpture; an angel, derived from the antique — not by any copy, but from sentiment — argues with one hand and points with the other; the Virgin moves the draperies of the Child.

The son of Pisano in Pistoia begins that beautiful motif for artists (the lifting of the covering of the Child), that will persist forever, and gives its name to Raphael's "Madonna of the Veil."

With Giotto in the Chapel of the Arena at Padua, we plunge fully into the art of painting, and we see the Madonna stretched out as naturally as if we had only looked at her to-day. She lifts herself a little from her mattress to turn or help the little Child; above them the angels almost tumble over the roof; the Shepherds look up outside, and although nearly violating the laws of perspective, they seem far away; even a great mistake in perspective, or in anything else, may not disturb an impression of reality.

The fascination of the camel began far back for the unaccustomed Western mind, to whom the beast even now is more symbolical than necessary as an instrument of travel or a carrier of burdens. Leonardo was happy in the possibilities of the camel, which is entangled in the following of the far-away worshippers, and in Giotto's "Adoration of the Magi" the ungainly beast snorts on the left hand of the familiar scene. Gravely and reason-

THE NATIVITY. (Giotto)

ably, as we might expect both from the picture and from the subject, the older king begins to kiss the feet of the swaddled Child, carefully held by the majestic Mother, who already seems accustomed to receive homage. The other two kings calmly wait to present their gifts. Joseph is absorbed in contemplation, and in the most practical way an angel has received a covered cup and holds it carefully.

We may smile, but the good sense of the representation amounts to poetry, and there are admirable matters of arrangement of balance in the composition. Destruction has attended certain parts; destruction has also, in the "Nativity," partly damaged the beautiful extended form of Mary, who in her bed begins to move the little swaddled Christ held up to her, possibly by Elizabeth. Her bed is within a covered space represented by a roof with supports — a type of the courage with which Giotto has handled architectural fact. Below her, Joseph dreams in the manner which before and after has been recorded. The ox and the ass look up as the sheep lie down confidently alongside of the shepherds, who are turned away from us, listening to a wondrous choir of angels above them, who whirl in many directions, but who all sing the great song. If a movement of line can give the impression of sound, Giotto has done it, and his manner of folding the cloak high up around the neck of the shepherd who turns his back to us indicates the slight chill of the morning air.

Again, the balance of the composition, and all those things that must belong to the better men are there and help us to see the other points. Italy will follow far and will carry out wonders, but never shall the place of Giotto be usurped. His "Adoration of the Magi" at Assisi has

certain elements of grandeur which seem chosen for
their majesty, and although real, as everything of the
master must be, there is a something of especial style, of
voluntary disposal, as if he had had ample time.   Here
the kings are reticent, and take proper places.   The
young one, draped after some antique fashion, waits
his turn with the next of age.   They are erect; the older
folds his hands; the younger watches him with an expression of waiting which would be extraordinary in
any moment of realism in art.   The Madonna sits
under some preparation of architecture such as Giotto
likes, brand new and elegant, upon a sort of throne or
high seat, attended by two noble angels who seem almost
like great ladies.   The little Child plays with the head
of the older Mage who is kissing his feet, and the Madonna
waits, seated like a reminiscence of the antique, which
may have come from Giotto's acquaintance with Rome
and its traditions.   Behind the Magi is a tumultuous
and not very respectful set of attendants, and with them
the camels thrusting their heads into the crowd.   All the
more noble appear the main actors of the scene.

In another of the paintings in the same place, the
Madonna again is majestic and classical.   She has been
stretched on the mattress and half rises to look at the
little Babe all wrapped up, while the angels sing and
fly in curving lines.   Outside in the night air the shepherds listen to them; the trees show that winter is
there; the sheep come tumbling in.

When we think of painting as a religious art, the
Angelic One comes at once to our minds.   So perfectly
was it understood that he was a "religious painter," that
for a long time ignorance of his development (and, indeed,

THE ADORATION OF THE MAGI. (FRA ANGELICO)

ignorance of the art of painting) prevented many admirers from understanding that the monk, apparently shut within his monastery, was also a leader in his art. (We realize, of course, that as a cleric he designs within the limits of necessities, within the limits of his calling.)

His Adoration of the Magi in San Marco is still within the mediæval feeling. The orderliness of arrangement, as well as a certain indifference to the setting, reminds us of Giotto; nothing tells beholders where the event is happening, but it is an event, though not an unexpected one. All the figures move steadily to the persons they have come to see — the Child and his Mother; the modest Mother and the Child who blesses them. The older king stretches out at full length on the grassy ground, and (a touch of realism worthy of Giotto) one feels the stiffness of his arms; he will not rise easily. His companions wait in the proper way of expectation and according to their age. All their attendants come up slowly; each has some special present; one man carries a terrestrial globe.

We recognize the probable visits of far-away people to Florence at the time of the good monk, by the long pigtail, the great sabre, and other varieties of unusual fact, including, of course, the necessary negro, but the younger king is of our own race. However interesting the attendants may be, the artist in Fra Angelico has not omitted to establish the central lines of his composition upon the arch of the tabernacle below, for (as we have just said) with all his piety and spiritual meaning, the Angelic monk was a painter also. The wise friar may have been learned or not, but he knew the traditions, and how the Magi became kings, for, as he has made them out, they are far from the shortcoated holders of religious secrets whom we see in the earliest representations. Their ancient names, Pudizar and Melchias, belong to that period, but already in the tenth century they wear crowns. The distinction of two standing and one kneeling, as in our picture, comes late, and as we now remember the story the Magi are called Caspar, Melchior, and Balthasar.

However beautiful pictures may be, the poetry of the hymns carries further than any realistic rendering. How can painting give the idea of the words of Claudian:

"Oh, man, the myrrh; Oh, king, the gold,
Oh, God, accept the incense."

In the old mosaics of Ravenna we are told that Caspar brought gold clad in a hyacinth dress, Balthasar brought incense in a yellow dress, and Melchior brought myrrh in a dress of many colors, and a long beard soon became inseparable from one of the kings.

Gozzoli fills the Riccardi Chapel in Florence with celestial creatures who sing and talk and preach and point, gather fruit and flowers, play with pet birds, and invade the landscape of Bethlehem with joy. Saint Joseph is no longer wrapped up in concentrated thought, but kneels and adores. The Child is surrounded by a glory of light. This representation of light will continue until we see it culminate in Correggio's "Night," and the supernatural light of Rembrandt, in itself a mystical creation as well as an imitation of reality.

In the picture by Fra Angelico in the Academy of Florence the shepherds come stepping carefully, and the angels are spaced as if around the Blessed Sacrament.

DETAIL FROM THE ADORATION OF THE MAGI. (Gozzoli)

We can do without the ass and the ox and the mattress and the place itself. The shepherds are there to explain the subject, but it is the religious meaning that is displayed for us, separated from any dramatic entanglement. There speaks the perpetual faith of the Church, as a moment ago we saw the joy of the faithful in the many angels of Angelico's pupil, Gozzoli.

In the beginning we may take the representations as just issuing from the obscurity of the catacombs, and in a doubtful position as to toleration or persecution. Whatever remains of the earliest moment is interesting to us as containing a reference to reality, and the costume of the Magi is poetic because it means innumerable relations to the mysteries of strange faiths. They wear short tunics and floating cloaks, narrow head coverings reminding one of Phrygian caps, and are still in connection with the extreme antique, and with the hidden things of the East, but for us the later Roman clothing is more impressive and the meaning more evident.

A few barbaric attempts pass very soon into our more modern and beautiful groupings. The Byzantine artificiality gives to the Virgin the look of an empress; the seat upon which she sits becomes almost a throne with steps. The Greek canon of painting[1] gives us this rule; "A house; the seated Virgin holds the Christ, blessing; the Three Magi offer gifts in boxes of gold; one, an old man with long beard and head covered, kneels, keeping his eyes turned toward the Christ, and with one hand he offers his gift, while with the other he takes hold of his crown. Second, very little beard; third should have no beard and, moreover, should belong to the negro race.

[1] Dedrion, "Guide to Painting."

They look to each other, showing the Christ. On the right of the Virgin, Saint Joseph should stand in an act of adoration. Outside the grotto a youth holds three horses by the bridle. In the distance, on a mountain, the Magi on horseback are returning to their own country with the escort of an angel."

The complication of the scene began in the oriental world and the West transformed the simple statement into a solemn reception, giving to the painting, as it were, the music and sound of the hymns of the Church for Epiphany.

Pisano recalls the barbaric images in a beautiful way: Mary is again an empress; the Magi are crowned and cloaked and booted and spurred; the Child accepts the gifts; an angel stands with the traditional staff. Except for that one mediæval detail, the bas-relief might belong to a Roman sarcophagus.

Later, again, with John of Pisa at Siena, galloping horses and the camel and dog tell us the story of the Magi's voyage, entangled with that of their further worship, which in Sant' Andrea at Pistoia becomes tender and intimate. The Virgin smiles sweetly down; the angel, who later wakes Joseph, is delightfully impressive, and the classical folds of the drapery do not interfere with the mediæval feeling.

Giotto has kept to the ancient simplicity, and has represented the Virgin with a thoughtful gesture, showing the Child to one of the Magi. The Child, princely here, welcomes the gentle homage of the elder king, while the others wait their turn.

Later in Florence the Blessed Monk will paint the scene on an artificial background of ornament, and we

ANGELS — DETAIL FROM THE ADORATION OF THE
MAGI. (Gozzoli)

shall see the Magi in the usual way, the elder prostrate, and the two younger with a modern fervency of adoration.

When we leave the fourteenth century these austerities pass into the representation of maternal love. In the painting of Gentile da Fabriano in Florence, the mediæval character, the Florentine anxiety for accurate representation, and the beautiful sense of ornament and of assimilation with the story, give an enchanting fulness of detail. From country to country the Magi pass; they go up mountains, they come down again; they pass over the drawbridges of castles; they are followed by their escort, sword in hand, and by hunters with tame leopards. The horses and the men become entangled together as they approach. All the more natural is the arrival of the large company upon a small scene. Thereupon all is graver; the older Mage kisses the feet of the Child, whose hand caresses the bald head; the other kings are clothed with gold and scintillating jewels, and the younger one's furs are being taken off.

As we come down the century the artist triumphs in every way; Botticelli and Ghirlandajo spread out proud compositions and bring in the costumes of Italian courts; symbolism disappears, and, as we noticed before, its ruin indicates the fall of the older world. In the fifteenth century all breaks up still more. The shepherds and the kings are no longer distinct; the story of the stable is put aside and the angels do not stand, but fly; Raphael touches the subject gently, and Correggio gives us a cloud of angels above the Madonna, who has bare feet, against the proper tradition.

We have left religious history to pass into the great field of art, an art not oblivious of sentiment, but with itself at the basis of the representation; we feel that the next day the painter will give himself with equal zeal to the story of Leda or some other enchantment of pagan tradition, or else to some merely human happening.

If we touch the North, we shall be both late and early; Albert Dürer, who comes down to Italy, returns to earn a living by woodcuts principally, and sometimes by engravings, which render the Gospel story accessible to a wide public.

If we look at these prints after the Italian decorations, they seem just what they are, spaces of black and white, but to us moderns they have a curious connection with our traditions, and perhaps even in their very frank and sometimes narrow statements we may feel that something which distinguishes Dürer, and which appeals to us of the less joyous races of the North, — that is to say, the touch of melancholy. When he shows us the black sun which illumines his "Melancolia," we have something that even the glorious sadness of Michael or of Leonardo has not for us. Perhaps we are too much influenced by Latin memories, and try to discern, in Dürer's frankly made statements, a more infinite revelation than his few fragments have to give us.

For he is certainly prosaic at times, as in the very beautiful print of the "Adoration of the Magi." He has little angels floating above, and there is a stile, and there are steps, broken with infinite care. There is a splendid Tartar in the distance, a record from nature, and the negro king is really African. All of this tends to prove that the design in itself is imaginative. The older Mage kneels stiffly but correctly; he is a great personage in his far country; and the next one, holding a vase with

THE ADORATION OF THE MAGI. (CORREGGIO)

three openings, remonstrates with his dusky companion, less high in position, — an image that takes us away from the mastery of the subject. Joseph is, however, anxious, and we feel a story in him and his face. He is holding a present in his hand, and the Mother is tenderly anxious about the proper behaviour of her Child — and yet we have spelled prose while we looked for poetry.

He gives us the shepherds in another woodcut. The first ones come in at the door, and commonplace, or, rather, vulgar as some of them are, they come with some important intention, and their astonishment is justified by the little fluttering group of angels gathered like birds around the Babe.

We are too severe, of course, because we cannot put the necessary business work of the great man in its proper place. We shall understand his meaning better when we look at the drawing in the Albertina. The pen and ink preserves to us the actual line of the master and that slight hesitation which belongs to handwork. The treatment of the subject is the same. The negro hesitates and is a real negro, with tremulous lips and retreating chin; he is booted and spurred, his barbaric ornaments jingle around his neck. He also is instructed by the middle-aged man who grasps him by the arm, and the older of the Magi kneels in an impassioned way. The Mother is draped as an older woman, beautifully and majestically, while Joseph looks on kindly.

We are now touching the real man fresh from his idea. Even the painting in the Florence gallery is not so great. It is beautiful; and the Child Christ sweetly accepts the offering of the older man. The negro is more princely, a man of middle age; he is a splendid creature, but something is missing, and we feel that it is important.

Rembrandt, the last great exponent of modern art, is also the last successor of the mediæval feeling. Some tradition, perhaps, may be there, some knowledge of Eastern countries remain, but as I said at the beginning of our study, it is interest in the synagogue which seems to have almost created Rembrandt. His New Testament is built out of the Old one, and is thus properly historical, and also ties together the past with the present and perhaps the future.

His "Adoration of the Magi" is one of the great pictures, but however wonderful as art, what is most important in it is its creation. Again we see what so rarely occurs, what shall not appear again until Delacroix comes in the nineteenth century — the representation of an actual vision. To-day we have the last expression of photography, which takes us at once into the momentary and accidental statement. In our painting the kings, or Magi, have come; the older one (for Rembrandt keeps to that necessary tradition) bends upon the stone steps outside of the thatched building which serves as a symbol of the stable, and which is lost in the Rembrandt mystery. Within it Joseph watches, perhaps, or dreams; we merely see that he is there. The Mother, draped in some Eastern manner, with a flutter of light around her head, uncovers the Child to the veneration of the old king. The Babe, in Rembrandt's way, is just a little newborn child all wrapped in swaddling clothes. The head of the old king almost touches the knee of the Mother — perhaps indeed it may. He has taken off his crown; its pressure is almost seen upon the forehead,

THE ADORATION OF THE MAGI. (Rembrandt)

where, indeed, the slight frown of veneration can be made out. In no painting, in no image, has that special look of worship been so completely understood and rendered; even the holy Angelic One is more abstract.

Behind the older king are two attendants, also not young. They, too, are filled with respectful belief in what they hardly see. They do not even look, but, as in the reality which we can see in the churches of to-day, they are drawn within themselves, within the contemplation of their own feelings. Behind the group another one of the kings, still crowned, stands. His left hand pushes back a younger attendant as he disposes carefully the vase which he intends to offer. Further back two strange figures step into the scene; one a bearded man with mitre and long cloak, and near him the strange swollen face of an attendant. Behind them again other figures, unaccounted-for occupants of space in the shadows which clothe them.

If ever there was a vision of mystery, of something unexplainable, whether religious as we mean it or not, we have it here.

The painting of the Magi is different, and of greater meaning than that of the shepherds, which is as it should be, for the meaning of the Magi is not clear. They are not made much of in the Gospel story, but the mere reference to them brings out a certain character of unusualness sufficient to make us understand the anxiety of Herod concerning these strange visitors. On the contrary, our delight in the representation of the shepherds is a feeling of pleasure over the actual realistic and truthful fact, as if it had occurred yesterday before our eyes. Of course there is also a wonderful arrangement of light and shade, and all that art which renders Rembrandt glorious in our eyes, although he was condemned and belittled, even within the memory of this last century.

The story is treated with some novelty: Joseph, as it were, almost explains it to the kneeling shepherds. His smile of pleasure at their coming is a curious study of human nature. He holds in his hand a light to show the little sleeping Babe, swaddled as usual. The Mother's arm stretches out toward him to fend off his arm and to guard from the danger of the light. The Madonna is ugly and older than necessary, but her hands uncover the Babe with a care belonging perhaps to an older woman. One might almost imagine that she is Elizabeth and not Mary, — but that is merely a bit of curious heaviness. The men appearing on the scene are no longer necessarily Jews; they are probably sufficiently Dutch. There, too, one must not press too far; those further back are strange enough for any Eastern story; the one who is carrying the lantern reminds us that Rembrandt never lost his curiosity about the East. Within the prosaic mystery, however strange, we recognize the forms of animals, and on some of the timbers of the strange building above is heavy drapery, probably carpets; on a cross-beam a bird of the night — certainly too strange for any ordinary barnyard fowl — grimaces weirdly.

Before Rembrandt, especially in Italy, or in the work of those who studied there, we still have the monuments of paganism represented; the fragments of the temples were there for everyone to use, and they appear in unfinished sketches of Leonardo, and in the carefully disposed stones and steps of Dürer.

However beautiful the many paintings of distinguished "religious painters" like Perugino may be, however perfect, however artistic in their promise of the form which Raphael shall bring to a triumphant close, we miss the feeling of anxiety to explain the Adoration, and the artist triumphs too much. To be sure, the suggestion of his day that Perugino was not a believer comes in somewhat as an explanation of his shortcomings, and he has in that case a right to interior reticence or scepticism as to accomplishing perfectly what he cannot quite feel.

In the North of Italy the Adorations and Nativities came to be elaborately composed upon lines which will remain forever; skill and distinction accompanied many of the smaller artists, and then appeared a painter of grace and sweetness who blended together the echoes of the songs of the Church and of the choirs of angels, who had a vision of the prophets, and brought human trust, penetrated by human devotion, to the Christian ideal. At first Correggio gives us a Nativity where the Madonna covers her right shoulder with a mantle as if to indicate the winter cold, and the moon, coming through antique rooms, sends down her silver beams. Even the trees below in the wind look as if the chill of Christmas night touched them too. Christmas is for us cold; while far off in the East, and far South in the isles of the ocean, Christmas is warm, sweet, full of fragrance and joy, and the shepherds of those countries need no more coverings than did a pagan faun.

In his famous "Night" the genius of Correggio finds its most complete development. The light which is born from the Child spreads all about and lightens the face of the sweet Mother, is reflected on the shepherds,

and on the angels that float in glory. This painting,
now in Dresden, is the synthesis of the representations
of the Nativity. As Leonardo in the "Last Supper,"
or Titian in the "Presentation" or the "Assumption,"
so Correggio makes the highest mark for the Nativity
with the "Night" and ends a long-beaten path of art in
a manner so Italian, so indicative of both the faith
and the affections of the people, that we realize what a
national art can be.

CHAPTER VII

THE PRESENTATION OF CHRIST IN THE TEMPLE. THE FLIGHT INTO EGYPT. THE REPOSE IN EGYPT

"And, behold, there was a man in Jerusalem, whose name was Simeon; and the same man was just and devout, waiting for the consolation of Israel: and the Holy Ghost was upon him. And it was revealed unto him by the Holy Ghost that he should not see death, before he had seen the Lord Christ. And he came by the Spirit into the temple." At that time the Virgin and Joseph were bringing the Child to Jerusalem to consecrate Him to the Lord according to the law of Moses, which prescribes the offering of a pair of turtle doves or pigeons.

Simeon took up the child and blessed God and said: "Lord, now lettest thou thy servant depart in peace." And Joseph and His Mother marvelled, and Simeon blessed them and said unto Mary: "This child is set for the fall and rising again of many in Israel, and for a sign which shall be spoken against; yea, and a sword shall pierce through thine own soul also."

Meanwhile an ancient prophetess serving God in the temple, and present at the ceremony, blessed the Lord and spake of Him "to all them that looked for redemption in Jerusalem."

In some early work, as in stories taken from the apocryphal gospels, angels accompany the Virgin. In ancient forms of sculpture Simeon received the Babe with veiled

hands, but later mediæval art dropped certain ecclesiastical features; the veil is omitted, a mere mantle being
sufficient for the respectful reception of the Child. The
first simplicity of rendering the story with four figures
changes to an accompaniment of angels and prophets;
Simeon in the character and costume inherited from Rome
takes the Child; behind him Anna, the prophetess, is
often studied from nature, and would be even to-day a
realistic treatment of passionate excitement. A number
of assistants are there, whoever they may be.

At length Giotto at Padua brings in nature. Near
the altar (upon which burns no fire as in Orcagna's
sculpture) Simeon, with long beard and hair falling in
curls upon his shoulders, holds up the Child, gazing upon
Him intently. The Babe — a real baby, more or less
struggling — stretches a hand toward His Mother. Mary
answers the Child with eager hands ready to comfort
and receive Him. While she reaches out her hands in
anxiety to hold the Babe again, Anna, quite wrapped up
in her mantle, holds the roll of prophecy and, bending
her head, salutes the Christ. Above them a floating
angel makes some sign.

At Assisi Giotto again repeats the story in another
variation of sentiment. The Babe merely looks at the
Mother with a smile of reassurance as she holds out her
hands to bring Him back, as it were. Anna addresses
the relatives, all listening attentively in different ways.
One of the attendants of the Virgin near her kneels and
stretches out arms for the cheering and helping of the
Babe, while Simeon looks up to heaven in thanks.

Giotto will carry us through until the end of the fifteenth century, when Francia and Carpaccio will tell

THE PRESENTATION OF CHRIST IN THE TEMPLE. (Giotto)

the story, and also with religious sentiment, but the scene has become a sort of religious ceremony and not the record of an event prepared by prophecy; hence, also, Anna is dropped from importance.

Luini places his Presentation within an antique temple, and the personages move freely and as if by accident, with reality and with the sweetness of Luini's character. Anna is an ancient crone; Simeon is absorbed in the Babe, who looks about for His Mother; the bishop's mitre of Simeon is carried by an Italian page; the turtles are brought in by some girls; and Joseph, a handsome, aristocratic personage, explains the story to the women of the family, one of whom holds her mass-book.

We have entered again into the kindly acceptance of stories that are beautiful, and there is no longer any necessity for insisting on any tremendous meaning; those methods are left to persons whose business it is to teach; painting is no longer a method of instruction, scarcely even of the lifting-up of the beholder. We must recognize that the Christian creed and all the teachings of the Church were now fully accepted, and also that the greater part of Europe was settling into shape, which accounts for the detachment of artists — they had other things to do.

The Legend of the Gospel of Infancy gives the story of the Flight into Egypt and its romantic details. As the Child passed, the idols of Egypt fell, music filled the air, fountains gushed beneath the sycamore trees, bad men and robbers fled, and all Earth smiled. Eastern fancy spoke in additional parables, bringing up changes of personality and marvels; the winds obeying the Child's will, dragons, lions, leopards, and wolves adoring Him. On the third day of their journey, the Virgin, suffering with thirst and heat, said to Joseph, "Let us rest under this tree in the shade." Joseph helped her from her saddle. As she looked up at the fruit above her she said, "I should like one of those dates"; to which Joseph objecting, the Child Jesus said to the palm tree, from the arms of the Virgin which held Him, "O tree, bend thy boughs and feed us with thy fruit," and the tree bowed its very top at the feet of Mary.

With time the early embellishments became fixed. The robber pardoned by the Holy One is the good thief on the cross. Peruzzi has painted at Sant' Onofrio in Rome the legends of the Flight, and somewhere the fall of the idols is recorded, which in a legendary gospel is said to have happened on the edge of Hermopolis.

In an ancient ivory at Bologna the Virgin rides triumphantly on the caparisoned ass. Joseph follows and guides, staff in hand, and the city, perhaps Hermopolis, personified in the ancient way, with hands covered as a mark of respect, bends forward to welcome the travellers.

At length Giotto gives us the elements of the past with the feeling of reality. The Virgin passes through the landscape, not ignorant of the future. One feels her silence; she meditates, as if knowing her own fate. On one of his paintings, in A sisi, the bending palm tree salutes the Virgin instead of keeping, as at Padua, its steady uprightness. Angels, in both pictures, flying above, indicate the way, or rush to the City in the Hills to open its gate. Joseph shows the fatigue of carrying necessary

THE FLIGHT INTO EGYPT. (Della Quercia)

food. The attendant girls converse together, as belongs to their age, and a charming youth leads the
ass. He does not understand why Joseph is so tired
and looks at him wonderingly. What we feel, without
knowing its mechanism, is that this is a travelling, moving party. They have come into the picture and they
will leave it. This is especially true in the Paduan
picture.

The subject pleased Rembrandt and he has tried it.
One etching, known as the "great Flight," gives us a
wide landscape, across which we look, with a winding
river far off and a tower and distant hills. The fugitives
are ready to go down into the river. The beast stops
at the brink. A woman is on its back; on the other side
a man, evidently young, holds it by the bridle and checks
it. It is again travel.

Another, which is unfinished, is at night perhaps.
They ford a stream. Joseph feels his way, leading the
ass, on which sits the Virgin, holding the Child to herself
with one hand; with the other balancing herself and
keeping a hold on the travel kit.

Not more natural, but more in keeping with symbolical
and historic meaning, is a sculpture by Della Quercia,
in the charming series at San Petronio in Bologna. It
gives us the passing of the travellers, the carefully hurry-
ing beast and rider, and the accompanying guardian
Joseph pushing and watching, for the road is heavy,
and dangers from men press also. The tired dog leads.
The Mother sweetly bends over the Child, pressed to
her and held by the long cloth that goes around His
Mother's neck. It is beautiful. This less-known man
precedes Michael Angelo, who worked in Bologna at

first, as we may remember. Della Quercia worked hard and found poverty or straitened means the reward of his labour. We have the full record of it all.

In the delightful sculptures at Orvieto a dragon at the forefoot of the ass bends down, perhaps reëntering his cavern in fear, as the legend tells, or (as the legend also tells) he may be crouching in adoration.

In a fantastic illustration by Lucas Cranach the Virgin sits under a tree. Above it play little angels, and a choir of them dance around Mary and the Child in an unbroken circle. Against the tree Joseph stands dreaming. It is a gawky but well-meant effort, such as we might expect of the master.

Seven years are given to the Repose in Egypt; then Gabriel called them back. The Repose, as the Flight, became a subject for art. Indeed we might believe that the innumerable images of sculpture and painting wherein the Holy Family are represented by themselves may have been, not purposely but unconsciously, begun from the Repose of the story; the image of their household life.

This suggestion of a halt in weary travel appealed to occasional artists. Rembrandt was sure to take hold of it, as he had the Flight, so we have a night landscape, with heavy trees; in the distance the towers of a town; lights in window openings; water in the foreground (the corner of some river); at its edge a wall of rock and cavern, and Joseph and Mary seated on the ground with the Babe. At a little distance from them a fire has been lit; a figure kneels and stirs it; behind him a group of cattle stands, and at a distance many others lie in

THE REPOSE IN EGYPT. (Correggio)

the landscape. Here and there, some shepherd by his sheep or cattle is touched with light. Certainly rest has come.

Much less natural, though in Rembrandt's "manner," is another picture in which we see the Mother with the Child in her lap, seated and extending a tired leg and foot; near her Salome is stretched out, resting on a tired arm and hand. All this is in full light, seen through the opening of a cavern. Joseph with his back turned toward us, and in the dark, sits on the edge of a rock. They are all shut in, the feeding ass included, and safe, for near them is the wall of a tower.

Before that Correggio had given us the moment of repose. The legend represents the Virgin, tired of course from travel, descending or coming off her saddle to sit in the shade of the palm tree, from which, as we know, the Child through a miracle obtained the fruit far above. Correggio remembers the legend and shows all together; water runs under the tree which gives shade to the Mother and the Child, and angels floating above seem to bend the branches of the palm tree, in which Joseph gathers the dates. The Virgin sits now at rest and smiles at the charming Child who takes the fruit from the fatherly hand in His own right hand, with the other stretched out to the cup of water which his Mother is just lifting up. We see behind the trees, at a distance, a child with a vase, presumably full of water. And Correggio has given us again the Mother and Child in the "Zingarella," which is certainly meant for a fragment of the scene of the Repose, for the angels above stretch out for the branches of the palm, and the Babe sleeps in the shade under His Mother's head bent over Him. Flowers grow about; and a little white rabbit has come to see what looks so beautiful.

Yet another "Riposo" by him in the Uffizi at Florence has the Virgin sitting against a great tree, gazing dreamily before her; the Child stands on her knee, stretching out his hand towards Joseph, who seems to be offering Him dates; and a monk kneels on the other side, in wonder and adoration.

CHAPTER VIII

THE DISPUTE IN THE TEMPLE. THE BAPTISM OF CHRIST

JESUS is already seated in the Temple, and on either side is a row of noble figures of ancient doctors astounded by His wisdom. Our Lord's figure has the expression of the teacher, the back severe and angular. One hand is raised in argument, slowly. Thereupon the parents come in. Joseph stands like the average onlooker, astonished at what he hears, while the Mother stretches out her arms toward her Son, happy to have found Him again.

Thus Giotto sees the Dispute. Earlier than Rembrandt he gives us the look of the synagogue. One listener draws back astonished, the other bends an attentive head, another seems to meditate over the words of the Boy as he passes his fingers through his long beard. Another has his hand up to his neck as if he does not quite agree with what he hears.

The pictorial representations of the Dispute vary in the place and in the arrangement. The occasion for composition is a fine one, but rarely does the expression of a spiritual event appear in the pictures, whether they are successful or failures. The Northern man, Dürer, in his set of engravings, has built the synagogue around the distant figure of the Christ sitting at a desk, and the Mother and Joseph come in almost casually, in contradiction to the care with which the Italians have always recognized the Madonna as an imporant personage of the story.   Her pursuit of the Child is a story itself, and even in Giotto the rigid composition accepts the influence of the two arms stretched out — the only real action of the painting.   As ever, Giotto is the man from whom everything flows.   His pupils and assistants at Assisi give us the story divided by columns, and with a number of figures whose backs are turned toward us, a novelty not quite successful and yet impressive as beginning a new departure.

The curious mind of Botticelli has placed among the listeners a clothed, monkish figure which is supposed to be the devil.   Everywhere in that land of the Madonna, and wherever the veneration for her extends, the tender presence of the Virgin is seen.   At times she is habited like a nun, at others in her usual draperies; but she always appears with her one idea of finding the Child.   There may be, but I do not remember it, some representation of the stern answer of the Boy to His Mother as to His employment in His Father's work.   Luini shows us Mary passing through the crowd of doctors seeking her Son, and He who, according to the text of the Gospel, should have answered severely, almost smiles at His Mother, lifting His hands on high.   As sentiment grows more and more in the painters, the persons present lose the character of listeners to moral law.   Giotto alone has kept in his first painting to what is the main statement before us, notwithstanding the tender speech of Mary; — that this is the voice of God speaking the doctrine to which all must listen.

Rembrandt's etching is too slight to be more than a reminiscence, though he has not missed the statement of the event being something important.

In early art the Baptism takes an important place. There are angels present, and in Eastern representations a suggestion of official assistants, as of deacons. At a fixed date (787), the Second General Council of Nicæa made the rule that Christ shall be in the centre, in Jordan, John to the left on the shore, the angels on the right, and over Christ, the glory of God. Even later than that the classical and beautiful use of a symbolical figure — the personified river — still occurs. In the thirteenth and fourteenth centuries we find representations of the water being poured on the Christ instead of His immersion; in ancient works both rites are represented.

With Giotto we have the double rite the attendant angels ready to clothe the Christ, John standing on the brink, according to the manner of the apostles, and a witness whose gaze seems one of mere curiosity. Christ is naked, but in order to meet the question of our feelings the wash of the water is spread over Him up to His waist. There is no attempt to make the water look as if it were real; it is merely a concession to Western and modern sentiment. Above, the blessing of God comes down; light is spread about; perhaps there are angels. Of course the merits of a Giotto cannot be questioned, but the face of the Christ is not of importance; however, the paintings were in such condition that they have of late been restored, so that our naturally severe judgment of any failing of the great master may not be in order.

We should, perhaps, have taken up the sculptures of the subject first, though in general our work is mainly among paintings. The sequence of thought, nevertheless, and sometimes of doctrine, is to be followed, and

sculpture has often marked some change of thought, as
it precedes painting usually in the development of art.

An early representation of the Baptism has the same
peculiar rendering of the water, showing it mounting to
clothe the Christ in part. The sculpture is childish in
certain ways; for example, John is quite an elderly person, bearded and strange. The Christ, also, is not young,
and meets the movement of John with a look of astonishment. Angels, too, fluttering in the foreground (or
rather, perhaps, kneeling) are full of anxiety; and from
above the Dove dashes down. Much later, in 1370, a
font of the Florentine baptistery is adorned on its six
sides with reliefs telling the story of baptism. It shows
an unaccustomed form of Florentine art, indicating perhaps Venetian influence. A curious and interesting point,
which may help to prove this influence, is that in the first
division the background is of a mountain upon which are
indicated trees with heavy foliage; a lion and another beast
roam about, and there is also a horse on the ground; the
trees which crown the scene throw their foliage beyond the
division and reappear on more than one side of the font.
The figures vary much in character, and show some
acquaintance with various Italian movements besides
the Venetian. We are passing from the ancient forms,
but there is an intention of doctrine which is interesting.

The first scene represents John baptizing the people.
The crowd kneel, after moving in a circle, partly in the
water, which is indicated sufficiently. The Baptist
wears the clothing peculiar to him. In the second
scene, John baptizes the Christ. In the distance there
is again a representation of landscape fitting into the
division and helping to separate the figures from the

distance. A stag feeds on the leaves of the trees, and angels descend as from the rocks. Already a full pictorial development is attempted from a specially technical point of view. This is again to be insisted upon as a new departure, following the manner of more Northern work. One feels the water flowing far back, although it is merely indicated. The Christ accepts the baptism of John with folded arms and an air of quiet; His feet only are in the water, and He is now partially draped. The Baptist kneels, the believers stand at a distance; the angels in the usual way kneel or stand ready to clothe the Redeemer.

The third scene has inscribed upon it "Christ Baptizes John." Again in the distance things happen which do not appear to have any bearing on the subject, but the complication of such matters is great, and it may be that the animals of the background have some relation to a hidden meaning, or perhaps to some text, although I have not been able to discover it. Under the trees a lion devours a stag, with rather successful realism. Two children gaze at the scene, evidently frightened. One of them stretches out his hands as if to climb into a tree. Two angels come on in full flight; various believers fold their hands in prayer, among them several women, who follow with devotion the baptism of John. One of them holds Jesus' dry clothing over her arms. The Baptist kneels, half clothed, upon a little indication of water, and the Christ pours water upon him from some cup or vase.

In the fourth scene Christ baptizes the apostles. Above, two angels drop in a half-circle from the distant mountain with the trees. One of the apostles kneels in the conventional water; the expression of devout acceptance of the sacrament is most beautifully given. Another takes off his principal coat or mantle, and two more in the distance do the same, drawing their sleeves over their hands. They look toward the angels, and perhaps address them, and the whole scene is remarkable as realism.

The drapery of the Christ, which is all that remains of His figure, is battered. Perhaps French invaders, perhaps mere unbelievers, perhaps German or Swiss troopers have done this as other things; as in France the Christs of the cathedrals, and thousands and thousands of beautiful windows, have been broken in the enthusiasm of new ideas; a sight more cruel even than the English destruction. Reformation in various forms has frequently wiped out what is most annoying to the reformers. So in far China the images of the Buddha have been broken by revolted Mohammedans in their momentary passage of barbaric triumph. That we are milder to-day, and that we no longer break church windows, is not a proof that the same unreason may not re-occur.

Two other divisions, by different hands, represent in a less successful way Saint Sylvester baptizing Constantine, and a priest baptizing children in the usual manner of the Church; both with realism having some interesting points of similarity to what we see anywhere to-day. There has been discussion as to the author of this font, notwithstanding the fact that Vasari (who should have known, but who is more or less inaccurate) gives the work to John the Pisan. This is what Vasari says: "He had worked at Orvieto with his assistants, certain Germans." (This statement about Germans may account for some peculiarities of style in the Italian art which they handled.) "John repaired to Florence after leaving Orvieto, partly to inspect Arnolfo's building, but also to visit Giotto, of whom he had heard great things related. He had scarcely arrived in Florence before he was appointed by the attendants of the fabric to execute the Madonna which stands over that door of the church which leads into the Canonical Palace." . . . "He afterwards erected a small baptismal font of Saint John, adorning it with passages from the life of that saint in half-relief." Our beloved Vasari is of course wrong here, for the date, as we know, is 1370, nearly half a century later than the death of John the Pisan.

Later, at Siena, Ghiberti the Florentine carries out for another baptismal font a decoration grander perhaps than that of his predecessors, but more artificial. An interesting novelty is the indication of a sky with clouds, cirrus clouds which break the apparently flat distance, otherwise quite empty. Here begins the search of the artist (by which we know him) for picturesque effects. Two women make some conventionally elegant gesture, while John, in a rather theatrical manner (compelled perhaps by the necessities of the composition) stretches out an arm violently. [I have spoken of the two "women" who hold some of the clothes of Christ, but they may be some form of angels.] The adoring angels above the Christ fly in the form of an arch, with hair floating in the wind, and with wings mingling with the clouds, as if sunrise would soon light the scene. Above the beautiful creatures, God the Father in a cloud, far away in space with seraphim, blesses the scene. Christ, whose drapery covers His shoulders in part, makes a gesture, graceful but uncertain, which again is not so far from the character of our artist.

In the next panel we see Herod sitting like a Greek ruler, helmeted and cuirassed, balancing on his knee a little globe representing empire, and ordering, not ungently, the arrest of the Baptist. The prophet raises his right hand in resentment or appeal as the soldiers lay hold on him. On the other side of the throne sits the unlawful wife of the Tetrarch, her hand upon her breast, quietly waiting for revenge. All of which is pleasing but somewhat irresolute, and although it is beautiful and picturesque, we recognize a tendency to diminish the force of the statement, which for us who follow the story is a need not to be replaced by the mere beauties of art. But the Florentine minds are already turning towards the new wonders, and Ghiberti is one of their great names deservedly; one of the glories of his city and of Italy and of the whole world. The search-light of our inquiry does not diminish him, for he did what he had to do; as a developer of the art of sculpture and a creator of noble pleasure he deserves his Florentine place.

Fra Angelico, at Saint Marco in Florence, gives us the Saviour as a tall, slight, graceful figure who stands looking upward in thought, with bare feet hardly wet by the supposed water. The Baptist steps violently forward to pour the water upon His head; His Mother kneels close by, in what I believe to be the only similar representation. Near, or behind her again, stands Saint Dominic, clothed according to his order, representing the meaning of the place and the patron of the painter, or perhaps even of the givers of the painting. Two little angels kneel with the

Lord's clothing, disturbing somewhat the solemnity of the story. Far above, in circles of cloud, the symbolic Dove appears, but the good painter (not so much a painter in this case as a believer) has not succeeded in separating his landscape from his figures.

In the Sistine Chapel Perugino represents the Baptism. In the centre of the long painting, with a little dove fluttering overhead, the Saviour and Saint John the Baptist stand in the Jordan. Saint John places his right foot on a stone in the water. He holds in his left hand the long cross, and with his right pours water from a gourd upon the head of the Christ, who prays with joined hands. Near them, at a sufficient distance on the shore, three kneeling angels carry the clothing. In the foreground, a mass of people, — all portraits of personages known to the painter. Further back, a number of figures coming to receive baptism, half clothed, or, rather, half naked. One of them has come quite close, and, seated, takes off his clothing. Above, in an artificial frame made of cherubim, God the Father holds a globe and gives a blessing.

The Spanish mark distinguishes the work of the Spaniards to a less extent than we might expect, considering its very strong character, and that it stretches from the time when Semites touched their shores on the way to far-away mines of tin and the strange islands of the North, up to the date of the Spanish painters coming to Paris, or London, or New York, when it gives again the same impression. The forms of their art, especially that of painting, have been derived from other nations, but quite innocently, which gives a type of expression that we recognize as honest.

A typical Spaniard is the Carthusian monk who painted in the Cartuja, or Chartreuse. His name is Sanchez Cotan and he may be considered to have a certain devotional feeling. Realism is carried far into the rather naïve representation of the edge of the shore and distant trees, and bits of architecture. The Baptist has apparently just clothed himself again, and makes a gentle gesture of pouring water from a cup or shell. The Christ bends, accepting the sacrament with the devotion of a neophyte; His head is Spanish, with long black curls. An angel or female figure stands ready, in a movement which is well known to us, to drop upon the Christ His garment of one piece. Above these two beautiful figures flutter little angelic forms, almost lost in the clouds, and the symbolic Dove is seen in part at the top of the painting. It is a case of the value of a strong feeling, worth more than mere art, as we have learned to recognize in our passage through history. As an illustration of the other side of Spanish character we may mention a realistic head of John the Baptist by the great artist Cano, a terrible representation, with gasping mouth and heavy frown and hair wet in the agony of death.

Murillo has painted the Baptism in the Cathedral of Seville. We recognize the special grace of the Master, almost too much perhaps, in the kneeling form of Christ, who leaves the water and kneels on the shore. He is naked but for a bit of clothing, and His long hair, with a Spanish wave, drops down. He is absorbed in the reception of the sacrament, and in that way the painter has carried out the feeling of his story. John baptizes with due reverence. He holds what sometimes annoys us of to-day as improbable, and what is merely symbolic —

the cruciform staff with the floating ribbon, upon which
is usually inscribed the text : "Bring forth fruits worthy
of repentance." Above, in the sky, two child-angels, with
little wings, such as Murillo loved, carry the Redeemer's
cloak, a great deal too heavy for them. They are respectful, however, and recognize the unknown meaning of
what they see. Above, a real Dove — a paloma —
makes a centre for the upper part of the curved painting.
We are far from the severity of the past, and nearly on
the verge of the next century's latitude. Notwithstanding, in his painting of "John the Baptist in the
Desert," one single figure against an uncertain distance,
Murillo has expressed what he might well understand as
a Spaniard, a frequenter of the desert or lonely places,
and the Baptist looks up expectantly, while an innocent
symbolic lamb gazes at him with curiosity. He also
holds the cross and the ribbon. Another Spaniard of the
name of Navarrete has given the Baptism with a singu-
larly realistic and imposing beauty. The Christ, almost
of feminine gentleness of face, but still noble, merely
bends the head enough to receive the water poured
upon Him from the two hands of the Baptist. Near
them three women stand on the shore, for the river is
hardly wide enough to make any difference. They are
angels, perhaps, and hold the usual clothing. Above
them, far up, more angels ; still further, the Father represented in drapery, and below in the middle of the picture, the Dove in clouds and light.

We are approaching more and more the verge of something not sufficiently respectful, and must look at the
curious Baptism of El Greco as the result of a somewhat
unbalanced mind, replacing sentiment by extravagance.

And yet one feels unwilling to judge the interesting master too severely (forced as he probably was to over-production) for often we do not recognize the business side of much that we think of as done in a spirit of noble competition. For us ultra-moderns exhibitions of paintings, such as salons and academy shows, seem to have existed forever. We forget that the famous "religious" pictures were usually done for business, just as much as the portraits that were produced in the gradual evolution of painting.

It is difficult to describe El Greco's Baptism. It represents the clothing of Christ on His coming out of the water. He is almost naked, and has just drawn up His foot on the rather steep shore. Strange guardian angels throw drapery over Him, while others take up the edges and apparently assist. One, however, lifts an arm in recognition of the marvellous sight above, where the Father appears in glory.

We must not forget a singular drawing by Rembrandt — a most realistic representation of the Baptism, if indeed we can call these slight scratches by that name; in the loose sketches of great men the meaning is as great, very often, as that of the most important finish, and here we see the vision of the actual scene. Christ has unclothed himself enough to enter into the water, which takes Him up to more than mid-leg. The Baptist also is plunging in, having lifted his clothes also so as not to get them wet. It is an astounding piece of reality seen by the visionary eye of the great man. What it might have been, carried out, we can only guess; we know that Rembrandt could always do what he wished.

The Frenchman Poussin has given us the Christ on

THE BAPTISM OF CHRIST. (El Greco)

shore, a beautiful, youthful figure, almost feminine, very much draped, bending, as it were, to Himself, and the Baptist coming to Him from behind carrying water in his two hands, to pour upon the head bowed low in humility. It is a very beautiful, almost pastoral, representation, and, like all the works of the Frenchman, respectful, and done in remembrance of the teaching received in his Italian life.

CHAPTER IX

THE PREACHING OF JOHN THE BAPTIST. THE DEATH OF
JOHN. THE TEMPTATION OF CHRIST

THE Baptist's life has naturally been a subject for
art, whether religious or for art's sake. The Gospel of
Saint Luke begins with the story of his birth, of the apparition of the angel to Zacharias and Elizabeth, and the
visit of the Virgin to Elizabeth. Saint Matthew tells
us of Saint John in the wilderness and his exhortation
to the people. The miraculous escape of Elizabeth and
her son from the massacre at Bethlehem is recorded by
tradition; also that he went to the wilderness while yet
a child, died at Machærus, east of the Dead Sea, and was
buried at Sebasto in Samaria. His severed head was
said to have been brought to Europe in the fifth century.

Saint John the Baptist is often pictured in child-
hood or youth, and his appearance in the desert is represented in various and very different ways. Sometimes
he is a tall figure, sunburned and haggard, his hair
and beard dishevelled, and scantily covered with a garment of camel's hair, his legs and chest and arms bare;
at others he is a youth, so near mere beauty that it is
doubtful whether one of Leonardo's studies represents
Bacchus or Saint John, and we see him pointing up in
many lovely pictures, merely because the painter did not
let such a chance escape; the painting by Leonardo in

THE PREACHING OF JOHN THE BAPTIST. (REMBRANDT)

the Louvre, where he holds the cross and points upward, is an instance of this.

Memling has given him with proper severity, and Van Eyck in his great altarpiece has shown him wearing over his arm a garment bordered with gold and jewels, and with his hair and beard long and dishevelled; these two carry out the tradition, and as yet artists had not seen their way to bring greater freedom into their treatment. Raphael has given him as the patron and witness, as well as the beautiful boy and the charming youth. The Spaniards take him as a child and place him with lambs, and suggest the pastoral meaning of his retirement, and of his already beginning life as a hermit.

When the priests and Levites send messengers to question John, asking, "Who art thou?" Murillo paints him with a mantle over his camel's hair tunic, and holding his reed cross. Three men are before him, one of whom wears spectacles; a lamb lies in the foreground; above are angels, scrolls, and the emblem of Saint Mark, from whom are taken the texts inscribed on the scroll: "The voice of one crying in the wilderness, 'Prepare ye the way of the Lord.'"

In the statue by Michelozzo at Florence, Saint John is treated in the same way, with the hair tunic, the cloak covering it, and the staff with the cross. The artist has varied the expression and action of the two angels; one is addressing many others, the other arguing to himself as if still to be convinced.

Rembrandt's etching of the "Preaching of John the Baptist" is, like that of the Annunciation, the realization of a possible scene, something of which we may judge if we have in our own lives heard the out-door discourse of some revivalist, some preacher for the open-air people who do not assemble in churches, who have no previous acquaintance with too many comforts.

Not that the people to whom the Baptist speaks are merely the poor, or people who are ready for listening. Many of them come together in rather a surprised way; we recognize groups of men and women settled into positions; there are many who do not listen; there are strangers from far away, a coloured woman or so, monkey-carriers, here and there a pleasant face. In itself this little group of the caravan is beautifully suggestive of the passing crowd, an appeal to minds that are on the wing. These people may carry the good news very far; it may reach the Indies, and nations that only slowly shall be known to us as having heard the story.

In the foreground three wise men stand in argument; one evidently holding to the proper observances, perhaps some Pharisee with phylacteries around him. They turn their backs to the preaching, but not from any want of interest; it is the natural manner observed by Rembrandt in the crowds addressed by some great mover of minds.

A cautious pursuer of the truth is trying to follow in a book; near him is a crowd of children and women; the children are being told to keep quiet and not disturb the preacher. Many of the audience do not care, and others have come for the outing; quite in the foreground children play. The Baptist is in strong light, with the curved shoulder and outstretched hand of the preacher convinced of his truths; his mouth opens with his steady call; his eyes are the least important part of his face.

THE DEATH OF JOHN THE BAPTIST. (Donatello)

It is a wonderful story; something tells us that this is important news, and something unutterable separates the great man's view of the scene from the vulgar scene itself.

In his treatment of the Baptist's death Donatello had his usual success in every department of the bas-relief. Indeed, he may be said there to have carried out the four effects which Ghiberti, in speaking of his own work, lays down as necessary. He said that every such work should contain four representations well made out, or the effect of four representations, and Donatello has placed his figures on several different planes. In the first, the Baptist's head is offered to Herod by Herodias during the feast; further back are musicians; far away, on another plane, we see through the windows the executioner showing the head to outside figures, who may be Salome and her mother; in the foreground a soldier, kneeling, presents the head of the prophet to Herod. The evidently drunken tyrant draws back in fright; two children hurry away; Salome interrupts her dance, with a frown difficult to explain. One of the guests covers his eyes. The entire group rise to their feet, taking hold of one another, and even the dishes are pushed away in disorder.

The tragedy is a grand one, and here the artist begins the full use of all the powers of sculpture, so that the bas-relief has quite the scope of a painting; indeed, as we have said before, Donatello would have been a great landscape painter.

There are musicians also in the painting of Quentin Matsys at Antwerp, he whom love "de muliebre fecit Apellem." There we have an ugly tyrant, bearded,

and frowning like the Wandering Jew; Salome pushes
the plate containing the head upon the fair white table-
cloth, and her lady mother already cuts at the tongue
of the Baptist. We feel as if a memory of mediæval
atrocities had passed into this otherwise graceful and
gentle picture. It is a pretty scene, notwithstanding
its subject, and not so far away from the habit of mind
that gives us the painting wherein the Persian king, Cam-
byses, seats a young judge in a chair draped with his
father's skin, torn from him while alive as a punishment
for bribe-taking.

In a painting by Filippino Lippi, Elizabeth is bending
over her son and resting her cheek upon his head as she
presses him to her, presumably before he goes into the
desert; it may have been suggested by seeing a boy taking leave of his family before departing for his service,
so natural is it.

A bas-relief by Andrea Pisano represents John's disciples carrying his body to burial, and there is a tradition that he waited in Hades or Limbus until Our Lord's
appearance there.

The representations of the Temptation are few. It
may be that Mrs. Jameson is right in suggesting that it
was not a subject liked by the Church, a reason which
might be sufficient. The association of ideas would not
appeal to the devout, nor would its rendering be followed
by the prayers and thanks of the faithful.

It is shown, however, in one of the set by Tintoretto
which forms the decoration of the Scuola di San Rocco
in Venice. These pictures are among the very greatest
triumphs of the master. They are based on landscape,

THE TEMPTATION OF CHRIST. (TINTORETTO)

and take hold of our imagination because they have been imagined, not made up, and look as if they had really happened.

Our Lord has had built for Him just enough shelter to protect Him from any sudden change, for the climate, though not Italian, is not that of Palestine. Some bits of wood have been fastened to the growing trees; Jesus sits there and listens with remonstrance to the offer of Satan. And it is a real Satan, a real tempter, that rises to address the Christ. With all the beauty of woman, like some Greek god, the demon half kneels, half rises, from the ground and offers to Our Lord the stone which He is to change into bread. Satan's fair hair blows in the wind; his eyes are wet with joy; we are confronted with an unknown power, evidently not of earth. The wings are ugly, and perhaps meant to be so, but that is all that can help one to know who it is, except that from the entire figure disengages something that is not right, something that is out of place : it is the real and only incarnation of the devil ever put into painting. And the painting is beautiful; it would be pleasant to look at all the time, were it not that the eye must go behind this devilish beauty which has no other meaning than that of ironical enticement. Satan does not half believe in his chances, but, as we have said, angels were supposed to enter deeply into the meaning of their earthly occupations, and our Satan is a fallen angel.

We have in the background of Botticelli's fresco of the Sacrifice of the Leper, in the Sistine Chapel, another representation of the Temptation of Christ. It comes near being extremely important, notwithstanding that it is merely a fragment of the distance, nor is it easily connected with the entire story, unless one knows that the meaning of the painting was a vindication of the apostolate of the Pope, who therein triumphed again over his political adversary. The Pope was Sixtus IX; his enemy, Andrew Zamometic, Archbishop of Krain, who called a general council at Bâle and otherwise attacked His Holiness. Zamometic's end, as we know, was bad; he was put into prison and committed suicide there.

On the left, high up on a mountain of arbitrary shape, Our Lord is accosted by a monk. The monk puts a question to Him by pointing to the stones at His feet, and Christ puts away the question with His hand, gently raised in remonstrance. In the middle of the picture, also high up, is a temple, a Renaissance building, recalling the Pope's special interest in architecture, and in the uppermost part, where a cupola might have been, Christ again is asked by the same monk, evidently now a devil, to cast Himself down, while the answer, "Thou shalt not tempt the Lord thy God," is signified by the simple gesture of the Redeemer. A third scene on the right shows us the minister of Hell disrobed, his monk's vestments flying away from him as he plunges over the edge of the precipice, followed by the passionate gesture of Christ; the translation of the words "Get thee hence, Satan." At the same moment three sweet angels — Botticelli's angels — place a table covered with a cloth, and with wine in the proper flasks; a suggestion of elegant home life which is delightful; we feel that the trial is over. On the left Christ is coming down talking to the same angels, perhaps explaining to them what has happened, as He stretches out a hand to make His statement more distinct. It is an idyll; that is all.

As Milton tells us in the beautiful lines of the " Paradise Regained " : —

> " So Satan fell; and straight a fiery globe
> Of Angels on full sail of wing flew nigh,
> Who on their plumy vans received Him soft
> From His uneasy station, and upbore,
> As on a floating couch, through the blithe air;
> Then, in a flowery valley, set Him down
> On a green bank, and set before Him spread
> A table of celestial food, divine
> Ambrosial fruits fetched from the Tree of Life,
> And from the Fount of Life ambrosial drink,
> That soon refreshed Him wearied, and repaired
> What hunger, if aught hunger, had impaired,
> Or thirst; and as He fed, Angelic choirs
> Sung heavenly anthems of His victory
> Over temptation and the Tempter proud."

CHAPTER X

ONE of the earliest sculptures gives us Christ and the woman of Samaria on either side of a draw-well. They are both idealized; He is young and meant to be handsome, and wears the cloak of a philosopher; she has drawn up the bronze bucket, and Christ extends His hands as one speaking. It expresses the meaning of the words of our Lord, "I am the living water; whoso drinketh of the water that I shall give him shall never thirst." One likes to think that this sculptor is one of those of whom the Fathers have spoken as giving his work to the Church. We, to-day, can in our modern wanderings reach the sacred places readily, and see the well where our Lord sat with the good woman, a very different well from the pure ideal of our sculpture.

The Samaritans were fragments of colonies long settled, of different races, but established by Assyrian power. The Jews looked upon them as strangers, and were divided from them by a stern hatred, reciprocated on the other side. These schismatic half-believers were excommunicated by the Synagogue, but business interests and consequent relations kept up a manner of acquaintance. As our Lord crossed this land of Samaria He stopped at the gates of a town called Sychar, feeling weary (St. Augustine tells us that His journey in the form of the flesh was taken to meet humanity).

His disciples passed into the town for food, as their habit was not to carry any with them, and Jesus sat down on the brink of the well. Abraham had raised an altar in ancient days at Sychar, and there Simeon and Levi, sons of Jacob, had killed many Shechemites to avenge their sister Dinah. Jacob having bought land for his flocks had bequeathed it to Joseph, and had there dug a well which was known by Jacob's name.

There came a woman to draw water, and Jesus said unto her, "Give me to drink." She hesitated, and asked how it was that a Jew asked a drink of a woman of Samaria.

"Jesus answered and said unto her, If thou knewest the gift of God, and who it is that saith to thee, Give me to drink; thou wouldst have asked of him, and he would have given thee living water.

"The woman saith unto him, Sir, thou hast nothing to draw with, and the well is deep; from whence then hast thou that living water?

"Art thou greater than our father Jacob, which gave us the well, and drank thereof himself, and his children, and his cattle?

"Jesus answered and said unto her, Whosoever drinketh of this water shall thirst again:

"But whosoever drinketh of the water that I shall give him shall never thirst; but the water that I shall give him shall be in him a well of water springing up into everlasting life.

"The woman saith unto him, Sir, give me this water, that I thirst not, neither come hither to draw.

"Jesus saith unto her, Go, call thy husband, and come hither.

"The woman answered and said, I have no husband. Jesus said unto her, Thou hast well said, I have no husband:

"For thou hast had five husbands, and he whom thou now hast is not thy husband; in that saidst thou truly.

"The woman saith unto him, Sir, I perceive that thou art a prophet.

"Our fathers worshipped in this mountain; and ye say, that in Jerusalem is the place where men ought to worship.

"Jesus saith unto her, Woman, believe me, the hour cometh, when ye shall neither in this mountain, nor yet at Jerusalem, worship the Father.

"Ye worship ye know not what; we know what we worship; for salvation is of the Jews.

"But the hour cometh, and now is, when the true worshippers shall worship the Father in spirit and in truth; for the Father seeketh such to worship him.

"God is a spirit, and they that worship him must worship him in spirit and in truth.

"The woman saith unto him, I know that Messiah cometh, which is called Christ; when he is come, he will tell us all things.

"Jesus saith unto her, I that speak unto thee am he.

"And upon this came his disciples, and marvelled that he talked with the woman; yet no man said, What seekest thou? or, Why talkest thou with her?

"The woman then left her waterpot, and went her way into the city, and saith to the men:

"Come, see a man which told me all things that ever I did; is not this the Christ?

"Then they went out of the city, and came unto him.

"In the meanwhile his disciples prayed him, saying, Master, eat.

"But he said unto them, I have meat to eat that ye know not of.

"Therefore said the disciples one to another, Hath any man brought him aught to eat?

"Jesus saith unto them, My meat is to do the will of him that sent me, and to finish his work."

There are two beautiful etchings by Rembrandt, one called the "upright plate." As usual, he has *seen*. The well is a half-ruined fragment of the past — it is square on the outside and round within, and stones have been put against it to hold it up, for it is Jacob's well. Christ is sitting on its edge, and His hand covers the further rim; behind Him are parts of an old building against whose ruined wall is set the well-sweep. The Samaritan woman, amiable and anxious, holds the rope hesitatingly, and her bucket stands on the upper edge. She is listening astonished; Christ, with one foot raised, is arguing; He is a Jew, and a doctor of the faith; behind them both opens a city some way off, and coming up the hill toward them are the disciples. But a still more extraordinary etching is the "plate in width." Here the Lord is even more a Jew; He stands, and we see only a part of Him behind the well; He speaks, His hand is pressed against His heart, the other lies against a stone of some ruin, and His face smiles with a look kindly and good, but still indoctrinating; the woman stands on the other side of the well, her bucket balanced on the edge, her hands crossed on her waist, listening patiently; slowly the apostles (if it be they) come up the hill, and behind them again opens a wonderful creation, a city on a hill, seen evidently, and a likeness, but of what city? Did Rembrandt, with his extraordinary memory, and his painstaking habit of getting any information possible, have documents for each of these many scenes?

He treated the subject again in a painting which formerly belonged to Rudolph Kahn. Here is a distant view: there is a wall outside a town, the large arches opening on the sky; from the town come various persons curiously looking; they may be the disciples, or they may be men of Sychar. Christ and the woman are behind the well, or, rather, she is on one side of it, and He is seated alongside in half shadow; she has dropped her bucket halfway down, and holds the chain with

two hands, looking at Him, and evidently not believing;
over the edge of the well a curious child, partly hidden,
looks up.   The Christ, again a Jew, we see in half shadow,
and He talks with uplifted hand, explaining.   No description can give the extraordinary accuracy of this tran-
scription apparently from nature.   Compared with this
curious vision the very interesting, but less poetic, painting
at Saint Petersburg is more of a set composition.   There
Rembrandt has again put a child listening and following
the conversation; we merely see his head, and he is
evidently a stranger.

We may give, in comparison to the Rembrandts,
a painting of that serious and religious man, the so-called
Jansenist Philippe de Champaigne, which follows the
classical French teaching and tradition of meeting all
the points of the story.   The woman standing both
accepts and rejects — she is astonished, but not inimical;
behind her we see a classical well and a classical urn;
Christ, seated on the edge of the well, leans with one
arm on a bit of stone, that arm and hand pointing up,
while the other hand is spread out in expostulation or
explanation; His face is handsome and dignified, worthy
of the serious mind which elaborated the picture and
filled in the architectural distance, in all probability
made up of Eastern recollections and bits of old France.

In the graceful poise of all the lines, in the simplicity
of the intention, there is something dignified, which has
made me choose it in preference to more picturesque
representations.

We may forget how our Lord passed from one place
to another, and on what exact mission, and what its

CHRIST AND THE WOMAN OF SAMARIA. (Philippe de Champaigne)

end, but we remember His parables and sayings, and their messages. Within our narrow compass we can only give the parable of the Prodigal Son. He who thinks that he can state the Story of the Gospel better than as given in the text has not understood it. The text is better than any commentary.

Rembrandt has painted the return of the Prodigal Son definitively. We see the father looking toward us, bending over the ragged creature who, kneeling, hides his face in the fatherly bosom. Pity and love pour from the father's venerable and yet over-sensitive face; his hands press with a sort of hesitating encouragement upon the shoulders of the prodigal. For him all else has disappeared — there is but this one event, the return; the prodigal, too, has but one expression: he is back again at last, and his closed eye dreams of the past which is happily over. The bystanders do not approve. The brother looks down on the weakening of the father, and each line of his face, from uplifted eyebrow to drawn-in mouth, objects to such want of principle. Every detail of the face is a study, and the hands, too, are part of the protest — one thumb has passed over the other, and will again go under, and the first come up. The other seated figure is rather curious, but looks at the scene dispassionately; he also is not a partner in the welcome; behind all some woman's face and shoulders appear, perhaps the daughter, or daughter-in-law; she, too, has a look of curiosity, and not of sympathy. The old man is a squanderer of the good things that belong to him. The painting is in itself a parable.

There is another Rembrandt, an etching, done many years before the painting: it is dated 1636. However great the artist, however inventive, however intelligent as an observer of human nature, the older man who painted the first picture would understand the subject better, and perhaps might himself have felt the feelings that he painted. Still, as invention, the famous etching deserves its place. The father comes rapidly out of the house to meet the half-naked son who kneels and presses his head against his father's heart, the father frowning upon him with anxiety as he realizes the miseries crowded into the body of his son; his emaciation, his cramped legs, his trembling arm, while he himself is comfortably robed and slippered. Higher up some one brings the necessary clothing down some steps; perhaps it may be the brother; there is no good-will, and the woman who opens the shutter and looks out is also not in favour of the old man's weakness; we might say even more, as we note her savage frown and the ugly eye that lights up her face.

THE PRODIGAL SON. (Rembrandt)

CHAPTER XI

CHRIST IN THE HOUSE OF MARY AND MARTHA. THE
MARRIAGE OF CANA

The Lord had rebuked the Pharisees, thereby giving a lesson to His Church, so that the illusion of a false idea of justice should not corrupt the truth. There have been Pharisees among Christians, because all vices belong to the human race, but nothing is more opposed to the Church than Phariseeism in doctrine or in manner.

Passing by Bethany, Jesus rested in a certain village; "and a certain woman named Martha received him into her house. And she had a sister called Mary, which also sat at Jesus' feet, and heard His word. But Martha was cumbered about much serving, and came to him, and said, Lord, dost thou not care that my sister hath left me to serve alone? Bid her therefore that she help me. And Jesus answered and said unto her, Martha, Martha, thou art careful and troubled about many things; but one thing is needful: and Mary hath chosen that good part, which shall not be taken away from her."

Tradition holds that Mary was the Mary Magdalen forgiven at the banquet of the Pharisee Simon. Of what Jesus spoke that day the Holy Spirit has preserved only this word of the "better part" which explains the one thing necessary for the happiness of the soul, the one thing without which all is fatigue or only momentary pleasure. Martha is not blamed, for she wishes to help, but she learns that work done for the Lord is to be done in peace and humility; that it is especially through love that He is to be served. Thus the teaching goes into the question of the contemplative life. The saints have looked upon God in contemplation. Martha has served the Lord, but Mary will be at the foot of the Cross.

Two famous painters have given us that visit. Velasquez painted it in his earlier days in what we might call a vulgar way, because we cannot in our modern falsity of impression get rid of the idea of pictures in galleries, and the competition of exhibitions; we forget that religious pictures formerly served in the ordinary household as reminders; a dining room might have pictures taken from the Gospel or the Old Testament or the lives of saints, whereas now we should have only the Banquet of Simon or the Marriage of Cana, and so forth. If there be one thing in which I can help my readers, it is by recalling to them this fact. Then at once the idea of "the commonplace" will disappear, because we are only looking at something meant for the home life of every day. Occasionally the treatment of such texts passes into splendour, as in the great Paul Veronese and other beautiful canvases; but there must have been small people who needed small things; so Velasquez painted a kitchen scene. The cook is at the table, or, rather, probably, a young kitchenmaid. She is seen at half length, using a pestle and mortar. On the table there are some uncooked fish, a plate of eggs, and a water jug. An elderly woman close behind her touches her on the shoulder and points, giving her some order or reproof, and she listens indifferently, with the usual unwillingness to obey. In that way the painting is all that it can be. It belongs to a class which the Spaniards called "Bodegones," that is to say, kitchen and tavern scenes, at a certain moment the fashion throughout Spain, as we remember in thinking of the novels of that period: this is one of the results of the new movement. Pacheco, Velasquez's father-in-law, said of him: "He disliked plebeian art, and yet are we to hold these Bodegones as of no account? No; they are certainly to be valued; these, when painted as Velasquez paints them, deserve high esteem, for with these elements he discovered the true imitation of nature." And the great Palamino says: "Velasquez in his early days took to representing with singular fancy and notable genius, beasts, birds, fish, fishmarkets, with perfect imitation of nature; also all manner of household goods, or anything necessary which poor, beggarly people in low life make use of."

All this explains the naturalness of certain early works of his. But now comes the wonderfully realistic and yet noble representation of the story. We are, as I said, in the kitchen, but in the background, in what appears to be an inner chamber, seen through a door, the Saviour is addressing Martha, who has come forward to protest concerning Mary, who is kneeling before Him. The scene is Spanish; Mary is a young Spanish woman with long, loose hair, and of an absolutely different type from Martha, with just the expression that we need for a suggestion that she may possibly be Mary Magdalen, and yet not too much. Martha is what she ought to be in every language and in every race, and the Christ, though not very spiritual, is still a preacher. He speaks with the manner that Velasquez must have seen in religious

Spain; the same that we know in all countries. The
story is perhaps all the more real from that simple scene
in front. Indeed, if it were not for our prejudices, it
might almost be Martha who, in the foreground of the
picture, addresses the indifferent kitchen maid.

Far apart in one sense is the Tintoretto. We are in
Italy; the costumes of the two women are purely Venetian.
One of them, Martha, is in her best dress to receive a
visitor, and we feel that Mary should also attend to the
reception of their guests. Christ is not alone; there is
some one at the table, there is someone else coming in,
and outside is the group of disciples in the sunlight.
We should think of the scene as more enclosed, in more
of a chamber perhaps, but Tintoretto paints a Venetian
habit of hospitality for us. We do not know for what wall
it was painted, in what home it was meant to remind the
household of something beyond the dinner or supper at
which they were gathered. The meal, also, in the Italian
way, is prepared within sight. We are in the best room,
but the curtain is partly drawn and we can look into a
generous kitchen where a maid is at work, and where on
the wall, on long shelves, are arrayed the plates which
are both for the pride and for the use of the household.
Below there are other things for the table, and white
napkins and a tablecloth. Christ argues, teaching and
explaining, but much more as addressing Mary than as
rebuking Martha. He, too, is of Venice, as far as His
gown and His cloak, and His hand argues in the Italian
way. Mary does not exactly kneel; she seems to be
rising under the rebuke of her sister and hesitating while
listening to the words that save her from blame.

The painting is, of course, a grand composition, but

CHRIST IN THE HOUSE OF MARY AND MARTHA. (Tintoretto)

that we expect from the great man whose faculty for letting himself go brings often to our minds the great Rembrandt.

Another remarkable man, not a genius, but a person of much nobility of character and of expression, almost within the influence of the meaning of religion and the influences of the Gospel, but with the defects due to the regularity of the French mind, has painted the subject very differently — I mean Le Sueur. Here we have the tendency of his moment, which could not be further from that which moulded the art of Velasquez. We are in the presence of what is called "the academic," and yet there is throughout a sense of the real scene, especially in regard to the persons of the background, such as the men bringing down baskets and being told where to go by the major domo, and (seen through the high-arched door of the French convention) the maid servant spreading the tablecloth on a noble table. Back in this large hall stand the apostles, a noble group, quite indifferent to the scene, and apparently seeing nothing of it, but beautifully posed and all within the French tradition which was just beginning. In the middle the Saviour sits on the classical seat, with one foot on the footstool offered to the guest : He points with one hand upward as referring to "the better part," and with the other He expostulates with Martha. His is a noble figure, but still academic. Martha is a Frenchwoman of the period — that period floating between Jansenism and the opposite — and her gesture, which is quite right, belongs to a respectful and orderly France. Mary kneels, listening, absorbed in the saying of the Christ ; her hands are clasped, as one who listens to a lesson. In that way we have a splendid presentation and yet, relatively to the simple statement of Velasquez, it is not filled with reality.

"And the third day there was a marriage in Cana of Galilee; and the mother of Jesus was there.

"And both Jesus was called, and his disciples, to the marriage.

"And when they wanted wine, the mother of Jesus saith unto him, They have no wine.

"Jesus saith unto her, Woman, what have I to do with thee? mine hour is not yet come.

"His mother saith unto the servants, Whatsoever he saith unto you, do it.

"And there were set there six waterpots of stone, after the manner of the purifying of the Jews, containing two or three firkins apiece. Jesus saith unto them, Fill the waterpots with water. And they filled them up to the brim.

"And he saith unto them, Draw out now, and bear unto the governor of the feast. And they bare it.

"When the ruler of the feast had tasted the water that was made wine, and knew not whence it was (but the servants which drew the water knew) the governor of the feast called the bridegroom.

"And saith unto him, Every man at the beginning doth set forth good wine; and when men have well drunk, then that which is worse; but thou hast kept the good wine until now."

It was not only in such a case as the meeting of the Jew with the Samaritan that the Pharisee was shocked — a perpetual watchfulness followed the Saviour in His journey, as to what He said and did, and as to His mingling freely with persons of easy life, and so we have records of the feastings. We have noticed the use of certain paintings in dining halls and in refectories to bring in some pious feeling at mealtime, as if asking a blessing on the meal and also making formal recognition of the propriety of religion. The great people who have

been able thus to decorate their walls have invariably
represented the particular way of thinking of the period.
We have gained by this some marvels of painting, especially in Venice, when the blending of business, religion
and enjoyment of the best in every way marked the full
flowering of its splendour.

Titian has not painted the dinners that he gave,
for his were private and artistic; the great banquets of
the Doges and Senators were different. Paul Veronese
has painted the "Marriage of Cana," a rival of his other
great painting (which is still in Venice), the "Feast in the
House of Levi."   The "Marriage of Cana" in the Louvre
is almost too well known for further description.   Looked
at in a print or in the gallery, the wise critic will remark
that there is "too much architecture"; it seems so because we are no longer accustomed to live in noble buildings, and we modern painters have been forced to become
Pharisees and keep to a manner of decoration which
will not disturb modern walls.   And what is sad is that
this curious narrowness of feeling has had place more
especially in examples of the best art of our day.   There
was a time when the painter took up and continued the
architectural forms of the wall beside him, and the great
Paul Veronese is now in a foreign land of art even in
the grandeur of the Louvre.   His clear and sane architecture looks like a final condemnation of the modern
French curved ceilings, and the mean openings of the
doors through which we pass to look at him.   The huge
picture was not returned in 1815, like so many others,
for it seemed cruel, even to the spoliators of Paris, to
risk the gigantic canvas across the Alps a second time.
Its great size was quite in place in the triumphant archi-

tecture of joyous Venice, where the high buildings which
fill so much of the painting carried up to the ceiling the
lines of doors which were in the real walls enriched by this
noble decoration.   Paul Veronese studied at once painting, sculpture, and architecture, working in each of these
divisions of art with the good nature and good sense
which marked the centuries that preceded our modern
scientific division of feeling from thought, so that Veronese,
the architect, has built in his paintings architectural
decorations equal in their nobility of taste to the creations
of Sansovino or Palladio.   As a sculptor he built his
figures solidly from within.   The foreshortening in his
ceiling decorations is as easy to him as to Correggio, yet
all his science disappears in the joyous and easy surface
work of the great Venetian.   The Marriage is difficult
to describe; the Christ, the disciples, and the Mother
are (as they should be in such a space) a small part of
the enormous scene; even the guests of all kinds are more
or less hidden by the musicians in the foreground, whom
we know to be portraits of the friends of the artist.   Notwithstanding the crowd one can distinguish the governor
of the feast, who tries the wine; we have dogs, a parrot,
and above us many attendants working in the open
air instead of in a dark cellar; the tables covered with
gold and silver, and then, in the clear sky, between the
great columns, the flying pigeons of Venice.

The Feast at the House of Levi is another chance
to fill a great space with many figures.   The scale is
real and the splendid architectural ornamentation of
a real building in the same Venetian sky is given with
astounding accuracy.   The painter has placed the Christ
in the distance at the long table so that our eye, following

THE MARRIAGE AT CANA. (VERONESE)

all the lines as it would do in nature, comes to Him as
He converses and explains merely by an inclination of
head and shoulder. The realities of the photograph
are there invented.

This picture occasioned a curious incident in the story
of painting. It was not made for an ordinary dining
room, but for a church, and its magnificence and appearance of earthly joy seemed insolent to the Holy Office
of the Inquisition, so that Paul Veronese was brought
up before it on the eighteenth day of July, 1573, and
was reprimanded for having placed in this picture of the
Feast at the House of Levi, " buffoons, dogs, and German
halberdiers."

Another spirit, and a dramatic one, breathes through
the similar festival compositions of Tintoretto. One
realizes sometimes, but only for a moment, that the
great man admired another even greater than himself.
Tintoretto bowed the knee before the gigantic Michael
Angelo, and something of this adoration has passed into
his work without any imitation, without any wish to do
more than indicate as a student the grasp of a man who
was perhaps the farthest away from Venice. Tintoretto
has also painted the Marriage at Cana, and, through a
trick of perspective has devised another way of making
us see the Saviour. We are at the end of a long table,
and are trying the wine, as is the maid servant who is
arguing with the governor of the feast; but the guests,
of course, are seated, in the absence of knowledge of
any trouble, and talk to each other, the ladies on one
side and the men on the other, in the proper way which
Tintoretto knew; one of the ladies at the corner of the
table turns around to inquire what the delay may be.

The big hall is again, as in the other houses of Italy, partly occupied by the preparations for the feast. There is no separation of the means and the end which we have learned to observe, and so a big crowd gathers in the distance to watch how the feast goes on. These special moments of our story belong to Venice; all other images are abstract.

CHAPTER XII

THE ENTRY INTO JERUSALEM. CHRIST BIDS FAREWELL
TO HIS MOTHER.   THE LAST SUPPER.   THE WASHING
OF FEET.   THE DISPUTE OF THE EUCHARIST.

THE Entry into Jerusalem was a great symbolic triumph, but its simplicity does not give to our minds, trained
in Roman views, an adequate sense of external importance.
Our Saviour rode, as we know, upon an ass, whereon
never man sat.   From the distance that we of the West
are now from the East, it is plausible, at least to me,
that the intentional humility of the Entry has prevented
its popularity with art, however great the opportunities
might have been.   In various pictures we see people
casting palms and spreading their garments before the
gentle King, coming into His Kingdom, but none are very
convincing.

There is a separate subject, Our Lord weeping over
the city.   Saint Luke says, "As he drew near the city
he wept over it."   There is on one of the porches of
Amiens a bas-relief of this scene; a very wonderful
adequate statement, which we understand in a singular
way, without even knowing exactly its reference to the
Gospel.   It is evidently deep sorrow, expressed only by
the slightest motion; there is no attitude of grief, nothing
but that intangible agitation of the entire human form,
by which we feel that the body is impressed by a sorrowful thought.

The Farewell of Christ to His Mother, a subject taken from the apocryphal gospels, appears late in the development of Art. Correggio gives the story in an evening light, wherein are four figures. In the distance we see the streaked sunset sky. The Christ kneels before His Mother, bending His head, with arms crossed, as if waiting for her blessing. The youthful figure of Saint John looks at the Christ sadly, as if about to break into helpless speech. The Mother, lost in grief, dares not turn toward her Son; her mouth is trembling, her eyes are unseeing — one arm is helplessly lifted just a little, the other rests on those of the Magdalen who supports her.

It is a late Italian subject, Venetian also, but not peculiar to Italy, for one of Dürer's finest woodcuts in his series of the Passion gives it also.

There is but one Last Supper — the "Cenacolo" of the Italian painters. All others fade before Leonardo's injured and vanishing masterpiece at Saint Maria delle Grazie in Milan, although we must remember and be just to some other paintings of the subject which tell the story either piously or conventionally.

The record of the Last Supper as later art imagined it does not appear directly in the earliest images, as we may remember with regard to the famous painting in the catacombs, the Breaking of Bread, which is a representation of the real solemnization and not the symbolical image of doctrine. That the last survivors of the Supper may have looked on that very painting in the catacombs — for according to tradition Saint John lived to a very great age — is enough to give to the almost accidental picture a connection with the Last Supper that we hesitate to put aside. And yet, of course, the doctrinal picture or image is entirely different. The earlier representations are not important, indeed they trouble us as we get into the full mediæval practice, by certain details, such as Saint John leaning on the shoulder of Christ, or even lying in His lap. We dislike to be reminded of these smaller points. The very importance of the subject has kept it from frequent treatment. It is not a part of the Passion of our Lord; it is the beginning of an institution carried through the centuries, both in doctrine and practice, and marks the actual permanence of Christ Himself. Respect for the importance of its meaning also protected it, in the earlier days, from any theatrical representation, although the Supper at Emmaus was one of the subjects given in the theatres.

Leonardo's difficulties were great. There was the mechanical difficulty of grouping a number of people together, yet indicating that One alone was all the picture; that had remained a problem to all who had attempted it. And then, how was it possible to tell the story of the sadness of the scene, to give the echo of His words, "Verily I say unto you, one of you shall betray me," and yet bring together the ordinary images of men at table? Nor could it be splendid, as in the great feasts of Tintoretto or Rubens, — and by some means the terrible story of the treachery of Judas must be told.

By a curious good fortune we have Leonardo's own notes:

"One who was drinking leaves the cup in its place and turns his head toward the speaker. Another folds the fingers of his hands together and with unbending rigid look turns to his neighbour:

that other, with open hands, shows his palms, lifts his shoulders up to his ears and gives the expression of marvelling with his lips. One speaks into the ear of another, and he who listens turns toward the speaker, while he holds a knife in one hand and in the other his bread, already half cut. The other on turning, holding a knife in hand, pours with that hand from a cup upon the table. Another places hands upon the table and gazes; another swells his mouth; another, to look the better at the speaker, shades his eyes with his hand. Another turns just the other way from him who bends, and looks at the speaker between the wall and the one turning."

We read with some satisfaction the prosaic analysis by Leonardo of how he should dispose the movements of the disciples. He has not suggested in his crude notes what he proposed to do for the great figure; he might, indeed, have indicated it by one of his curiously intellectual abbreviations. However, the figure of Christ means all the more to us to-day because the unfinished, faded face brings back to us the hesitation of the painter, who found it impossible to carry out in full the intention of his portrait.

The appearance, the vision of a *sacrament*, has been placed by him before us, and this meaning is given by his manner of rendering the text.

The Saviour bends His eyes down; His thought is on Himself; He is abstaining from looking, so as not to see the traitor Judas, which tells the feeling of the Divine Sufferer. That knowledge of the treachery or the dereliction of the friend is to us all the one cruel thing, the sorrow which makes Him one of us, and us one with Him. He has just spoken and is now silent. His two hands on the table represent the previous attitude of speech; the one is open, the other turned away, and

THE LAST SUPPER. (DA VINCI)

those hands are near to the hand of Judas — "Behold, the hand of him who betrayeth me is with me on the table."

Around the central sad peace of the Christ, we see the agitation of the disciples, their indignant expression of abhorrence, and the terrible anxiety of the traitor. That has to be, because it is in the story, but it is only the fringe of the subject, which is the sorrow of Our Lord.

It is not unfitting to quote directly and in full from Vasari. He has described the picture, wonderful then, in his own accustomed way, and he gives us the history of how it came to be painted :

"For the Dominican monks of Santa Maria delle Grazie at Milan, he also painted a Last Supper, which is a most beautiful and admirable work; to the heads of the Apostles in this picture the master gave so much beauty and majesty that he was constrained to leave that of Christ unfinished, being convinced that he could not impart to it the divinity which should appertain to and distinguish an image of the Redeemer. But this work, remaining thus in its unfinished state, has been ever held in the highest estimation by the Milanese, and not by them only, but by foreigners also. Leonardo succeeded to perfection in expressing the doubts and anxiety experienced by the apostles, and the desire felt by them to know by whom their Master is to be betrayed; in the faces of all appear love, terror, anger, or grief and bewilderment, unable as they are to fathom the meaning of their Lord. Nor is the spectator less struck with admiration by the force and truth with which, on the other hand, the master has exhibited the impious determination, hatred, and treachery of Judas. The whole work indeed is executed with inexpressible diligence even in the most minute part; among other things may be mentioned the table-cloth, the texture of which is copied with such exactitude, that the linen cloth itself could scarcely look more real.

It is related that the Prior of the Monastery was excessively importunate in pressing Leonardo to complete the picture; he could in no way comprehend wherefore the artist should sometimes remain
Q

half a day together absorbed in thought before his work, without
making any progress that he could see; this seemed to him a strange
waste of time, and he would fain have had him work away as he could
make the men do who were digging in his garden, never laying the
pencil out of his hand.   Not content with seeking to hasten Leonardo, the Prior even complained to the Duke, and tormented him to
such a degree that the latter was at length compelled to send for
Leonardo, whom he courteously entreated to let the work be finished,
assuring him nevertheless that he did so because impelled by the
importunities of the Prior.   Leonardo, knowing the Prince to be
intelligent and judicious, determined to explain himself fully on the
subject with him, although he had never chosen to do so with the
Prior.   He therefore discoursed with him at some length respecting
art, and made it perfectly manifest to his comprehension that men
of genius are sometimes producing most when they seem to be labor-
ing least, their minds being occupied in the elucidation of their ideas,
and in the completion of those conceptions to which they afterwards
give form and expression with the hand.   He further informed the
Duke that there were still wanting to him two heads, one of which,
that of the Saviour, he could not hope to find on earth, and had not
yet attained the power of presenting it to himself in imagination,
with all that perfection of beauty and celestial grace which appeared
to him to be demanded for the due representation of the Divinity
incarnate.   The second head still wanting was that of Judas, which
also caused him some anxiety, since he did not think it possible to
imagine a form of feature that should properly render the countenance of a man who, after so many benefits received from his master,
had possessed a heart so depraved as to be capable of betraying his
Lord and the Creator of the world : with regard to that second,
however, he would make search, and after all — if he could find no
better, he need never be at any great loss, for there would always
be the head of that troublesome and impertinent Prior.[1]   This made

[1] The jesting threat of Leonardo has given rise to the belief that the head of Judas
was in fact a portrait of the Prior, but the character of Leonardo makes it most unlikely
that he could have offered this affront to an old man who was merely causing him a
momentary vexation by a very pardonable, if not very reasonable, impatience; we
learn besides that Padre Bandelli, who was at that time Prior, "erat facie magna et
venusta, capite magno, et procedente ætate calvo capillisque canis consperso."

the Duke laugh with all his heart; he declared Leonardo to be completely in the right, and the poor Prior, utterly confounded, went
away to drive on the digging in his garden, and left Leonardo in
peace: the head of Judas was then finished so successfully that it
is indeed the true image of treachery and wickedness; but that of
the Redeemer remained, as we have said, incomplete. The admirable
excellence of this picture, the beauty of its composition, and the care
with which it was executed awakened in the King of France a desire
to have it removed into his own kingdom, insomuch that he made
many attempts to discover architects who might be able to secure it
by defences of wood and iron, that it might be transported without
injury. He was not to be deterred by any consideration of the cost
that might be incurred, but the painting being on the wall his majesty was compelled to forego his desire, and the Milanese retained
their picture."

Needless to say the painting is wrecked and has
been wrecked over and over and over again by official
carelessness, repainting, and brutality, such as the cutting
of a door through it. A drawing (also a mere shade)
in the Brera gives again Leonardo's attempt at the
expression of the Christ.

The painting by Fra Angelico of the Cenacolo is
remarkably successful, and suggests that large upper room
where the disciples assembled and which was mysteriously
prepared for them by their following the servant carrying
a pitcher of water, and making the goodman of the house
understand that the Master should eat the Passover
there. In that upper room they were to find the
requisite tables and couches, and there they made ready
the Passover.

This brings us to the question of the necessary attitudes
of the personages. Cushions on couches, each large
enough to hold three, were placed around three sides of

one or more low tables.   The seat of honour was a central
one.   This, of course, was occupied by the Lord.   Each
guest lay at full length, leaning on his left elbow, for the
custom of eating the Passover standing had long been
abandoned ; reclining had taken its place because it was
the habit of free men.

Thus we understand how at the right hand of Jesus
lay the belovèd disciple, whose head therefore could at
any moment be leaning on Jesus' bosom.   And Simon
Peter beckoned to him that he should ask who it was
of whom He spake.   He then, lying on Jesus' breast,
asked the question.   I mention this because there is a very
beautiful painting, by Moretto at Brescia, in which the
two apostles, John and Peter, form a composition of
the same movements on either side of the erect figure
of Christ, which separates that part of the story from the
meaning of the attitudes of the other disciples.   Perhaps
Moretto knew the Leonardo at Milan, for behind the
Christ a window opens with a division of two columns,
very beautifully emphasizing the erectness of the figure
of our Lord.

[We may realize how far from the possible fact of
the time is that long line of table, so natural to us
from association in the great Leonardo.]

The strife caused by the apostles taking their seats
and insisting on their privileges brings in the office of
the Washing of Feet and the lesson of humility taught
by Our Lord.

Saint John mentions the washing of the feet of the
discip'es, telling us how Christ rose from supper "and
laid aside his garments, took a towel, and girded himself.

THE LAST SUPPER. (Moretto)

After that, he poured water into a basin and began to wash the disciples' feet and to wipe them with the towel wherewith he was girded. Then cometh he to Simon Peter. Peter saith unto him, 'Thou shalt never wash my feet.' Jesus answered him, 'If I wash thee not, thou hast no part with me.' Simon Peter saith, 'Lord, not my feet only, but also my hands and my head.'"

This is a moment which art has not adopted, nor has it followed the text which described the Christ as having put aside His garments, thereby rendering Him naked to the waist. The meaning of words has changed, for us especially, and we, to whom the past and the East are not familiar, need not trouble about the question. There is a curious and rather striking representation on a very old sarcophagus found in the Catacombs, where our Lord stands with a long cloth around His neck, reaching far below His knees.

Naturally, from the text, the artists took up the fact that Peter was not the first, and so, in Giotto's painting, in the Arena Chapel, Christ kneels before Peter, holding one of the feet of His servant, and He holds out the other hand, teaching, as it were. The great man conceived this chance of expressing the higher meaning at the same time with the humble and prosaic occupation. Our picture gives it well enough; we see one of the disciples (presumably Judas, from artistic tradition) fastening his sandals. In contrast, two young disciples carry water and help to give official service to the Christ. In fact, they look like attendant angels.

Fra Angelico has made a more realistic rendering, and has, by some arrangement of space and intensity of movement in the few figures, given an importance to his

treatment which brings up, even more than Giotto's, the
idea of some sacred action carrying spiritual meaning and
benefit.   Christ offers His service — His hands show
that — and His face is earnest, yet expectant of
the obedience of Peter. There is a look, also, of per-
suasion, of kindly offering, which assures us of the importance of the act, in connection with what has gone
before and what is to come after.   In that way, the good
Brother has created an extraordinary figure as mere art,
for even without action of the disciples we should have this
sense.   Peter, as we see, is troubled and withdraws, and
another of the disciples watches the Lord anxiously with
an expression of inquiry.   He knows that it is something
more than a usual kindness.

Raphael's fresco of "The Dispute of the Eucharist,"
in the Stanze of the Vatican, is one of the celebrated pictures of the world, a triumph of knowledge, of intelligence,
an assemblage of many meanings, and, in fact, a sort of
encyclopædia of almost everything except the actual
realization of a vision, which is, after all, its intention.   The reason seems to me to be that the necessity
for a great arrangement of the architectural disposition
has taken mental effort, and that is opposed to what I
call "vision."   We know that an architectural arrangement remains an intellectual problem, and does not appear
to the mind's eye as a part of nature.   It is necessary
to notice these few objections before treating of the
enormous success.   Let us see now what Raphael
has accomplished.   In the opposite painting, "The
School of Athens," he wished to signify the triumph
of intellect, following successfully the pursuit of philo-

THE WASHING OF FEET. (GIOTTO)

sophic truth. The moment in Italian development is just the moment for this great record. In the Dispute we have a symbolical description of the relation of man to God by the redemption through Christ and the mystery of the Eucharist. The Eucharist is the subject of the painting. Below, in the very centre, above steps of white marble, on a square, simple altar is placed an ostensorium containing the Host, encircled by rays of light. On either side, grouped in a half circle, are Fathers of the Church, saints, and illustrious persons, legendary or contemporaneous, forty-two in all. On the left, seated on a classical bench ornamented with chimeræ, is Saint Gregory, looking up, crowned with the papal mitre. Near him, further back, Saint Jerome spreads and opens the leaves of a great book, and is deep in search. His young clerk looks up at him as if expecting some speech. Behind, as if speaking to Saint Jerome, and telling him where to look, a priest in an embroidered cloak points with both arms to the solution of all diffi-culties — the Eucharist itself. His long gesture continues the line of the altar and the lines of the landscape, and gently brings back the meaning of the entire composition to one idea, and in that we see a triumph of meaning and of technical arrangement. Quite near us, on the first step, is the figure of some philosopher and another of a saint, from whose hands a couple of books near him have dropped. We feel that he looks directly to the Eucharist, absorbed by it. A youthful, saintly figure, partly clad in white, kneels with devotion, stretching leg and foot to the higher step. His hands indicate admiration or adoration. Next to him is another whose arm, extended, makes a wide gesture of recognition, as of listen-

ing to some statement.   Behind them are bishops with
mitres, waiting, as it were, for more discourse.   Another
bishop converses with monks and bearded hermits;
others we see listening or talking, in a long line.   Leaning
on the balustrade in front, Bramante, erect in a long
coat, shows pages of an open book, arguing with a young
man of classic, Raphaelistic beauty, who leaves him,
stepping toward, and pointing up to, the Eucharist, as
if it were a sufficient answer to Bramante's incredulity.
The figure might be Raphael himself — if not his portrait,
at least his suggestion.   His life was one of the most
charming and successful of all existences, and he is well
named "The Divine," which in Italian has something
more than a spiritual meaning — it signifies the successful
also.   While these two talk, two others dissertate behind
them, one pointing to some passage in the book held by
the architect.   On the right-hand side of the painting,
seated and clad in sacerdotal dress, Saint Augustine,
turning sideways, dictates, with closed book and extended
arm, to a young clerk who bends over the scroll upon
his knee.   (The dictation is supposed to be from the
Saint's book, "The City of God.")   Saint Ambrose, also
seated, with bishop's mitre, looks up to the heavenly
vision pointed out to him by John Lombard, Bishop of
Paris.   Duns Scotus, in monkish frock, stands near
them.   Behind the two fathers stands Pope Anacletus,
palm in hand.   On either side of the Pope, Saint Thomas
Aquinas, in Dominican costume, and Saint Bonaventura
in his cardinal's dress, reading carefully in a book.   Nearer
to us, Saint Innocent III blesses all those present in
the accustomed papal way.   Quite near, an elderly man
in antique costume points to the Pope while he speaks to

THE DISPUTE OF THE EUCHARIST. (RAPHAEL)

a youth who leans on the wall.   The corner of the painting
is the wall which runs, like the opposite balustrade, out
of the picture and carries us into further possibilities, for Raphael has always taken great care of the
accessories of his paintings, so as to imply something
beyond the mere frame confining the subject.   Between
these figures, further back, is the head of Dante, crowned
with laurel, and a portrait said to be Savonarola.   Above,
in the sky, are the three persons of the Trinity, God the
Father carrying his symbolic globe and giving His blessing.
Around Him spreads an artificial but beautiful arrangement of rays of light, through which one sees the seraphim
and cherubim between two groups of angels, half seen
in luminous clouds, who are flying toward the Lord.
They are far away, and the reality of their distance is
one of the great triumphs of the painting.   Below the
arrangement of cherubim in the centre is seated the
Christ, opening His hands pierced with the nails.   He
is naked to the waist as if just stepping from the Cross.
On either side are the Virgin and Saint John, who is pointing, in the usual manner, to the Virgin bending in adoration.   Below, in a luminous disk, the Holy Ghost in the
shape of a dove comes down toward the altar between four
little naked angels, who each bear a book — presumably
one of the four Gospels.   On either side, seated in a
circle made of clouds, are the saints and the prophets;
on the left Saint John the Baptist talks with Adam, who
has crossed his legs and holds his knee with his hands, in
naturalistic listening. . Near them, Saint John the Evangelist is writing, perhaps on the Apocalypse, and smiles
at his work.   Toward him turns King David with his
harp.   Further on, Saint Stephen, a deacon, addresses

one of the ancient Sibyls (whom one hardly distinguishes) and points to her and her successors below.   On the right-hand side of the clouds which carry the Saviour, Saint Paul leans upon his sword, Saint James meditates, Moses holds upon his knees the tables of the law, Saint Lawrence a palm-branch, and between them is Saint George, helmeted and cuirassed in antique elegance, a patron of Liguria, whence Julius the Second came.   The name of the "Dispute" is a modern one, and the meaning, of course, is just the contrary, as has been wisely re-marked many times; it is not a dispute, but a concur-rence and agreement, and one of the great historical successes, crowning a long series of efforts by generations of painters in the many directions which have made modern art.

THE AGONY IN THE GARDEN. (Ferrari)

CHAPTER XIII

THE AGONY IN THE GARDEN. THE BETRAYAL. CHRIST BEFORE CAIAPHAS. JUDAS RECEIVES HIS PAY. THE REPENTANCE OF JUDAS.

MATTHEW, Mark, and Luke describe the Lord's sorrow and His praying three times and thrice returning to His sleeping disciples. Saint Luke tells us of the sustaining angel. We have from each and all the simile of the cup — which, indulged in by artists, has destroyed sometimes the very meaning of the story depicted. The subject began to be represented when art allowed, or was directed into, symbolical statements, which are often misleading — for instance, some of the South Sea Christians whom I knew believed that when the sword pierced the Virgin's heart her suffering was physical.

Here is the picture by Gaudenzio Ferrari. At once we have every combination of error — the sleeping disciples almost touching the Lord, and He adoring His own cup, instituted only just before. Could anything be more impossibly wrong, and both artistically and religiously foolish? Perhaps some devotee may have suggested it, for Gaudenzio elsewhere is more reasonable. Let us turn to him for a moment; he certainly deserves notice, and I regret that we shall so rarely use him in our story, because his main charm lies in single representations of the Madonna and Child, and also in ideal subjects, which

are splendidly, if somewhat conventionally, treated; perhaps by no fault of his, but of the time and place.

We must always remember that the creator of religious
subjects, even to this moment, is not the free artist of
sentiment and feeling that we should wish. He is a form
of merchant, and on some sides a degraded one, as we
see all about us in what the French call "*bondieuseries.*"
But Ferrari is one of the victims of Leonardo, partly
through the glory and light of that great man. It is largely
through others that Leonardo's manifestation takes
place. We all feel him and are told of him — but only a
few phases of him we know, and in many more we can
scarcely believe.

Gaudenzio at the end, more than others (Luini for
instance), escaped into what I take to be the real North
Italian nature. Of course he himself as a unit had
personal gifts. He had the faculty of vision, and a
sense of the moving line, not the outline of the "linists,"
as ours of to-day, but that which the sculptor has, who
grasps the sense of form not seen and brings the impression of the next movement into the present immobility.
The gift is extremely rare — a little more and our Gaudenzio would have been a great genius.

He also had religious feeling, and his poetic sentiment
was influenced by the Franciscan sweetness. Thus, in
his attempts or successes in the history of our Lord or
in any other works, he wished to give the impression of a
reality both divine and human and express his dreams in
terms of beauty. It may be that we do not recognize
sufficiently in his later works the Northern influence.
Not only was some of it latent in that Northwest of Italy,
but artists possessed the actual knowledge of Germanic

art, through Dürer and others. This may be imaginary as to Ferrari, but so lovely and pious, and high-minded a nature cannot be left out of the illustrators of the story.

Strangely enough, we shall be able to approve a most modern treatment of this subject in the middle of the last century, when all feeling seemed gone from any religious paintings.

Delacroix gives us this episode of the Passion; it is imperfect, perhaps, and certainly almost invisible, in the Church of Saint Sulpice. It is despised and rejected by the great patrons and critics, but if I remember it accurately, it is wonderful in giving the *loneliness of abandonment*.[1]

The double sympathy of Delacroix for form and also for feeling led him at times to religious subjects, and he alone in our day seems to have been fitted from our point of view for the continuation of the development of art in sympathy with the memories of the Church. Strange as it may seem to those of us whose habit is to divide contradictions in humanity as they do in school books, this reader and admirer of Voltaire, this quiet, rather cold gentleman remained, during all his life in France, in touch with religious story and feeling. Indeed one whole year of his more than busy life was devoted to religious subjects — studied all for himself — hence we have some sketches for the Passion, and one dark, dismal, and probably neglected picture in a distant Paris church. That last, although new in expression and composition (*i.e.* placing of figures) is the least valuable. As happened with Rembrandt, for instance, and must happen with any genius struggling in poverty or straitened means, the

[1] Owing to its position, this cannot be photographed.

sketches or studies seem greater than the finished works,
immensely important as these are.   It is a law of human
nature, not recognized or insisted on by dealers.   The
drawings or half-paintings of the life of Christ by Delacroix are but little known (and also have been badly
reproduced) because hidden away.

In each a novelty occurs, or rather forces itself in,
though often the great man tried to meet the conventional
composer halfway, as he had friends in that camp and
disliked to shock them.   The figures of Christ fainting
from sheer emotion are probably the finest ever suggested; they alone, in the history of art, express the
solitary distress of the prophetic vision, and the others of
Pilate and the courts have also the same religious insight.

Twice at the extremities of the art of painting has
the turning point of the Divine Story been given in adequate telling.   In the Arena Chapel at Padua, Giotto,
the "Father of Painting," tells the story as he saw it,
from experience of life, and with the power and imagination which we call genius, the "*dédoublement*" of a
noble or exceptional mind.

There are other more or less noble representations,
because they are by noble artists.   Fra Angelico gives one,
but it is too intentional — "*voulu*" as the French say;
spiritual feeling certainly moved the painter, and it is a
religious work of art (indeed that is its defect as a
story); and Duccio tells us perhaps better, because he
is less mystic and deep.   But Giotto is there — and
makes us see how Our Lord is the only one who is not
anxious; how He accepts Judas's embrace or serpent coil
(both meant for capture and for possible self-protection),

THE BETRAYAL OF CHRIST. (Giotto)

and how the Victim bends to the traitor, with calm and searching eye. [It has been said, according to a tradition accentuated by some passage in a revelation to Saint Bridget, that Judas was much smaller, so that the Captive bent toward him willingly.]

The rabble around them is uneasy, as in any capture of a dangerous criminal. The high priest is all concern; what to-day would be a policeman blunders in stupidly. A blast from a horn announces the capture to those outside.

The great Van Dyck is not sufficiently known. Now that there are more travellers for Spain, and we can see other great Van Dycks here, our attention may be drawn to the wonderful blossoming of the new art in him, with the sentiment, the touching sentiment, of the old. Little of that shall we see after him, fine as some painters may be, although contemporary Spain may have something, as always, of appeal to the heart.

In Van Dyck's Betrayal there is a great rush of lines and of the people who make them. It is as if the lacing of ropes thrown over our Lord were also repeated in the crowd of captors, all anxious to secure the Unresisting One. Judas, of whose face we see little, ends the long serpentine uphill movement.

He steps on the Saviour's cloak, again in a sweep of lines, as if to prevent Him from moving or slipping away. The practical old man concealed behind the traitor has his rope ready in case of blunder, but that is unnecessary.

Over the Lord's head swings the rope. His arm and shoulder are clutched, partly in fear, by another captor. Meanwhile the Captured One allows His hand to be taken by the traitor. It lies gently in that tentative grasp,

and the Lord looks down at him with the gentleness almost of indifference, yet as if aware of the awful crime.
"Was ever grief like mine?" says the pale face, the only
peaceful spot, for all, even the trees and moon and the
lighted torches are wild with the rush and turmoil. "On
the edge of the picture is the armed leader, with his directing hand. In the lower edge, out of the main subject, we
have the episode of Peter and Malchus, properly subor-
dinated, as if necessary to the record but not to the
drama.

Caiaphas was he who gave counsel to the Jews that it
was expedient that one man should die for the people.
On this account Dante has placed him in hell.

In Giotto's story this is the first tribunal pictured,
that most impressive and evil one. Two function-
aries occupy the seat of Justice. This doubtless arose
from Saint Luke's speaking of Annas and Caiaphas being
high priests conjointly, and is seen as early as the
eleventh century, on the doors of the Cathedral of Bonaventure.

Giotto has chosen the moment when Caiaphas has
adjured Christ, by the living God, to say whether He
be the Son of God, to which Jesus answered in the affirm-
ative. Caiaphas is seen tearing open his robe, showing
his bare and hairy breast, his lower lip pulled up tight,
expressing contempt and superiority, saying, "He hath
spoken blasphemy, what further need have we of witnesses?" Annas has long hair upon his shoulders, and
extends a hand of command. The order goes forth to
take the prisoner away — an officer hastens to obey.
Behind the Christ another officer, with the exact ex-

THE BETRAYAL OF CHRIST. (Van Dyck)

pression that we know in the official guardian of the peace, raises a hand to strike Him, a motive repeated in various pictures, before and after. Two ugly, glaring heads behind are the witnesses who have testified falsely; one or two of the younger men are disturbed by the evident evil intention of the magistrates, and place a hand on the soldiers to prevent any hurried violence. Within these narrow limits the story of a charge before a magistrate is told, with the addition of the theatrical gesture of the high priest. Meanwhile, the Christ stands in thought; He waits, and His eye turns upon the ugly face of one of the witnesses. Already a sense of the atrocity of the calumny has touched Him, but He waits; His hands are tied before Him.

In the fresco of the same subject by Gaudenzio Ferrari His hands are tied behind Him; He is all the more defenceless when the servant of the high priest, a fierce, brutal, turbaned creature, strikes Him violently; behind Him another ugly being has hold of Him; He smiles gently and kindly at the man who is striking Him, and His bound arms give still more the feeling that He accepts the cruelty; the soldiers stand with natural indifference, for they think it is a Jewish quarrel into which they need not enter. Caiaphas sits on high arguing, with crooked fingers which resemble the wicked horns of a devilish soul. The beautiful background is filled with flowering plants, and above hangs a triple canopy of oriental suggestion.

Many painters show us the mocking of Our Lord before Caiaphas. Giotto seats the Christ, who again patiently waits. His hands now are free to receive the

mockery of a sceptre; the same insolent brute pulls
His hair, with a look of triumph; some youngster behind
strikes Him, another boy pulls His hair, another merely
puts out a tongue of contempt, a cowardly creature
kneels in derision before Him, and behind them all comes
a negro, with a stick ready to strike.   In the same room
the Roman asks the wrangling Pharisees, "What manner
of man is this?"

The only representation of Judas receiving his pay
of which I know is by Giotto in the Arena Chapel.

The priests of the temple, venerable bearded persons,
confer with Judas, who receives a bag of silver.   Two
of these Levites reason about the matter, as if saying,
"There is the man who engages to do it" — one points
with reversed thumb.   The older priest has just placed
the bag in Judas's hand, and lifts his own, with the
necessary recommendation to be sure, to take precau-
tions, and he promises, for "then entered Satan into
Judas, surnamed Iscariot, being of the number of the
Twelve," and we see Satan entering — an awful black
shape with a claw for hand, and a grin of possession on
his beaked and bearded shadow of a face, strangely carica-
turing some Jewish original, so that we feel that even if
visible, it might still be a shadow.   His one leg seen is
the long thin stick of the traditional Devil's leg of bird
or goat.

Judas is transfigured; he gazes into the face of the
priest, with eyes and lips intent both to know and to
show that he understands it is a bargain; consciousness of
cleverness spreads all over the countenance of the man
who has found his place.

THE PAYMENT OF JUDAS. (Giotto)

The repentance and death of Judas occurred apparently while our Lord was being led from the palace of Caiaphas to that of Pontius Pilate. Saint Matthew alone says that Judas, when he saw that Christ was condemned, "repented himself, and brought again the thirty pieces of silver to the chief priests and elders, saying, 'I have sinned in that I have betrayed innocent blood.' And they said, 'What is that to us ? See thou to that.' And he cast down the pieces of silver in the temple, and departed, and went and hanged himself."

In ancient ivories he hangs by a rope to which he puts his hand, a manner of saying that it was his own act. On the Bonaventure doors the indignation of the artist has put Satan upon the shoulders of the traitor, as if to weigh both soul and body down.

In his youth Rembrandt painted Judas kneeling in the temple at the feet of the priests, with hands clasped in pain, and speaking with closed and blinking eyes, through which, however, he sees spread out upon the floor the thirty pieces of silver cast down by him ; the clergy standing above him are indignant at this additional annoyance. The high priest looks stiffly indignant at the injustice that allows such trouble when all had been settled ; his hand takes hold of a curtain which half conceals the sacred books ; another, seated, turns away in contemptuous wrath, reversing his hand ; scholars, farther away, rise from their desks looking on curiously at these insolent priests seen in the distance, and are just a little disturbed by an incident which they scarcely understand. The painting is an early one, and consequently hard, lacking the consummate rendering of experience in life, but it has all been seen, and these are records of

s

the synagogue.   We notice that by the very fact that we
do not quite understand them; the synagogue is not to
us habitual, but it is to Rembrandt, who moves at ease
in it, and has through all his work repeated the Bible,
in and out, both Old and New Testament, as no one
but himself has done or could do.

CHAPTER XIV

CHRIST BEFORE PILATE. THE DENIAL OF PETER. CHRIST
PRESENTED TO THE PEOPLE. PILATE WASHES HIS
HANDS. THE FLAGELLATION. ECCE HOMO

"When the morning was come, all the chief priests and
elders of the people took counsel against Jesus to put him
to death, and when they had bound him they led him
away and delivered him to Pontius Pilate, the governor."

Before Caiaphas Christ had been charged with blasphemy; before Pilate, and subsequently before Herod, with
treason to Cæsar, in styling Himself a king. The Jews,
therefore, had no power to put Him to death without the
order of the governor, for within the Paschal week it was
forbidden by their customs.

Jesus stood before the governor, and the governor
asked Him, saying, "Art thou the King of the Jews?" and
Jesus said unto him, "Thou sayest." Glad to get rid
of Him, and learning that He was a Galilean, they sent
Him to Herod.

Christ has been brought before Pilate in the painting
of Gaudenzio Ferrari; He stands patiently waiting, His
hands tied behind Him. Pilate wears rich clothing and
heavy fur; he inquires with disdain as to the charge
against the prisoner. The governor has come outside of
a palace, upon which is written in Latin that it is his,
because, on our Lord's being first brought, the Jews
refused to enter lest they should be defiled; therefore

to humour them Pilate went out to them, that they
might eat the Passover. One of the soldiers who has
brought the Christ tells the story, with lifted hand, and
an ugly Jew watches to see how it will be taken. The
scene is almost modern in its realism; we are far from
the religious rendering of Duccio or Fra Angelico.

It may be well to notice that the chief priests who speak
to Pilate, and of whom he says to the Christ, "Thine own
nation and the chief priests have delivered thee unto me,"
are Sadducees. They were apparently the conservative
party, and were said to be able to persuade the rich
that the populace was subservient to them. It was not
merely the Pharisees who wished the death of the Lord,
it was also the men who were superior to those narrow
opponents of a wider and more generous life. That they
were of aristocratic, ecclesiastical origin is marked by
their having been named after the Zadok who anointed
Solomon. Ezekiel speaks of the sons of Zadok, and ex-
pressly describes them as the special priestly family,
to the exclusion of other Levites; "the priests that are
sanctified of the sons of Zadok; which have kept my
charge, which went not astray when the children of Israel
went astray." Hence the sons of Zadok were singled
out as the priestly line from the captivity, and they were
still the priestly party in apostolic times. To us, usually,
they represent the unbeliever. It has been supposed
that their views were coloured by the influence of Greek
thought — they are said to have held that there was no
resurrection. We have no remains of their literature,
but perhaps their sacerdotal pride is contained in the book
of Ecclesiasticus. We are therefore in the presence of
intellectual and free-minded opponents of the Lord, and

THE DENIAL OF PETER. (Rembrandt)

in the picture by Giotto we recognize, however cruel
their look, the presence of a relatively superior and cold
opposition, — that of the governing mind.

Then comes, in most dramatic succession, the contrast
of Peter's denial. Rembrandt has painted it twice.
In one picture the story is told by three or four personages
— the maid servant, a couple of soldiers and Peter.
The maid, the usual person of no particular importance,
lifts a hand of remonstrance, and points to the Christ,
saying, "Art not thou also one of this man's disciples"?
The light coming from her candle (not from the fire at
which they warm themselves) falls upon Peter's cloak
wrapped around him, "for it was cold," and on his troubled
and doubtful face; he has not spoken yet, he is merely
surprised, and one hand is ready to make some gesture
putting aside the question; nearer to us, and watching
the scene sits a soldier in armour, his helmet on his knee;
he holds an enormous flagon, one hand is around the neck
ready to put it to his mouth, but he stops and grins at the
confusion of the disciple. His sense of enjoyment of the
discomfiture of Peter contrasts with the expression of
another soldier who thrusts out lips of disdain — the rest
is lost in the dark.

Later Rembrandt has told us of the contrite Peter in
an unfinished etching which gives in a mysterious way
Peter kneeling; he leans on his staff, holding one of the
keys of heaven, the other hand holds out another key.
He looks at it with an indescribable expression of doubt
and reminiscence.

Tintoretto's "Christ Before Pilate" in the Scuola di
San Rocco has been dignified with much fine writing by Mr.
Ruskin, and all visitors to Venice know what he thought

about it.   Not even the most florid praise can hurt this, one of the wonderful paintings of the world.   It is not necessary to know the story; if ever there was a portrait of a just man before some obscure power, here it is.   Out of the gloom the figure of Pilate appears, if you wish to see it, just enough to tell the story.   That judge may well forget how many similar cases he has dismissed, or turned over to the law, or to a clamouring mob of accusers.

The etching by Rembrandt of "Christ Presented to the People" is perhaps more important than his painting. Apart from the subject, the picture he gives is the picture of a *crowd*, a furious crowd.   Not even the photograph of to-day is nearer to the rendering of a multitude. There are not many figures, one can easily count them — there are not many more than a dozen — and yet it is a great, great crowd.   That is the effect of genius, and that faculty of *sight* of the subject, of creating an image all made, for which we ought again to use the word imagination.

Also there is a trick or method of the painter or designer, which we saw in Raphael's Heliodorus, and in the Heliodorus of Delacroix, and may see in another of the latter's works, the "Massacre of Scio."   It is the massing of the multitude outside the edge of the picture — that is to say, beyond what we directly behold.   This sense that we are not able to see them all gives the psychological impression of *a crowd*, and some men have instinctively noticed this visionary fact and made use of it.

In the Rembrandt, the sense of a surging sea of people pouring through some distant archway fills our imagination.   Little seen, they yet are there.   Two figures, one far back in the gloom, and the other nearer, keep back by gesture the unseen mass. "Patience," they seem to say, — "we shall soon have Him." Then close before Pilate we have the Pharisees, the believers, the real fanatics. Behold the awfully earnest face of the kneeling Jew, with the look that it is impossible to have "no" for answer. To that question the delicate hands of Pilate — an oriental Pontius Pilate — answer in a gesture. The guards are guards — they are already annoyed by the presence of these Jews, and one or two already look at the prisoner with an eye of doubt. From Him spreads the light. His face alone is not disturbed; it is even absorbed in prayer — prayer to the Father — prayer for them who thirst for His life.

With the washing of his hands, Pilate passes away into relative obscurity. Troubles with the Jews had followed his last experiences; he must have been happy to escape from the responsibilities of ruling over a people he never understood, and would be glad to forget.

In Anatole France's story of the Procurator of Judæa, Pilate is one of two old friends who meet long after their sojourn in Palestine. They sit far into the night at table and recall this or that. The other Roman, formerly an official, speaks well of the Jews, describing the beauty of the women of Syria and of one especially who was very lovely and who joined certain men and women who followed a young Galilean, a worker of miracles. He was called Jesus; he came from Nazareth and was put to death for a crime which the Roman cannot recall. He asks Pontius if he recollects that man, and Pilate frowns in silence, hunting in his memory, and says at last, "Jesus, — Jesus of Nazareth — I do not remember."

In his later or "golden" manner Rembrandt has given us "Pilate Washing his Hands," in a painting formerly in the Kahn and now in the Altman collection. Pilate, in a rich semi-oriental dress, sits out of doors, in a sort of loggia, holding out his hands, over which a beautiful boy pours water from a golden ewer. Behind Pilate stands some priest or Jewish official, apparently commending the course taken by him, and beyond a wall we see the helmeted heads and the spears of a group of Roman soldiers. Pilate has a mild and dreamy face, and appears to be half indifferently fulfilling an accustomed rite. If the picture did not inspire France's story, it seems like a foreshadowing of his idea, besides being in itself most beautiful and full of imagination.

"Then released he Barabbas unto them, and when he had scourged Jesus, he delivered him to be crucified."

With Pilate the flagellation was a proposition of satisfaction to the Jews, thus: "I will therefore chastise him and release him." The commentators are not clear whether scourging was the usual prelude to the Roman death upon the cross, as beating often is in Chinese executions, but there are Roman stories of sufferers who perished under the infliction. Tradition has represented Christ attached to a pillar or column, perhaps because of the Roman habit. But another tradition, not accepted by artists, placed Him prostrate on the ground, according to Levitical law and to fulfil a passage in the Psalms, "The plowers plowed upon my back." Again, some have thought that Pilate would not have permitted any excess, but that the Jews bribed the Roman soldiers to treat their victim with unusual cruelty. However, the column has remained, hence the "Christ of the Column." In some early cases His face is turned from us or the column is interposed, but in the few final representations the reverse is the case, because it is more beautiful and reverent.

Rembrandt has given us the preparations for the flagellation : Christ stands by the column, not clearly seen ; one of the torturers pulls His arms, which are fastened together, upward over a pulley ; another arranges the ends of a chain around His ankles and fits apparently at the same time the other end of the long rope so that the Victim becomes bound in all directions. Meanwhile the Christ stands firm, His legs apart ; He is stripped to the waist and His body begins to yield to the strain ; already His face indicates the beginning of suffering, however patient He may be ; He sees with half-closed eyes the movement of the executioner pulling down the rope.

Like all the great Rembrandts, it is the vision of a real scene ; whether Rembrandt ever did see it may be a question, cruelty to the punished not being yet abandoned. In the Italian or Spanish renderings, or in any others of the Middle Ages where the subject represents a form of cruelty, the painter may give us what he has seen, for we know that the law and its practices allowed things which appear monstrous to us. One feels this often as a side issue in mediæval Italian memoranda of actual facts, and it is not so long ago that in the England of Christianity and justice similar things might have been seen, attended by still more cruelty ; one need only read the terms of the punishment of the Catholics or of the followers of Charles Stuart.

In Gaudenzio Ferrari's picture the column is one of

many that support the arches of a loggia, delicate and
dainty. The Christ is fastened by His arms, which are
tied behind His back, to the base of one of them. He
looks upward in patience, and receives the stripes of the
two executioners, one an ugly creature triumphant over
the weaker being, and the other a mere machine repeating
blows in a mechanical way. The charm of the picture
lies, besides the points of art, in the vision of the Christ
which seems to cover all the space and appeals to us,
without our thinking of the story, as a victim, a martyr.
The sense of injustice pours out from it. Far back, a
figure looking like a woman, but probably some superior
dressed in an extreme oriental manner, holds a rod and
watches the scene. It may be Pilate, though it seems
not sufficiently prominent or important.

In Rubens's picture of the Flagellation in the Dominican Church at Antwerp he has turned the Saviour's
back to us on account of the lines of the composition
and also for the question of the drama. It is a terrible
representation of the scene.

When our Lord had been scourged the Roman soldiers took Him into the common hall and stripped
Him and put on Him a scarlet robe and plaited a
crown of thorns and put it on His head and placed a
reed in His right hand (His hands were tied) as a manner
of sceptre, and they bowed the knee before Him and
mocked Him, saying, "Hail, King of the Jews!" Then,
as a manner of revenge upon their own false homage,
they spat upon Him and took a reed and smote Him on
the head.

When Pilate considered that Christ's sufferings were

enough to satisfy the Jews, he left the Prætorium and said
to them, "I bring him to you." Then he made Jesus
come forth wearing the crown of thorns and the purple
robe, and Pilate said, "Behold the man!" In every
language the words "Behold the Man" (in Latin "Ecce
Homo") remain as the type of all that is sorrowful and
touching, not only in the story of our Lord, but for all
human beings who have passed through the Via Dolorosa.

The Ecce Homo has given to the painters a subject
covering all the personal feeling and interest apart
from doctrine which began to flood the human mind.
The purely religious feeling, of course, continued and
was probably marked in the givers of the paintings, but
the subject by itself, the suffering of the just, in its singular unity was sufficient for the deepest feelings of the
artist.

In Italy the Ecce Homo appeared first at the finest
moment of art, and Ferrari has painted it at Milan in the
Church of the Madonna delle Grazie. The Lord stands
at an opening of the railing, and two indifferent attendants, evidently not enemies, but soldiers or officials,
dressed in the Germanic manner, pull off the cloak so
that He may be better seen. A rope hangs around the
neck of the Christ and down to His feet; His hands are
not tied, but crossed on His breast and He holds the reed
sceptre. He looks down in lassitude.

The Ecce Homo by Correggio in the National Gallery
of London is perhaps the greatest of all. The scene is
imaginary, for the fainting Mother is not in the story, but
she adds to the meaning, by supplying a representative of
our own pity, carried out in the ideal of womanhood, whose
name for centuries has lifted woman from abasement or

intellectual contempt by placing before the minds of men
the infinite capacity for sympathy and help which belongs
and has belonged in every form of life to woman.   Here
it is sublimated.   The Christ's head is what we might
expect from the master of expression and sweetness,
who was also a great student and draughtsman, a magi-
cian as to light and especially a composer, a man working
within the frame, and thus within the problem set before
painters when they attempt to solve the mysteries of
light and shade.

The expression is difficult to define.   If it were otherwise, the art of painting would not exist, but one may say
in an attempt at definition — or, rather, suggestion of
definition — that the Christ is pitying the creatures who
force upon Him this agony.   A soldier looks at Him
with the usual curious momentary derision of the official;
on the other side a figure who may be Pilate or some
other judicial personage offers Our Lord to the multitude.

CHAPTER XV

THE MAN OF SORROWS.   THE PASSION OF CHRIST

Not even guards or cruel fanatics attend the Saviour after His flagellation.

The painting by Velasquez is pure invention, I take it, but the Spanish feeling fills the work.   There is no making out of the Victim a weakling.   His body, bent over and exposed to the waist, is of the healthiest and cleanest, and on it lines of blood tell the story of the brutality of the last moments, though, as we know by the story, the Roman governor thought that the accused might escape further punishment.   What at bottom did it matter ?   He could not have believed in the charges. It was as it is to-day when we attempt to escape from taking any real share in questions which can be avoided. Velasquez comforts us with a little child — a donor's child attended by its guardian angel — who kneels in adoring reverence.   The ray of light which blesses the little kneeling figure seems to us, in our habit of thought, a spiritual act.

In the Man of Sorrows, Dürer has given us an image of Christ which both tells the story and appeals to our pity.   In a certain way the seated figure sums up the entire Passion; His feet and His hands are pierced, therefore it is not exactly the Christ waiting for His Crucifixion, as we see in that most touching painting of Velasquez of which we have just spoken, where, by great good fortune and mere chance, a little child appears to pity the Saviour — a detail entirely contradictory in one sense, but deeply true as a matter of feeling. It is a manner of carrying out the question of pity, which in the history of art began to mean more and more in the figures used to specify religious requirements, while before that moment the doctrinal side of the representations must have been the main one.

Let us consider the type of what shall be the Christ of Pity: Jesus naked, worn-out, is seated on some rock or mound; His hands and feet are tied; a crown of thorns tears His forehead, and His blood, already largely shed, pours down slowly; He is waiting, and sadness fills the half-closed eyes. There are a number of these representations made in the innocence of their hearts by the early artists, or those of whom we think as early artists — for already they have come to the end of expression through story, and therefore to the extreme limit of art. On the Cross Christ is dying, and has already lost the capacity for suffering, but while waiting for the Cross He thinks and He suffers; hence, it was necessary to express the deepest moral grief joined to an extraordinary exaggeration of physical suffering. As we noticed, the simplicity of soul in these men allowed them to attempt what no one had ever dared — to represent the agony of a God. To show a god worn-out, even covered with a sweat of blood, would have been beyond the grasp of the greatest of the Greeks; nor would they have felt sympathy with pain; their heroic understanding of life took away such sympathy. For them suffering was servile, because it destroyed the balance of body and of soul; the order was therefore that it was not to be made eternal

THE MAN OF SORROWS. (Velasquez)

through art. Pity, force, serenity are what should be offered to the contemplation of man. Thus the work of art becomes kindly and offers that model of perfection to which man must tend. The young man is told by these Greek heroes, "Be strong, and like us control your life"; a great and noble lesson, which later, with the Renaissance, has made man hesitate. Michael Angelo was a Christian, and very deeply so, but he too has not dared to give to his Christ the look of a sufferer; Michael, like the Greek, teaches us to despise suffering, and so the Christ is represented as a hero who has a contempt for death. However, do not let us mistake the feelings of those older artists; they do not mean to say that suffering was the teaching of the Gospel. What they wished to represent was not suffering, but love — the suffering of a God who should die for love — so one forgives the want of pity in some of the imagery of that last moment of the Middle Ages.

There is a statue at Troyes, in France, among the most pathetic of all the works of these men. The crown of thorns has been so driven down upon the head of the Christ that it looks like a turban, hair and beard are heavy masses made stiff by hardened blood, but the eyes express astonished grief, as if the man in Christ is only just realizing the brutality of the sons of Adam. At the same time the head is lifted straight, and tells the story of continuing to the end and accomplishing the Sacrifice.

Then appears another figure of the suffering Christ, which is usually known under the name of "The Christ of Pity." It is different, really, from the one we have spoken of, though resembling it at first. The Christ is sometimes placed against the Cross, and seems still to suffer, and yet He has gone through death; His hands and feet, as with Albert Dürer, are pierced, and His side wounded; sometimes He is half placed in the tomb. It is a manner of dream; it was, in fact, probably a vision. We remember how Christ appeared in some such way to Saint Gregory the Great, at mass. It is not an old tradition, and was not recognized even as late as the thirteenth century. A picture in the Church of the Holy Cross of Jerusalem at Rome may have given the beginning to all this tradition; so said some early engravings, said to be copies of it. But strange to relate, the painting badly copied by the engraver was the work of a Byzantine artist, for a Greek monogram and inscription are upon it. It may be that this strange image, brought back from the East in the twelfth or thirteenth century, was important from its very strangeness, and in the end people believed that Pope Saint Gregory had it painted to represent his vision, which would add naturally to its importance. In those far-away times such images formed part of what may be called the ordinary business habit of religious men and women (besides appealing to sentiment) before the woodcut and the engraving came in and gave to big people and little ones what they had been wishing for, and what was a rarity before. The Christ was frequently supported by two angels, who held the body half out of the tomb, or else the Virgin and Saint John took their places, a favourite theme with Italian masters. It is the idea of the eternal Passion of Christ, the Passion which continues even after death; the Christ of Pity became by degrees that marvel of sentiment which we have seen in the Italians, and in the masterpieces of John Bellini, where Saint John, with mouth half open, seems to give forth a faint note of pain, while the Virgin in anxious tenderness leans her face against that of her Son. This contemplation of the sufferings of Christ went into various details of this suffering; some words of Saint Bernard (not really his) compare the Passion to a bleeding rose, and Saint Bonaventure describes how Christ, draped in His own blood, appeared as if wearing the pontifical purple. More and more the divine blood pours forth; Saint Bridget, Saint Gertrude, and other saints see the blood run, and the artists so represented it, and thus the idea of suffering gives us a number of historical works wherein is exhalted this power of the blood of Christ. We shall have sacred edifices named from it, the Knights of the Round Table will look for it, at Bruges we shall have the Precious Blood, and so we shall be brought to such a strange, mystical composition as that of the "Fountain of Life," a painting in the Church of Pity at Oporto in Portugal. There the crucified Christ is between the Virgin and Saint John, and the foot of the Cross, instead of meeting the rock of Calvary, is plunged in a great basin from which blood pours and fills another lower one. Around it there are a number of persons, either givers of the mystical painting or holy believers of every kind. We cannot, in the quiet of our studies, follow this violent poetry of the mystical fountain, the strange work of artists wherein breathes the feverish pity of the end of the Middle Ages.

We are so accustomed to speak of Our Lord's Passion that we do not wonder why the term came to be applied to the suffering of Christ, His acceptance of misery, pain, humiliation, of the meanness or weakness of His friends, of all that makes even ordinary life sad ; and then to His reign from the Cross. We know that at a certain moment in Italy the fervour of the monastic orders, called into life by the great saints whose names they bore, brought into play every form of appeal. Before this the outward expression is restrained or lost in the stress of the times. Then comes the rendering, in dramatic action, of the story. At first it seems strange that over twelve hundred years had to pass before a dramatic representation was given, but we know what difficulties must have intervened before the theatre could become instructive and be welcomed as a religious expression.

In the end it was universally accepted, and we have the mysteries, and the prolongation of more or less respectful versions of the story, even to our very day in the Bavarian Tyrol. It is well that this example remains, even if it is becoming somewhat commercial at this late instant. It shows us, by the concomitant life of people joining in a pictorial agreement with the Church, how the finer sides of the idea existed side by side with the more degrading tendencies that follow all attempts to amuse. The good Northern people may not have begun it, but they kept it up, and we may sympathize in the relief of the theatre after the too realistic life of earlier mediæval effort.

But we are going out of our way. Let us turn once more to Giotto, as the greatest of all those who represent the history of Our Lord. What he might have done, had he lived later, we cannot even surmise. No one has beginnings from himself alone, and the little boy who drew in chalk for immortal fame had beginnings, as we shall see, notwithstanding Leonardo, who declared, according to Vasari, that Giotto owed nothing to his forerunners.

It is interesting to remember (as an example of what must have happened over and over since his time) that Giotto's memory was probably charged with stories depreciating the very monks and orders for whose glorified founders he gave to the world of his day and also to ours such beautiful records as make us even now converts and special believers in the graces of Saint Francis. For now we begin again to entertain that guest who comes to our mental door and knocks as the living man did centuries ago — as the Christ in Fra Angelico's picture called up the monks to know Him.

In the Arena Chapel at Padua Giotto has given us the history of Christ directly, simply, as if stating for us what he knew. There is no gainsaying it — nothing can be better. Nobility of statement, sufficient accuracy, soberness, and yet fulness of poetic vision. We can understand why the great architect Richardson should have spoken as he did to the writer of these pages, when he and Bishop Phillips Brooks walked around the chapel. Said Richardson, forced through the statement of fact by Giotto to express something of the feeling of which he was full : "And do you believe all this ?" For that was the proper effect and result of such a connected, pictured statement, or record, by a hand and eye certain of that record and its previous vision.

(And then the Bishop told him that he believed, and followed with words I dare not quote because inexactness would be doubly wrong to the memory of two men worth remembering.)

But realistic as Giotto is, his real value, one beyond

his imitators and successors — one which explains the difference, and maintains him as the head and fountain and also the glory of Florentine developments — is this, that the double vision and thought are there. The subjects are no common happenings. That story you see *must* mean much. This is of course in his mind's view, and in his feeling of sentiment and propriety. But with this, and so completely interwoven with it as to be inseparable, is his study of the real play of the human form, its meaning or intention, and this so much so that even to-day the modern man, with all his knowledge, is usually mute beside this beginner who is stuttering the first words of our language of painting.

For a long time Giotto seemed to have sprung from the unknown, as Minerva from the brain of Jove Almighty, but now we know that Florence and Rome held men whose training, whose intentions, whose sentiments were already developed, and from whom the greater man derived impulse and training, and we return to our early appreciation of how Rome naturally received the ancient Roman language of art, preserved or encouraged in the more pagan or less Christian south.

This should in no way derogate from our masters. We all derive from others — only there are many ways of inheriting.

Leonardo said of Giotto : —

"The painter shall certainly find his painting of little value if he picks for his foundation the painting of others; but if he makes use of natural things, he shall produce good fruit. As we see in the painters after the Romans, they continually imitated the one the other, and from age to age they handed down art to its final descent. After these came Giotto, the Florentine, who, born in solitary mountains inhabited only by goats and such-like beasts, looking at the image of nature to make a similar art, began to draw on stones the actions of the goats of which he was keeper; and so he began to make all the animals which he found in the country in such a way that this man after much study stepped ahead not only of the masters of his own age, but of all those of many past centuries. And that art declined because all imitated the previously made pictures, and so from century to century it went on declining until at length Thomas the Florentine, nicknamed Masaccio, showed by perfect work how those who had for guide something else than nature, which is the mistress of masters, labored in vain. Thus I wish to say of mathematical things, that those who only study authorities and not the works of nature are creatures and not sons of that nature, which is the mistress of all good makers. I do hate that greatest foolishness of those who blame the others who follow the law of nature and put aside those men who are the disciples of that nature.

"And it was in truth a great marvel that from so rude and inapt an age Giotto should have had strength to elicit so much that the art of design, of which the men of those days had very little, if any, knowledge, was, by his means, effectually recalled into life. The birth of this great man took place in the hamlet of Vespignano, fourteen miles from the city of Florence, in the year 1276. His father's name was Bondone, a simple husbandman, who reared the child, to whom he had given the name of Giotto, with such decency as his condition permitted. When he was about ten years old, Bondone gave him a few sheep to watch, and with these he wandered about the vicinity — now here and now there. But, induced by nature herself to the arts of design, he was perpetually drawing on the stones, the earth, or the sand, some natural object that came before him, or some phantasy that presented itself to his thoughts. It chanced one day that the affairs of Cimabue took him from Florence to Vespignano, when he encountered the young Giotto, who, while his sheep fed around him, was occupied in drawing one of them from the life, with a stone slightly pointed, upon a smooth clean piece of rock, — and that without any teaching whatever but such as nature herself had imparted. Halting in astonishment, Cimabue inquired of the boy if he would accompany him to his home, and the child replied he would go willingly, if his father were content to permit it. In a short time, instructed by Cimabue and aided by nature, the boy not only equalled his master in his own manner, but became so good an imitator of nature, that he totally banished the rude Greek manner,[1] restoring art to the better path adhered to in modern times, and introducing the custom of accurately drawing living persons from nature, which had not been used for more than two hundred years. Or if some had attempted it, as said above, it was not by any means with the success of Giotto. Among the portraits by this artist, and which still remain, is one of his contemporary and intimate friend, Dante Alighieri."

[1] What we now call Byzantine.

CHAPTER XVI

THE CRUCIFIXION

At the beginning of the third century one of the young slaves at the Palatine scratched upon a wall a joke or insult destined to become historical. His design was that of a crucifix with the head of an ass, toward which a man looked, and alongside was a Greek phrase meaning "Alexamenos adores his god." Here in this insult of the little pagan is the oldest form of the crucifix, and the old accusation of crime in adoring a god with the head of a beast.

At first no material representation would easily occur, from many reasons, one being the non-necessity of external manifestations to the spirit wrapped in God and holding Him in the heart. The symbolical images of mystical importance, the Good Shepherd, the Lamb, and so forth, left the idea of the Redemption in a glorified form, so there was no need of dwelling on the atrocious suffering of the Cross. At length, with the triumph of Christianity in politics and morals (as testified by the Labarum of Roman legions) the Cross appears crowned, to recall Constantine's vision and proclamation. Imagery, as early as the beginning of the fourth century, adorned churches which we do not know with the eye, but which are described for us. Images gave the meaning; aureoles surrounded the Cross; the apostles were symbolized, and so the Dove came down with them as doves; the peacock was of oriental meaning, and the hart's searching for water brooks signified thirst for the water of life.

But in course of time came the need of asseveration and the natural craving of the people for something more than signs. And so at Santa Sabina on the Aventine, in the sixth century, the Crucified appears, not in the exact meaning of replacing them, but taking the symbolical place of Diana and Juno, for the church was built on the foundations of these pagan temples. It is a fragment, a piece of a wooden door, barbarous and inelegant. The Christ appears between the two thieves, He has the long hair of the Eastern Christian, and stands in the formal attitude of praying (orans); a narrow cincture, as small as it can be, covers the middle of the body. The Crucifix is implied, not made out distinctly, by the attitude of the Christ and the bars of the architectural background; the figures of the thieves are also "orantes," and therefore pray. This is symbolical, of course. The whole meaning of the Gospel tragedy on the crosses, as to the two thieves, is that of the choice of one and refusal of the other.

All is yet indefinite and barbarous, and what is apparent to us now was not so then, nor did the mind need it. So instead of the Crucified One, the mystic Lamb was put in His place in some examples.

In 692 the assembled Greek bishops brought up the question of the symbolic Lamb as representing the crucified Saviour, and decreed that the image of Christ should be placed in the holy places. This is the text: "With the addition of the Precursor is painted the Lamb, symbol of Divine Grace, which signifies, according to the

Law, the true Lamb, Christ our God. Such ancient types, such allegories, transmitted to the Church we can honour as sketches (or attempts) at the reality, but we prefer the reality itself, which here gives the proof of the law. And so, that such perfection be expressed in pictures to the eyes of all, we order that instead of the Lamb, the Redeemer of the world, Christ, should be represented in His human form."

Nor could the most critical expression of to-day be more laudable. But already the Crucifixion had been portrayed. In the Syrian Codes of the monk Rabula, of the year 586, the scene of the Crucifixion is represented. It is often quoted in the history of the subject and sometimes the date is doubted, because of the excellence of the rendering. Here we see the Christ dressed in a sleeveless tunic, the sun and the moon hanging over the Cross, the two thieves crucified on either hand, Longinus piercing the side of the Crucified, a soldier offering the sponge, and then the crowd of the pious women, the Virgin and Saint John, and the soldiers drawing lots for the garments of the Lord. The Virgin takes the antique way of covering the head with the mantle. An explanation of this dropping of the crucifix itself while all of the Crucifixion is given may be found in this; Constantine chose the Cross as a symbol of victory, rather than as a memento of ignominious death. Over all the Oriental and Western world the crucifix gradually appeared with the Christ in all varieties of ornament, and with the image of the Lord are associated figures coming from what is known as the Acts of Pilate in the gospel of Nicodemus. In the end of the sixth century, or in the seventh, we come to the literal translation of the Gospels into art. Matthew and Luke had spoken of the sun darkening at the death of the Redeemer. So the artist pictured the sun and moon above the Cross; the sun on the right has streaming rays, beautifully reminding us of the Apollo of earlier days; the moon on the left is not full. Sometimes a female form, another reminiscence of the pagan world, bears the half-moon on her head. The Gospel tells us how Jesus spoke from the Cross to his Mother, saying: "Woman, behold thy son," and to the disciple: "Behold thy mother," and so art placed the Virgin and Saint John at the sides of the Cross. Gathered around the Virgin are the women of the story; and later, Aquila Lamento has the crosses of the two thieves. Then it became necessary to distinguish the one from the other, and so the penitent began in the early images to look toward the Saviour and the impenitent to turn away. All these figures were naturally balanced, as coming from the subject, which by its severity brought in the laws of symmetry. Next to the Cross, sometimes less important than Mary and John, Longinus bearing his spear represents the Gentile converted, or else the executioner holds the sponge, which recalls the obstinacy of Judaism. The Christ at first is calm, and has no expression of suffering. He extends His arms, without an effort, horizontally, placing His feet on some little step without bending or displacing them. Thus He appears as superior to pain and triumphing over death. The Cross even comes to be a symbol of the tree of life, as we see very late in some works of Northern Europe. The legend of its origin appears in the gospel of Nicodemus. Father Adam spoke to his son Seth, telling him to relate to his sons, the patriarchs, and (because apocryphal) to the Prophets the things he had heard from the Archangel Michael, when he went to the gates of Paradise to beg for oil from the tree of mercy, so that he might anoint the sick body of Father Adam. So Seth, coming to the Prophets, told them: "I prayed to the Lord before the gates of Paradise, when the Angel of the Lord, Michael, appeared to me and told me: 'God hath sent me to thee; thou canst not have the oil of the tree of pardon to help thy father Adam, because I cannot receive it until thirty-five hundred years have passed, at which time the Son of God, full of love, shall come down upon the earth and shall resuscitate the body of Adam and of the dead.'" The legend goes on with the story of the Cross, more and more in detail, the one coming naturally from the other. Seth or Abraham plants or sows something — branch or seed — taken from the terrestrial paradise, and from that tree came to Aaron and Moses their magic staves. Then, cut down for the building of the Temple of Solomon, the tree was not used by the architects, but was part of a bridge over a river, erected by the Queen of Sheba, who, looking into the future, beheld and foretold the destiny of the world. Later, thrown into water where the flocks drank, it gave forth healing, and then, thrown out of the water (which had dried up), it became the Cross for the hanging of Jesus, and was hidden with the crosses of the two thieves after the death of the Redeemer. Helena, mother of Constantine, brought them back from Calvary (on which at that time was a temple of Venus), having learned from some ancient Hebrew the tradition of the place, but the three crosses could not be distinguished one from the other because the notice on the Saviour's had been torn from the tree, so the Bishop of Jerusalem proposed placing on the crosses three sick people, to recognize which was the sacred one by seeing which brought the good fortune of cure.

Later than the seventh century, the Lord appears in full dress, as it were with a churchly meaning, in sacerdotal kingliness. He also appears, according to what is told in some apocryphal gospel, stripped of His clothes and wrapped around with a linen cloth, and then another legend arose, also pictured, which told how the Virgin took off her veil to cover her Son.

Just as art was beginning to accept any pious fable, the great struggle of the iconoclasts came in, and the crucifix and the crucifixion were especially the objects of persecution; and, on the other hand, were made more holy by it. In the Carlovingian period we see the ancient elements, but with other new ones. A penetrating idea pours through the material image, and human piety now bends the body of the Martyr, and hides with mantles the faces of sun and moon, as in the golden crucifix of Luther. A celestial hand passes down from heaven, extending a crown towards the head of the Son, and within it often comes the Dove, symbol of the Holy Spirit. At the foot of the Cross sometimes appears a horned snake, giving us the symbol of the struggle of the wicked one against man — of the Prince of Darkness against Christ. Christ bends His head towards the right of His shoulder, and more and more we feel that He is ready to give up His soul to death. The Virgin, as always, comes, and seems a pious and heart-broken visitor. In an ancient poem, once attributed to Gregory Nazianzen, the Virgin is asked not to weep, because all this fulfils prophecies, and then she regrets that she could not give her own life for

His. With the ninth century we see the images of the
church and the synagogue on either side, the church
receiving in a chalice the blood dropping from the wound
of Jesus, the synagogue, on the contrary, moving away
from the cross. Sometimes, below, Adam appears, the
dead rise from hidden tombs or open the doors of mauso-
leums, and we see the ancient guardians of the earth and
ocean, figures of children and of crawling reptiles, with
the image of Neptune riding on dolphins or monsters
of the deep.

Rome herself, in a barbaric diptych of Ravenna,
appears in the form of the she-wolf suckling Romulus
and Remus. She indicates the West, to which, according
to a popular belief, the Christ turned as He breathed
forth His life. In these images the Mother of Christ
approaches the cross, pressing her head against her
hand (as does Saint John also in balance), and extending
another towards her Son; she is calm, makes no cry,
nor faints, as she is described as doing in false gospels.
This manner of covering the face with hand or drapery
was used to represent the great emotion which art felt
without being able to do more. Angels come down
towards the Christ, stretching out hands also, and, as
we have said, the divine blood was received in chal-
ices by the church, or sometimes by Father Adam; even
Joseph of Arimathea also collects it — he who was the
guardian of the Holy Grail, as we know by the legend
which tells us how the Knights of the Round Table
learned of the death of the Redeemer. So through the
Carlovingian period art stumbles along with great intention, but a prey to barbarism, as is the outside world.
Sometimes along the Cross the twelve apostles appear

U

in the shape of doves; below, hands are stretched out from the clouds, and at the foot of the rock upon which the Cross is placed pour out the four rivers of Eden, leading the sheep to the fold of Christ. This design in mosaic covers the apse of the basilica of Saint Clement in Rome. (We are now at the end of the eleventh century.) The base of the cross is represented in foliage; birds sing upon it; a serpent curls away, and over the great space of the wall of the church green branches of pure ornament spread forth.

In curves and centres are images, flowers and birds again, and holy beings, so as to give the sense of the happy world of the new faith and salvation brought to the universe in every way through the passion of the Redeemer.

Bishop Paulinus of Nola described the design on the wall to please his life-long friend Sulpicius Severus, and also another friend, between 1410 and 1431. The Bishop tells us how the base and the walls under the vaulting of the apse are decorated with "an illusion of mosaic — a joyful sight." Then he describes the painting, or, we should say, the mosaic.

"In full sweetness of friendship streams the Trinity.
In the form of the lamb stands Christ
Whose father's voice thunders from heaven,
And in the form of the Dove sweeps down the Holy Ghost.
The cross gives the crown in pure victory,
And of this crown the apostles are the crown,
Whose image here is shown in a chorus of doves.
The Holy Trinity becomes one in Christ,
Who in himself unites the very essence of the Trinity.
The cross and the lamb point him out as a holy sacrifice,
And purple and palm show a rule and a triumph.
Upon a rock he stands, himself the rock of the Church,

From which, high above us, are four pouring sources —
The evangelists, Christ's living rivers."

Elsewhere the good Bishop wrote :

"Behold the unadorned cross in the holy halls of Christ ;
The precious gift is for the hard and courageous battle.
Carry the cross upon thyself if thou wishest to obtain the crown."

The crucifix, then, is the symbol and the teaching in these images, and in the confusion of war and religious development that is as should be expected. A moment came for the relief of the world when feeling began to have its place in the expression of the arts. The old fear of some of the saints (which still pursues certain parts of the entire Christian world), namely, that all worldly things are the work of the devil (which is a putting aside of art), passed away in the need of comfort and in the surety that the death upon the Cross was a reproof of pride and also a cure. Then portraits of the Christ came from the East; from ancient sources; some said to have been painted by the apostles themselves. To those old images some miraculous virtue often belonged, much strengthened by many legends; pilgrimages came to them and copies were made. Of course they are Byzantine; they came from the East, and the Oriental type of the Christ, often with a majestic and kindly expression, lasts long before the Western mind and eye. What wonder that in the poor chapel of Saint Damian the crucifix spoke to Saint Francis during his contemplation of the bitter sufferings of the Lord ! And so the Christ upon the Cross is rightly given as supported by Saint Francis in later art; it is the record of an earlier story.

Murillo's painting shows Christ still nailed to the Cross by the left hand, but embraced and supported by Saint Francis; the Lord is still suffering, but sweetly looking down upon His devoted lover and passing a gentle hand around the faithful saint's neck.

Still in Siena is kept, in the house of Saint Catherine, the crucifix which spoke to her. With the Franciscan worship of the suffering Christ, the Christ of glory and power is put aside for the Christ of agony and pity. The body bends, the arms are drawn in pain, the head with half-shut eyes leans upon His shoulder; it is the Christ who died for the sins of man and whose sad image should convert the sinner. We realize to-day, through every form of historic belief or doubt or opposition, that a large part of what the entire world has of freedom and of kindness and of belief in fraternity dates from Saint Francis and the mystical love and passion spread by him, bringing the poor and the unhappy and the downtrodden, the victims of the great and the sufferers by war, to some place in the world, to some release from suffering through the oppression of others, or what we call the necessities of politics. We have not quite reached to the ideal of peaceful humanity, but no one is contradicted who speaks for it, and perhaps the world may be moving in that direction. Painting marks the beginning of the change in the world. In the Northern arts there are a few stories in sculpture, but they are not yet touched by the spirit of pity; on the contrary, Italy shows both the feeling and the image. In the North it will be through other representations than the crucifix that we shall have a part of our story. Meanwhile we pass through some wonderful paintings of the early men. Occasionally

CHRIST SUPPORTED BY SAINT FRANCIS. (Murillo)

in smaller details we find a few noble images, and coming
at length to two beginners, we meet the brutal crucifixion
of Nicholas the Pisan, where, however, the story is told
with sympathy for the real scene. Christ is crucified
according to a manner which in certain eyes, probably
not those of the sculptor, had special meaning. The
Cross is a sort of tree and its arms spread upward; along
them the arms of the Christ are nailed. The body
bends; the head sinks low upon the chest. Already the
knowledge of the body which we shall inherit begins to
show. Near by the Mother swoons. She is supported
by some weeping women, and John weeps gently beside her. Then we shall have the other great man
Giotto in a representation which is a type of the passing
from the Gothic to the modern idea. It has the elements
of compassion and tells the story with respect and with
half doctrinal statement. It is partly real, partly ideal,
and has a sense of not pretending to be anything more
than this combination. But it is true so far as the
figures are separately taken — the Mother faints, supported by her usual attendants; John is anxious about
her, the Magdalen is at His feet, even now wiping them
with her hair. The Christ is dead, His form has
dropped, His knees have given way, His head is upon
His breast. On one side the crowd of Jews and soldiers
is to some extent kept back by Joseph of Arimathea,
who points upward; he has had a vision. Two
soldiers, wearing the cuirass in the realistic way so different from the fittings of elegant art, are about to divide
the seamless coat. Some one interferes, suggesting that
they cast lots. Above in the sky the angels flutter in
suffering. Some bit of theological meaning appears,

for three of them gather the blood, two from the hands and one from the body. Their meaning is beautifully given, but not what he has done elsewhere. The head of the Saviour is of an extraordinary realism, but unfortunately, like most of the work, injured by restorations. Through it all, and the damage of centuries, one can recognize the power of appreciation and observation of the "restorer of painting." The Christ has gone through some awful moment. It is not necessary to know who He is, nor even that He has been crucified, nor is it exaggerated. It has been observed by the painter at a moment of the world when the results of brutal or ingenious cruelty could be seen without going out of his way.

The "great Crucifixion," as it is named, by Mantegna, now in the Louvre, recalls some of the half-ancient, half-classical feeling of the other still greater Italian. In it the beautiful landscape counts for much, and also the beginning of a serious study of every part which marks Mantegna perhaps too much, for we have almost nothing from him wherein he has let himself go. Here the thieves are represented, one more suffering than the other. The soldiers cast lots, the centurion looks up; all of that is relatively commonplace, but the old Mother held up by the women is worthy of his fame.

A hundred years before, the painters had already begun to represent the passage of the souls of the good and bad thieves, the one to angels and the other to devils, and Gaudenzio Ferrari has beautifully echoed for us the cry of despair of the angels.

The hymn of the "Stabat Mater" deeply impressed the minds and hands of artists, and it was evident that

THE CRUCIFIXION. (Giotto)

the sorrow of the Blessed Virgin must be told. When, however, the painters too often allowed her to fall into the arms of her friends, theologians found such a misapprehension of the courage and love of the Mother of Christ unworthy, but nothing could take this away from the wish of the painter and beholder. The moment came when more was necessary to relieve the mind than the mere story, and Fra Angelico opens the world of mystical painting. His crucifixion is evidently a sermon; the Christ recalls Giotto, and the good monk in his wisdom and from a habit of sight connected himself with Giotto whenever the opportunity came. The good and the bad thieves are each marked out, but now throughout the steps of the scene we have saints of the past and of his own day in attitudes showing their special character and their importance to the pious painter. The patron of his order — Saint Dominic — kneels at the foot of the cross. Learned doctors stand and point; Saint Francis is lost in adoration. Another weeps, unable to behold the suffering of the Lord.

In an earlier disposition, a group, beginning with Moses and Saint John, takes the other hand, but the realistic story of the suffering of the Mother occurs in the centre of the painting. She stands supported by her two faithful attendants, and her arms, spread out, have been seen perhaps in actual nature, they are so true to the physical agony of the heart giving way. Before her, turning her back to us, with a passionate gesture worthy of artists less calm than the sweet monk, Mary Magdalen throws herself against the Mother, half upholding, half imploring, wholly pitying her. We see her from behind a long line of gracious figures, and we must guess at what her expression would be if she rose. The great picture is, as we said, a sermon, but a tender one, and one realizes the happy life of the saintly artist in his cloister, absorbed in the contemplation and the love of the Lord.

An old man kneeling is Jerome, whose cardinal's hat lies on the ground beside him. A picture of the church appeals to Him who is our strength against the temptations of this life. The great and learned doctor is confident and contemplates. Two bishops stand behind Jerome; one is sometimes called Ambrose and the other Augustine. Augustine writes and meditates. Ambrose seems to follow the text wherein the Prophets have foretold what now is there. Then three founders of orders kneel; Saint Dominic, Saint Francis, and Saint Benedict. Over the face of "the poor beggar of Christ" spreads an unspeakable yearning, as if to take upon himself the sufferings of the Lord. Benedict weeps, a hand covering his eyes, for in his order the sufferings of Christ have left the greatest marks. Behind them, Saint Bernard stands; Bernard, whom Dante saw in paradise with his own eyes. Then Romuald and John Gualbert. They express in their look of abstraction the sorrow of their lives.

Then we close with two more of the Dominicans. Peter Martyr kneels. Upon his head are the wounds which opened to him the sight of this mystery. And then, still further back, Saint Thomas Aquinas, who has written of and explained sin and Redemption.[1]

[1] The writer from whom I have taken the names of the assistants explains the redness which covers the sky of the painting (a matter usually attributed to changes in the blue) to a recollection of the poet Dante when he tells us how heaven looked at the moment of the death of the Lord.

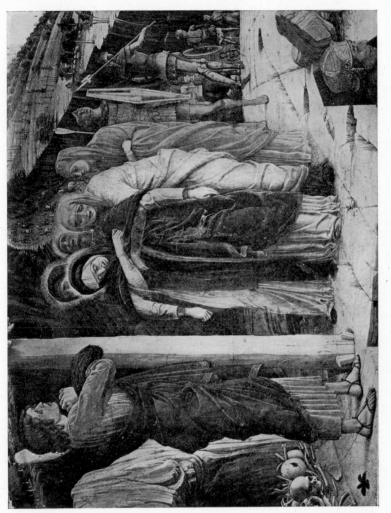

DETAIL FROM THE CRUCIFIXION. (MONTEGNA)

Later the learned artist Perugino, who, we know, was perhaps unjustly accused of not being a true believer, has spread before us the result of his Umbrian training. We begin to enter the learned world of beauty wherein the tragedy will be lost. Still, with other more Northern artists, as with Luini in the great page of fresco at Saint Mary of the Angels at Lugano, and in Ferrari's at Varallo, we shall have the lyric outburst. Luini has filled his painting with the scenes of the Passion as if seen from a distance. They follow a long procession, as if several stories were happening at the same moment. Separately, they are both beautiful and ingenious. Far above in the mountain we see the Lord kneeling alone while His apostles sleep, and an angel ministers to Him. In that ingenuity referred to, the forms of the sleepers are reflected on a wet space. Further down, the outrages to Christ, the insults, the bearing of the Cross, the procession of the soldiers, the thieves and the Mother; and then, to the right of the Cross (we will return to the crucifixion itself), the Christ extended on the knees of the Mother, upheld by John, is embraced by the Magdalen, while Joseph and another friend prepare the shroud. Incidental figures all about belong more or less to the story. On the right, within a marble hall, again Thomas kneels before the Lord in a last good-by, which is repeated far up the hill on this right-hand side by the kneeling crowd of apostles witnessing the Ascension.

To the traveller, coming from Northern paucity to the wealth of Italy, this page of what seems infinite detail is a surprise and a relief. Knowledge and joy and feeling and sorrow; the whole of the Italian nature and habit and learning is spread out upon the beautiful wall, injured somewhat by time.[1]

The Christ is placed high above, a noble figure fastened to the Cross, the face bent just a little, almost in sleep; around him is a chorus of weeping angels in the dark sky. In that sky one sees the spirit of the good thief carried off by angel hands, and on the other side a devil fastens upon the struggling soul of his companion. The figure of each thief on either cross shows the learning accumulated in Italy. The science of anatomy, and the instruction and influence of the great Leonardo had turned the world of painting into one of greater splendour than that in which we now live. Then below, in the foreground, the motley crowd, the men on horses, the executioners and soldiers, the Pharisees on the glistening mules which distinguish them from the Roman cavalry, — in fact, all the story. The struggle for the coat ; — the realistic, ugly scene is made beautiful by that training of the Leonardo environment. John stands by the foot of the cross absorbed in the contemplation of his Master. The Magdalen kneels with arms outstretched in an agony of feeling. The Mother is about to faint, or perhaps has fainted, but still stands upheld by her women. Further away the usual crowd, men and women, wonder what is happening.

In our superiority as foreigners we pass over a work of art which is beyond the power of any modern man, nor do we know enough to realize that it is not the work of the greatest man of his time.

---

[1] Here and there appear the marks of the under painting, giving us some explanation of the economies necessary to the moment when ultramarine blue was handed separately to the artist by the givers of the painting.

THE CRUCIFIXION. (Fra Angelico)

Signorelli is a man whom it was once rather the fashion to forget; a grave and somewhat disagreeable painter and draughtsman. He has painted terrible scenes; the Last Judgment, the waking up of the dead, the consternation of the damned, and the joy of the elect; and he has also shown existence on earth previous to that as the reign of anti-Christ, a beautiful moment where only a few suffer. In his great painting at Orvieto we have the portrait of his friend Fra Angelico. Signorelli, as I say, has been neglected. In his life he was not fortunate, and we may remember how he had to borrow from Michael Angelo, whose letter we have. Perhaps he was not so far away from the great master. Twice he has painted the Crucifixion, with little regard to tradition, as if for himself or the donors. One which we now see as a picture was made for the banner of an order, the Brotherhood of the Holy Spirit at Urbino. It was to be painted on both sides, and its value was to be judged by some master painter. Signorelli, who was more frequently called Luke, has given us the Christ already dead, alone on the Cross, which comes out strongly on the azure sky. The learning of the artist shows in the drawing of the Saviour, whose body stiffens while the legs part, a detail extremely rare. The Magdalen stands by the Cross with arm and hand passed about it. On either side, the two centurions on horseback look up as they guard the dead body. One of the soldiers points carelessly, perhaps in insult; the other one looks from under his hand with an appearance of compassion. Below the Cross the Mother is stretched out, dead to everything. Two of the pious women have taken charge of her, but she is oblivious of all. Other women about

her look down in pity, and then, a little apart, Saint
John, quite young and quite Italian, looks up in absorbed
contemplation. Far back are men and horses, and a
solemn landscape with buildings. It is a wonderful
painting from the mere fact that it is not large, only
about forty-five inches wide; a poetic and learned work,
which was studied carefully by the great Raphael, who
has imitated it.

On the other side of the banner the master painted
the Descent of the Holy Spirit, but of that we need make
no further record.

He painted another banner for the town of Citerna,
and it was again for a brotherhood. It is said that it
was given by him in thanks for the care given him in the
hospital retreat next to the little church, but, as often,
that story is uncertain.

Jesus is again dead on the Cross. Again we recognize
the master in anatomy. The same point is insisted upon —
the bending of the legs so that we see the cross between.
Every detail is slightly different from the other representation. Again the Mother has fainted below, and is
stretched out on the ground, her head resting in the lap
of one of the women, who lifts the Virgin's veil to give
her air. Her right hand rests listlessly in that of one
of these good women, a beautiful touch of observation
from nature. John stands behind them looking up,
absorbed in the past. On the right, another holy woman
— which one is not indicated — looks up also in quiet
compassion. An ancient man gazes at the Cross and the
Redeemer. (He is the patron of the brotherhood, who
asked that he should be represented as Saint Anthony.)
In the distance the later story is told; the three crosses

THE CRUCIFIXION. (LUINI)

are there in the distance, the Christ already taken down, while the other crosses keep the bodies of the thieves.

A still more singular Crucifixion, also somewhat passed over, was known under the name of another painter for a long time. It came from the Florentine convent of Santa Maddalena and its special and separate meaning may, of course, belong to some particular request or need. Here in a field with flowering plants, Christ, already dead, half hangs, half stands, because supported by the bracket to which the feet are nailed. There is the same curious detail of belt, of hair, and of arrangement of the crown of thorns, which we know elsewhere, and also the same representation of a powerful man. The Christ half slumbers in death. The great arm of the Cross, with the inscription above it, cuts against the sky. At the foot of the Cross kneels the Magdalen in sorrow and expostulation, as if appealing against such a monstrous crime. At the foot of the Cross a skull indicates Golgotha and serves also to help the master's composition. That is really the story, but further back two different scenes are told. On the elevated slope we see the apostle Peter denying the Lord to Pilate's servant, who, turning away from us, invokes the testimony of another man, and we recognize their unbelief in the protest of the apostle. Far away again, on the top of a hill, the Virgin lies fainting, while the divine Body is taken down from the Cross. Then, a little further down, the Body of the Lord is carried, followed by the Mother and John and some compassionate women. Meanwhile, also, Peter sits in despair in a corner, in repentance of his cowardice. A great depth of distance, probably copied more or less from the spaces that Signorelli actually looked at, stretches behind the scene. It was also thought that the very flowers spread all about have a meaning, as has everything in this remarkable painting.

We might call up the North again and remember that Albert Dürer has not carried out in his engraving of the Crucifixion the success of so much of his work. The big painting, with all manner of strange events, is still not complete, but very near the representation. The single figure of the Crucified, with a suggestion of landscape below, is also disappointing. Van Dyck (in Berlin) is partly terrible and partly commonplace. Rubens gives us a great painting which we cannot forget. We have passed entirely out of the ancient world, and he has said good-by both to the past and to the future. His arrangement is, however, full of good sense, as may well belong to a master whose balance of mind is perhaps the greatest ever known in art. He has managed to bring the crosses into some perspective, so that what after all we see is the Christ, whose powerful body hangs partly fastened in unreal pain, but with the illusion given by the splendour of knowledge. The picture, which has part of the nature of the heavy Fleming (who is also a great man), gives us the head of the Christ, dead or almost so, and contemptuous of death. The head droops down, the beard falls on the chest; around Him are the terrible figures of the thieves whose legs are being broken by the executioners. Mary Magdalen protests in fear as Longinus, high upon his horse, pulls up to drive his lance into the body of the Lord. John leans his head upon the shoulder of the weeping Mary, not more grieved than is neces-

THE CRUCIFIXION. (Signorelli)

sary to recall the story.   Such is the power of art that
this mistaken effort shall always be remembered.

Van Dyck gives us the mere crucifix; very beautiful, because the loneliness of the figure, looking up
to heaven, is a part of the story.   One need not insist
upon the beauty of the landscape and cloud of the
learned and graceful artist, the favourite of men and
women.

Far different is the painting of Velasquez; the Christ
is almost standing and the head hangs down, the face is
scarcely seen, and a few streaks of blood pour from the
wound.   We have elsewhere spoken of the Spanish craving for emotion of a physical kind, and of the answer to it
in the figures of the Crucified.   And then, these are
paintings not for the idle public, but, in some cases, for
convents or churches or private owners who wish something more than a mere portable crucifix.   We must
never forget that some of the great masterpieces are
nothing but business answers to business needs.

Again comes the sketch of Rembrandt.   Here the
story is told of other days, and also to interest himself,
for the singular appreciation of the Old and New Testa-
ments, the contrast between the synagogue and the
Christian belief, is equally felt, as if balanced, as it
were, in either hand.   This is a picture of Jewry.   The
Jews disappear from the scene.   They may be believers
or unbelievers.   Some argue; we see the movement of
their arms, and we can distinguish the face of the re-
flective and sensitive man who turns away, as well as
the hard outline of the priest.   The sense of punishment, of exile, of passing away, is extraordinary with
these people, who are, as it were, banished.   The two

near the front may be believers or may not; we hesitate, but they fly.   The Cross is far back; the Christ
looks up.   Indistinct as the sketch is, the appeal of the
face is visible.   At the foot of the Cross are grouped
Mary Magdalen, perhaps, and some other Mary.   One
is embracing the Cross; the other has turned from us
stretching out her arms.   Mary the Mother has fainted,
and we see her taken care of by some women.   Behind
them is the group of the insulters, "wagging their
heads and saying: 'Thou that destroyest the temple,
and buildest it in three days, save thyself, and come
down from the Cross.'"   These figures are mere outline, but all the meaning of contempt and insult is
there.   On the contrary, the soldiers are indifferent,
all except Longinus, who has left his horse and kneels
before the Saviour.   But one figure remains to be
explained — two perhaps.   Who is that woman lying
prone upon the ground, all wrapped up but for two
trembling hands extended; and then above her another
woman who bends in sympathy with open hands?
Is that Mary Magdalen?   Carried out further, it might
have been one of the grandest of all expressions.   Then,
in what we call Rembrandt's special power, the light
comes from far above, in the centre of the scene.
The Cross of the Christ, the twisted forms of the
thieves, all the mass of horses and men and people who
belong to the story, are bathed in this light.   On one
edge the Pharisees and Jews pass away into the shadow.
The light of Rembrandt has made this a triumph and the
glorification of the Crucifixion.   The little sketch is
greater than almost any one of the great paintings.
Alone, perhaps, the doctrinal Angelico has given us a

THE CRUCIFIXION. (Velasquez)

similar sensation, not by what he has done, but by what he has suggested.

It is many years since I was in the Alsatian city of Colmar where my friend Bartholdi was born and has left his mark. The museum there has a Crucifixion by Grünwaldt which is a nightmare of reality. Done in the North, it would have met the Spaniard in savageness, were it not that, awful as it is, it is a statement, not an exaggeration of the devout.

The Christ in the centre of the picture is very near us, so that we are almost on Him, and his Cross passes out of our vision into space below. The Cross is a rude thing hurriedly chopped out. Its transverse branch bends with the weight of the Crucified, who hangs livid, torn, and bleeding from the rods whose ends still remain in the wounds. The nailed hands at the end of out-stretched and lengthened arms claw the air in stiffened death. The knees are turned in, and the feet are a dis-torted mass of blood and muscles. The very nails of the feet have turned blue within the curve of the forced twist which holds them by one great piece of iron. The head of the Christ hangs on one side, crowned with many thorns; the eyes are closed, the mouth gapes. The dead man is there. Had he seen such or invented Him? We do not live at a moment that gives such horrible sights, but the artist did.

At the right of the cross are the Virgin, Saint John, and the Magdalen. Saint John, a young man, very young, like some student, holds up the Virgin by her waist and strained arm. She, dressed in a white cloak, has fainted, white as her dress; her lips move, disclosing her teeth. Although unconscious, she tries to stand, bending forward. It is like a photograph from life. At their feet is the Magdalen in wild distress, bent like a bow, with hair dishevelled, a veil through which we see her eyes that notice nothing. The fingers of her hands are crossed and entangled. Why she is so small is a mystery, but perhaps it is only one of the cases of a painter changing his mind as to proportion.

On the left of the cross (our right), stands John the Baptist, holding an open book and pointing to the crucifixion. His book says, "It is necessary that he should increase and I diminish."

The Saint John is savage; perhaps he may have been created as a type of the desert. At any rate, he draws us into the picture of the Christ and the three others. In the distance is a river, and night is coming on.

This formidable painting echoes the words of Saint Bonaventure:

"Chastised as a base and unpardonable criminal, they accompanied him out, and after he had put on his clothes, they hurried him away, and loaded him with the heavy wood of the cross, which measured fifteen feet in length; thus he was hurried along by an enraged mob, in company with two thieves, who were condemned to death; these were his companions in suffering. Wherefore, as the prophet Isaiah saith, 'You are not only numbered with evil doers, but are used worse than they. Your patience, O Lord, is unspeakable.'

"His blessed and afflicted mother, seeing that she could not get near him, on account of the great concourse of people which pressed about him, went, with Saint John and the rest of her companions, a nearer way, to the end that she might meet him at the winding of the street. And when she perceived him coming, bowed down with the heavy load of the cross, which before she had not seen, she was like one beside herself, and half dead with grief, so that she could neither speak to him, nor he to her, by reason of the furious

DETAIL FROM THE CRUCIFIXION. (Grünwaldt)

mob which hurried him along with great violence and compulsion. After, however, he had gone a little way, he turned to the women that followed, weeping, and said: 'Ye daughters of Jerusalem, weep not for me, but weep for yourselves and for your children,' as is further contained in the gospel. And in these two places were erected two churches in memory of these things, as they report who have been there and seen them. And as Mount Calvary was distant from the city, he was so tired and faint that he was not able to carry his cross the whole way, but fell down under it with exhaustion. The wicked executioners, not willing to defer his death, lest Pilate should revoke his sentence, as he had before shown some inclination to release him, compelled one Simon, a stranger, to carry it for him, and Jesus they led unburdened the rest of the way, but bound like a thief, to the place of execution.

"From the hour in which he was first taken in the night, till the time of his being crucified, Christ was in one continual combat, and endured numberless reproaches and injuries, sorrows and detractions innumerable, and suffered the most cruel torments among them.

"When the Lord Jesus was now come to Mount Calvary, then he was extended upon the cross, as it lay upon the ground, and nailed fast to it. Still to add insult to the pangs he suffered, he was crucified between two thieves, and loaded with derision, contempt, and reviling from all parts. Some blasphemed him, others shook their heads, and said, 'Fie on thee, thou art he that wouldst destroy the temple of God, and build it up again in three days. Others he saved, himself he cannot save: and if thou be the Son of God descend now from the cross, that we may believe.' All this was acted in the presence of his afflicted mother, who stood near the cross. Thus stood the doleful mother beside the cross of her son.

"There were also with our blessed Lady the beloved disciple, Saint John, and Mary Magdalen, and the two sisters of our Lady, Mary of James, and Mary of Salome, and other friends, standing under the cross, who all, but especially Mary Magdalen, the beloved of Jesus, were very sorrowful, and wept bitterly, and could no ways be comforted, because of the pains of their beloved master: for their sorrow was renewed with his, in the words, or deeds, which were said or done to him.

"The Christ spoke seven times, as is written in the Gospel.

"And then our blessed Jesus began to fail in his sight, after the nature of dying men, and grew faint and languid, sometimes closing and sometimes opening his eyes: and bowing his head first on one side, and then on the other, till being quite spent, and life failing, he recommended his soul to his Father, crying out with a loud voice, the seventh time, saying, 'Father, into thy hands I commend my spirit.' With which he yielded up the ghost.

"At this strong and vehement cry of our Lord Jesus, a centurion who was standing by was converted, and immediately said, 'Verily, this man is the Son of God'; because he heard him cry so loud when he expired."

And now we come to a dangerous passage in art. A glorious painting of Tintoretto will serve as an introduction to the modern view; and as to this very painting we have the documentary story of its influence within a short time, for Velasquez studied it, and his great picture, known as the Lanze — "The Lances" — is the final record of that especial grouping and movement of the attendant soldiers. Van Dyck also has left us his studies, not used in his shortened life, and to us their every detail agrees with previous representations of inherent cruelty in the mechanical work of military obedience or legal enforcement.

The executioner who ascends the ladder to the Cross, brings up to us the same horror of his indifference. We know who the august Victim is, and we shudder again as the brutal ladder rubs against Him. He is All in All; and yet nothing but the ordinary criminal executed. Hardly does He differ from the two thieves. Even the group of the mourners gives way to the story as it appeared to the artist's inner sight that day. That is a fact of nature; our memory will perhaps call back that when

DETAIL FROM THE CRUCIFIXION. (Grünwaldt)

we were looking at the picture what we saw most was a red cloak just before us on the grass.[1] That to our memory is the picture, as it would be in real life, and one of the most realistic of all paintings carries with it the lesson of the invisibility of the great motive or purpose, and the power of the momentary or accidental or usual.

One feels, as in all Tintoretto, how deeply the Church holds these souls, whether, like him, they lead an existence of hard work, joyously carried, or like Veronese, or even Titian, apparently enjoy all there is of life.

We might put into our list now the Crucifixion pictures which will be henceforward in the possession of the vast multitude, like the crucifixes to hang on neck or wall. Little engravings, even if signed Albert Dürer, will carry to any home the work of art used as a sign. Very late, even to-day, the Spanish woman will confess to gloating upon the little tortured image she half hides. It is partly a physical sensation, partly a reminiscence of special "devotions." For the struggle, too big for me to describe or analyze, is now in full force; the Church is fighting the Reformation in both spiritual and temporal domains. Many of the paintings now, especially of Venice the reasonable, and Spain the fierce or dreamy, will have politics in reality for their basis. Only the Spaniard, however, will be absolutely successful in carrying out the real meaning. Rubens may praise the triumphs of his beloved Jesuits, Titian at the end will give us the vision of glory, wherein the ruler of Spain and all the Indies recognizes the powers which have given him help and to which he owes dutiful obedience.

---

[1] The uncoloured print does not give this note of colour sufficiently.

It is a fighting world glorified, and it is only Jack
Spaniard who can, in certain places, cause to pass into
whatever he has to plan, for show or splendour or the
devotion of the community, his own fierce or sweet personality of sensation.

Titian has some personal emotion, as who can avoid
feeling on seeing his dead Christ carried off by His
people in sorrow; it is great because it is true and
beautiful, but it is not especially our Christ. Nowhere
in the well-balanced nature of the great Venetian is
he torn by the importance of his subject. One turns
more easily to such wondrous balance as he expressed
in "Christ and the Tribute Money," where Justice is
enthroned.

Let us go back again suddenly and sympathize with
far-away people who have felt the agony of the Crucifixion. There are absolutely Teutonic examples as terrible
as anything of Spain; the suffering of the Madonna
(I mean, in German words, of Our Lady of Sorrows)
and the distress of the disciple John are so expressed as
to typify such anguish for ever.

When we turn to Central Europe, the mediæval charm
encompasses us; but not with the Crucifixion. The
saints are barbarous at first, and then so refined that we
feel more and more confident that Eastern Greek influences, perhaps actual teachings, have allowed the sculptor
at Rheims to rival the Greek. How shall we choose?
The majesty of the wondrous Christs of the French cathedral porches will never be equalled. The "Beau Dieu"
of Amiens is well named.

The "Elevation of the Cross," terrible in its realism
as treated by Rubens, is known to us; the swaying of the

THE CRUCIFIXION. (Tintoretto)

crucified body, the strain of the arms, the shrinking of
the tortured waist under the grasp of the executioners;
and also we know the horror of what is foretold by the
great painter's skill, the shock which the Victim shall
feel as the Cross is dropped into its socket; — and yet,
notwithstanding all these accuracies of horror, the main
appearance of the marvellous painting is one of triumph
and glory. Part of it may be owing to the knowledge
of form and the splendour of drawing and in the actual
painting the splendour of colour; but the great lines of the
Cross, supplemented by the adjusted lines of the men who
lift it, is too great an artistic invention not to be a triumph.
Music has these moments. Indeed, as we know musical
description and appeal in most of the great compositions,
the sound of triumph goes through the mass of sound,
fills every empty space, and leaves us no longer in the
ordinary sense of life but in a created atmosphere. So
in this example of what indeed is sometimes called the
musical expression in painting.

For we are late in the world now. Only the personal
religious feeling of the very great Rubens saves his painting from being mere art. The times are nearing when the
feeling of the motive will disappear. Only a great man,
or an extremely sensible one, will be an exception. There
is also little or no more struggle as to the rulings of
the Church, although Calvinism or other Protestantism
may stir the sea of thought or discipline, and always of
politics. Rubens himself has escaped from the poor
name of his father in religious circles; all that has faded
into acquiescence, and the Jesuits encourage the great man
and his disciples and followers and surrounding admirers,
who return all fourfold and fill churches, chapels, and

books with records in praise of the saints who have been chosen.

We are far off from our Italians — though this comes from Italy in doctrine and partly in training.

Something, as I said, is gone, not to return — but the Church has triumphed.

THE ELEVATION OF THE CROSS. (RUBENS)

CHAPTER XVII

THE DEPOSITION AND ENTOMBMENT

THERE is a name given to certain representations connected with the story of the Passion, that of the "evening" images or pictures, because they tell us the events of the evening after the Crucifixion. Of all these, the most important is the Deposition, or taking down from the cross. All the Gospels refer to this moment. In art, the subject was not treated early, but when once begun every religious feeling and artistic possibility inspired the ambition of the painter or sculptor to take advantage of the subject, from the religious element, which has more or less been kept to, and also from that human sentiment which has necessarily accompanied the idea of the death of the beloved and the grief of the survivors. Therefore, in this moment of the story of Our Lord, His Mother became a necessity, a pivot of the artistic disposition, as in the earlier moment, with greater scriptural reference, she became one of the supporters of the Cross with Saint John. The references to her in the Gospels are few or merely assumed, but we feel that we cannot separate her from the story; she typifies the feeling of all mankind, and if we refer to the story itself we understand that its words describe her as living a life composed of two impressions — joy and sorrow. As an illustration of this meaning

335

we may take a representation of the Christ and His
Mother, a sculpture attributed to Michael Angelo, but
very little known. It is in the Refuge of the Poor at
Genoa. There is nothing but the head and shoulders of
the Virgin, with a hand of hers pressed on the chest of
her Son. The beautiful head of the Christ lies on His
Mother's shoulder, and He is just not alive. He has
passed away. No sign of pain whatever are upon Him;
merely the closed eye and the slightly open mouth.
The Mother is no longer young. Life has acted upon
her face, and the movement of eyes and lips represent a habit of sorrow, and of care of others, such
as might belong to some saintly helper, some sister or
mother of charity. As a bit of design, we must admire
the wonderful running together of all the lines — a
masterpiece of ornamental meaning. Whether Michael
Angelo's own hand has worked throughout upon it, I
do not know the work sufficiently to judge, but the refinement of expression, if carried out by other hands, is not
to be attributed to any but a sculptor of great skill.

Byzantine art gives to the Virgin a heroic grandeur
necessary to the meaning of her watching at Calvary, the
tomb of Christ. She is represented in tradition as having
gone to find the disciple whose sepulchre was to be
borrowed, and wherein the body of the Saviour was placed
at her request. So she was described also as helping
to take Him down from the Cross; helping to take out
the nails and placing them in her bosom, and giving to
Joseph of Arimathea the shroud in which the body should
be placed in the tomb redolent of myrrh. Another legend
represents her as receiving the weight of the body while
Nicodemus takes out the nails, and she kisses her Son's

hands. So is she represented in some early pieces of
ivory, where one sees her taking the hand of her Son, with
the other Maries next to her, and in a later sculpture at
Milan she lifts the hanging arm and hand of her Son as
if to kiss it. In that ivory, the beginning of a great
understanding of the full meaning of the human figure
may come from some tradition of Southern Italy, bringing
in a memory of the antique. Nicodemus, who stands
just against a conventional Cross, lifts entirely the body
of the Lord, with an action as true as any later skilful
artist, with his great intelligence, shall be able to represent. Then below we fall back on a bit of realism half
useless with this amount of conventionality, but interesting in giving a homely effect — there is a small ladder on
which the right foot of Nicodemus is placed. Meanwhile,
some saintly person, clad short for work, takes out the
nails from the feet, which have been nailed to a wide
support. Saint John weeps on one side — a primitive
and stooped figure. Above, two angels, whose bodies
are half classical, fit into and finish the conventional outline
of the Cross. The undeveloped past mingles suddenly
with the development of the future. In another moment
of art we shall pass to a work of Nicholas of Pisa at Lucca,
wherein Mary and John each take an arm of the dead
Christ, lifting it carefully and bringing the beloved mem-
ber to their lips as they weep. Each separate figure has
a distinctive character, so that one knows that Mary
makes no sound while John is audibly weeping. Joseph
of Arimathea, a noble and heavy and elderly man, passes
his arms around the falling body and takes it upon his
shoulder. The sculpture is in every way the promise
of the great art that is to follow, and at the same time

z

it brings up our much repeated impression, — that of
the persistence of ancient art carried from Southern Italy
to the Northern and more Gothic lands.

This poetic treatment, that is so full of tenderness,
ends there. A more logical and reasonable art shall
reign. In an ivory at Ravenna, the lower division holds
the future treatment of the subject. Innocently barbarous as it is, it has the human statement fully made out.
The bed of the Christ, that is to say, some form of rock
probably, with a conventional drapery, holds Him
stretched out, and His Mother presses her face against
His and closes her eyes, the two faces almost making one.
She lifts His head with one arm, the other being round
His body. Joseph has stretched out the dead figure;
the Maries and the other actors of the drama stand about,
weeping perhaps. Angels dip down from the sky, and
each presses around the body with a drift of passion.
On this treatment the representation will be based for
centuries. We may take as a type the painting of
Giotto in the chapel at Padua, so often referred to by us
in our following of the story. There he gives us the
Mother, her arm supporting the head of the Christ
stretched out, or rather her arms around His neck,
seeming to watch still for a sign of life in the face closed
to any more expression. The women lift each hand to
kiss or hold. Others, grouped about, are rather silent
or adversely noisy in expression. John throws out his
arms in an ecstasy of grief. It is as if he had rushed in
suddenly. Joseph of Arimathea waits with a shroud
drawn around him. Above, angels sweep through the air
in excited circles of grief and surprise.

At every moment the individuality of the painter or

the sculptor breaks loose, except perhaps in the case of Fra Angelico, whose comprehension of the scene is pious and complete. Part is incongruous because of the portraits of friends of his beginning to be introduced in the more modern way, and also, in many cases, because they were the givers of the works. In his paintings the Christ is draped, and the helpers lower Him or receive Him, or hold Him up. We have the beginning of the pictures we shall consider later. In various ways the holy women group around the Madonna, who kneels almost by herself. Mary Magdalen kisses the feet.

And again in a more quiet painting Angelico has given us the outstretched body, the Mother, like some pious nun, embracing the Son, sweet women and saints gathered around, and above them the foot of the cross and a bit of a ladder. Very beautiful, very quiet, with much senti-ment, but not much more than a record. Were it not for the special effect we must always get from the work of such a devout soul, the painting would fall below the ordinary rank of his work.

In most violent contrast are the images of the story as told by Donatello, in sculpture now at South Kensing-ton. Shrieks of anguish seem to come from the figures of the bystanders surrounding the Mother and her Son, who is supported by her. Her face is distorted by grief. The women tear their hair, and spread out the joined palms of their hands in protest, while the great tresses of Mary Magdalen's blond hair float furiously about her. John alone keeps quiet by himself. Otherwise, it is one wild protest against the crime committed, and also against the mere horror of death.

In the pulpit of San Lorenzo in Florence a similar

ferocity of general grief beats through the astounding
artistic representation. Masterpieces they are, beyond
the reach of any but a genius not only of the first water
but of extraordinary capacity in every direction. There
is no problem in representation which is not met and
solved by the sculptor; so much so that in certain lights
they look like paintings. The landscape with its buildings
takes a look of distance. A great ladder of wood stands
up distinctly, a worn bit of much used necessity. On the
crosses hang the thieves, evidently with broken bones.
The guards of Rome have not yet left. Some of them
move away. Meanwhile, around the Christ rushes the
entire chorus of the weepers, arms tossed up, hair torn;
here and there a more quiet figure, but all combining in
some shape to express the general complaint of humanity and also Italian passion. Nowhere else on earth
has any such extravagance in art been carried out, and
yet the reality of actual fact is like that. Any one
who has seen, as I have, fierce distress in certain types
of the Southern world will find these arrested, as it were,
in bronze or in marble, — only one does not easily meet
in the realities of life such a number of creatures equally
carried away by pain and indignation and surprise and
sorrow.

At the same time, these sculptures of Donatello are
miracles of handling, as, for instance, that of the shroud
in one of the divisions. Every line of drapery is masterly,
and the boldness, the sense of the thing actually happening, is astounding. In one of these panels — and there
alone, I believe, in the whole field of art — Christ's head
has no longer been supported, and it slips back against the
Mother and her face.

THE DEPOSITION. (DONATELLO)

A similar fever is seen again in a fragment of Ver-occhio, a lesser man, but one of great skill and great talent. There again the women shriek or rather remon-strate, but the angels floating above are not so wild, and the body of Christ is like that of some beautiful young man.

Then Italian art begins to be gentle and mild. Peru-gino has given us twice a result of beautiful balance and proportion, and, as Vasari says : "He made there besides a landscape which was held at the time to be most beau-tiful" ; but Vasari rightly speaks of the Maries who, around the dead Christ, "instead of weeping (in the Italian way), look upon the dead with admiration and extraordinary love." The other Italians follow, less and less violent, less tragical. Francia gives us the Mother holding the Christ in peace. An angel holds His head ; His eloquent body is asleep. The Mother looks upon Him with quieted face. Later, the greatest of Italians shall tell the story in three different ways, but it is better perhaps to take them up as they can be brought together. Per-haps he may have spoken to Sebastian, or given him the sketch, or in some way made him great for the moment, for Sebastian del Piombo has recalled in the landscape, where only Mother and Child remain, the evening of tradition which fills the canvas. The Mother sits apart, as if alone with her grief, and prays. The body, stretched out, is of course a manly form inherited from or given by the influence of a great man. A noble treatment of the subject by another Italian, Signorelli, gives us the Christ as half asleep, the Mother tenderly looking at Him and supported or encouraged by the loving John. Nico-demus holds up the body of the Christ as if to show Him to His Mother. We have another of the same sculptor where the Christ is so brought down that He is, as it were, on two ladders, a difficulty which comes up even with the very great artists. It may be hardly worth mentioning except as a curiosity of art. The Venetians give us grand and noble representations, and Tintoretto shows us the Mother fallen into a swoon from sorrow, supported by one of the women, while the Christ in her lap has dropped away into the arms of John. In Venice we have again another great man at work on the subject of death and the lesson of the Deposition as his last work. (Michael Angelo also bade good-by to the world with this subject.) We know how Titian, at the end of his long life, was still painting, and the unfinished picture bears the inscription that Palma reverently finished it and dedicated it to God.

In the series of "evening" pictures occurs occasionally the carrying of the body of Christ to the tomb. Donatello has represented it, using (from an antique sarcophagus, or more than one) the body of Meleager carried by the other youths. Raphael gives an image of marvellous refinement — a proof, as it were, of how far the art he employed could reach in the purity and sweetness and elegance which his mere name implies. Beautiful is the dead body and the Magdalen; and the head of the Christ, who seems but half asleep, and admirable also is the group of women who uphold the fainting Virgin.

In the Deposition, the body is often watched and prayed and wept over by the friends, or else by the single figure of the Madonna. The latter is known by the Italians as a "Pietà," but the word is technical, and outside of Italy has no real existence.

A moment ago we spoke of the carrying of the dead body and the connection of some antique fragment of pagan tragedy imitated somewhat by Donatello. There the body is carried to the tomb. There is of the subject a beautiful etching by Rembrandt, "The Entombment," which, although perhaps as far as anything could be from the eloquence of Raphael's story, is still a reverent treatment in a most realistic manner, and, notwithstanding that it is only a large sketch, it acts as a touchstone to the wonderful Raphael, — one of the prodigies of Italy. One feels that the artistic position, the arrangement and the triumph of art, and the possession of some details of the knowledge of anatomy, have become so important with Raphael that the real story has disappeared. With Rembrandt there is no graceful display of the action ; the men bearing the body upon the rough bier are really carrying the weight. Meanwhile one feels their sorrow. The Mother is close to them, but of necessity not taking any part. She merely looks down on the dead figure whose legs hang out of the stretcher of the bier. All but Joseph are average persons ; the Mother's face, on the contrary, belongs to a nobler type than any of Rembrandt's mothers.

With him we are at the end of the general possibilities of the religious story. Here and there, of course, there will be, must be, astounding exhibitions. We shall see them come down even into the nineteenth century, usually appearing where we do not expect them, while, on the contrary, the professional attempts are failures.

As we return to earlier work, in comparison with the more beautiful but not more appealing examples of Southern art, we meet here and there extraordinary in-

dividual expressions — such as that in the Louvre, an
ivory group of three figures, in which Joseph carries
alone the body of the Christ.   The head and shoulders of
the Saviour fall over the back of the man of Arimathea.
He has as much as he can do in bearing this weight.
The arms of the Saviour hang down; one is lifted by his
Mother, who walks behind and somewhat below the two
men.   Joseph probably is stepping up to some entrance
of the tomb.   The representation of the Madonna is
quite equal to that of the Italians of the end of the
thirteenth or beginning of the fourteenth century, but
the face has that curious incapacity for a full rendering
which marks the Northern Gothic after it had passed a
little from its connection with the older teachings.   It is
a point difficult to state, because the slightest exception
will contradict it, but we know what we mean when we
remember something lacking in representations otherwise
wonderful both as to form and artistic disposition, and
continuing to us the antique, which is otherwise so
little connected with the pure mediæval — with the
thirteenth century, for instance.   But as we have seen
elsewhere, we know that either ancient tradition or connection with some particular past, bring out so close a
connection at certain moments that there are fragments
that could pass as Greek.   We have been slow in recognizing the fact, and it is only within a very few years that
the archæologist or the artist has had the courage to
assert this, all the more that the best examples occur in the
triumphant cathedral of Rheims.   There, the images of
the Annunciation and the Visitation give this; a broken
fragment might well pass for the work of more than a
thousand years before.   These traces are here and there

THE DEPOSITION. (FRENCH IVORY OF THE XIIITH CENTURY)

throughout Europe, but in the average habit of classifi-
cation which we all have, we cannot help thinking of
nationality as distinct, whether in the first stages of
human development or later; and we have also a way
of ignoring a possible change of locality.   Quite as much
as in our moment of easy transit, the artist of the Middle
Ages and of later time travelled through Europe.   The
Frenchman built and carved in furthest Norway and
Southern Spain, in Poland or Central Europe, and even
pushed into Italy among characters not ready to be
taught by minds of less tradition.   The converse is not so
until very late.   The Northern man comes down into the
South, as long ago his ancestors, the Goths.   We see
sculpture upon Spanish cathedrals which may or may not
belong to the soil, as regards execution, but which had
the direction of foreign guidance.

Our present subject is necessarily affected by the
ecclesiastical necessities, and the strong feeling of the
Northern races.   In the church of Xantin, in Rhenish
Prussia, the Germanic heaviness is quite in place, and the
sad figures of the women mourn far back in the mystic
shadows, while elderly men dispose the meagre, flattened-
out body of the Christ upon the shroud for burial, and
Mary Magdalen, so dressed as to show that she has not
always been so serious, is disposed in the foreground with
that terrible expression just referred to as belonging
to the Germanic mind.   But the sculpture is deeply interesting as a promise of a change into the more modern.
In the school of Cologne, which was supposed once to
have originated in Flanders, where the Van Eycks
had already appeared, we have representations of our
subject with the character of the place.   However in-

ferior to the Italian (for example, Angelico of the same
date), there is in this one and that one of these painters
somewhat contemplative which suggests living mentally in
a world of piety and of poetry.   We have left the ugly and
the commonplace when we look at them, even if we realize
the deficiencies, more insisted upon than necessary, and
never, as in the more favoured Southern race, cleverly
passed over.   When an Italian had to face too difficult a
question of art he did not hesitate, but let the matter go.
In the North the difficulty is struggled with, usually to
the disadvantage of the artist entering into this conflict
with himself, his ancestry, and his teaching.   But one can
understand Albert Dürer's attempt to get some teaching and instruction at first from the Rhine, and later in
Italy, for Dürer is another example of the travelling
student, and goes from one place to another for many
business reasons, but among others to get some secret
(as he calls it, some "secret of inspiration") from Mantegna, or from the Northern men.

There was still the tradition of the teaching of Saint
Bonaventure, who, writing about 1300 (he was born
in 1221), lays down in his "Contemplation of the Life
of Christ" a precise form of arrangement suitable to
the Deposition.   He says: "Consider carefully and
deliberately how Jesus was taken from the Cross.   Two
ladders were placed against the arms of the Cross at
each end.   Joseph mounts that on the right of the Saviour and endeavours to draw the nail from the hand.
This gives him much trouble, for the nail is thick and
long and deeply buried in the wood, and it does not
appear that it can be drawn without cruelly pressing the
hand of the Lord.   The nail being taken out, Saint John

makes a sign to Joseph to give it to him, so that Our
Lady may not see it. Nicodemus then draws the nail
from the left hand, and also gives it to Saint John. Then
Nicodemus descends and begins to take the nails from the
feet; while Joseph sustains the body of Our Lord. Happy
Joseph, who deserved thus to embrace Him! The right
hand of Jesus remains suspended. Our Lady lifts it
with respect, carries it to her eyes, caresses and kisses
it while inundating it with tears and uttering mournful
sighs." This last phrase reminds us especially of that
little figure of the Louvre, but the tradition of Saint Bonaventure's arrangement has more or less affected all of the
representations, even until very late. We must not forget
that the question of the nails had a certain importance,
as we have seen in the representations of the Crucifixion.
With Fra Angelico, a sentry holds the crown of thorns
and the nails in his hands, and shows them with sorrowful
gestures to several other figures. This action of showing
or looking at the nails seems somewhat of a conceit,
seldom becoming the occasion, but it had a purely devotional meaning at one time, separate from the work of
art, or else it pointed to some variation in dogma, if
one can so use the term, — perhaps religious sentiment is
a sufficient expression. The entire subject of the Descent
and Burial, and, as the Germans call it, "The Weeping
over Christ," was increased towards the sixteenth century
by the interest in the Holy Places and the worship of the
Sepulchre, and by the greater facilities of intercourse, so
that many of these representations are more or less wrought
on by these outside influences. The Northern men
especially have made a point of it, notwithstanding that
they were less successful, and there is something in their

manner of looking at the subject which implies a very
strong interest. As, for example, in the " Descent from the
Cross " at the Escorial in Spain, attributed to Van der
Weyden, wherein, against an artificial background, the
Christ is held up by the two older men, the women
weeping, while the fainting Madonna is supported by
Saint John and one of the Maries.

Perhaps the best type of not over-realistic representation is the great painting by Quentin Matsys at Antwerp.
The Calvary fills the distance. Two of the crosses still
bear the bodies of the two thieves; the third in the
middle is empty. Two women at its foot gather the
blood of the Christ which has run down the stem. Near
or below them two men are seated; one takes off his
shoes, the other takes out some food from a basket and
eats. A third, at a distance, descends the back of the
hill, carrying a ladder. On one side Jerusalem is seen;
on the other, in the side of a rock, the space opens in which
the body is to be placed, and under its vault, near an
old man, a woman holds a light for a servant girl who
sweeps the ground. All these facts of ordinary life
are in terrible, cruel contradiction to what is happening,
just as in our sorrows everything goes on, indifferent to
us. We feel the pain of the subject all the more in this
epic of reality because of that background of indifference.

In the foreground Jesus is stretched on the death sheet.
Nicodemus kneels and lifts the body, holding it under the
arms; Joseph of Arimathea holds the Saviour's head,
and draws together, with care and pity, the torn skin of
the forehead. He wears a rich dress, partly Oriental in
pattern. Nicodemus, solemn and bearded, is clothed in
a long garment. Behind them a man with Turkish dress

THE DEPOSITION. (Van der Weyden)

and turban holds the crown of thorns and looks anxiously
over the others.   In the centre is the Virgin, clothed in a
long robe, and on her head a hood that covers hair and
ears, like a nun's coif.   She kneels with folded hands.
Behind her John bends over, watching with careful hands
lest she faint.   Near him Martha gives a sponge to Salome,
about to wash the bloody hands of Christ.   Near her
an elderly woman, the mother of James, weeps, and Mary
Magdalen wipes again the feet of the Lord with her
hair.   Each one of the actors in the drama has a special
expression to fit his character.   The Virgin's face has
the swelled change which weeping gives.   Her eyes see
nothing; they are almost closed.   Her lifted hands
seem to tremble, as her body balances in her effort to
contain herself.   This is the greatness of the painter; it
is really the Mater Dolorosa whom we see, and John looks
after her who has become his mother from the Cross.

The Saviour is at the end of suffering.   The body has
given way, as have the cheeks — the eyes are closed,
but still not quite, and the swollen lips are still wet, like
the beard, with drops of blood.   The painting calls for our
pity, as it also expresses the pity felt by the actual beholders of the scene.

In the series of the Passion by that not too serious
painter Tiepolo (the last descendant of sea-going people
in that Venice so well described, to its disadvantage,
by Casanova or Des Brosses), we are conscious of a mind
touched by the story, and treating it from knowledge and
observation and with a wonderful human tenderness.
Moreover, the purely artistic treatment is singular,
novel, and important.   In his " Descent from the Cross "
the body, supported by two men, each on a ladder, is

slowly coming down toward us. We see the face to some
extent clearly, though the long hair falls around it and
leaves only part exposed; a noble face, and almost un-
touched by death, as if He had but fainted. He is so
supported that one arm seems to be almost placed by
Him over the shoulders of the men lifting Him, which adds
something of friendly tenderness to them. On one side,
just as a fragment of the design, we see the end of
another cross with the arm of one of the thieves. At
some distance back there is a third cross, to which are
hung two arms, with a hanging head below — another one
of the victims. All that is as realistic as that late school.
We are high up, and we look down on certain witnesses;
the horse of a Roman soldier is partly seen, and some
Jewish head, explainable as we please. Just before us
lies the Mother, still young, in a faint, supported by John
or leaning against him; he looks up to the descending
body with some doubtful expression of countenance, but
with hands nervously telling the pain of the moment.
Mary seems to slip into the repose of absolute forgetful-
ness. One arm lies in her lap, of which we only see a
part, for, as I have said, she is so near to us that the
picture does not take more than this lap, hand, and face,
wrapped up in the drapery of a Venetian. With the
Entombment again, the realist and the sentimental artist
join in one. The Christ is all bent up with the necessary
lifting. One hand still lies on His waist; He is all but
naked. His face is quite bared; He is asleep, but unto
death. The two helpers carry Him reverently and lower
Him into the tomb with the shroud already blessed. In
a moment He will be wrapped and passed in. We see
the Mother, who is unable to bear it, and has turned away.

THE ENTOMBMENT. (QUENTIN MATSYS)

So with some Mary, just visible. Above, two cherubs, like little birds, flutter in a Venetian manner rather gay for such a scene.

One can understand how, with this subject, the artist has occasionally, like Titian, bade good-by to the world. Thus Alonzo Cano, in Saint Jerome's Church at Grenada, places the Entombment over his own resting-place. The Christ lies at full length on a richly ornamented tomb, rendered as the Spaniards have always been able to carry out their ideas; a realization so complete as to appear the actual fact; a noble figure, and all the others of equal beauty, though the two men who are about to lower Him are represented in some costume that we feel has been absorbed from Judæa, and which has a certain strangeness often given by authenticity. Both Saint John, far back, and the two Maries attend the Mother, who appeals to heaven. She closes her eyes in a half swoon, supported by her two beloved friends — her adopted son and one of the Maries.

A similar gesture, but of his own imagining, is that of the mother in the Mary and Christ of Delacroix. She, too, appeals to the infinite mercy and help, but also she asks if ever grief was like to hers. With this modern painter, whom many of us have known, passes the last ray of the expression of religious feeling. It may come again at any moment; we may have it all about us without being aware of it, but in the nineteenth century, except in an occasional flicker here and there, the great light of feeling has but one or two torches keeping it alive.

The subject of the Pity is most natural, the manner of expression having personal feeling in contemplation of the other world, and we shall see Michael Angelo closing his long life with two Depositions.   Earlier, as a very young man, he made the Madonna of Pity — which is world-famous and the main adornment of Saint Peter's at Rome, for which it was not intended, and where it is somewhat disfigured by bronze angels that hang over it. It is his church, but how far from his meaning, and how far from that early moment when the young man, in 1498, closed the century and opened the future of our modern art with the statue. "The Madonna" (we quote from Condivi) "is on the stone upon which the Cross was erected, with her dead Son on her lap. He is of so great and rare beauty that no one beholds it but is moved to pity. A figure truly worthy of the humanity that belonged to the Son of God and of such a Mother; nevertheless, some there be who complain that the mother is too young compared to the son." Condivi goes on to quote the well-known answer of Michael, whose repartees are enveloped very often in irony, but whose general seriousness gives importance to anything that comes from that extraordinary being. Michael refers this youthfulness to the chastity of the mother, and says that besides being natural to her, it may be that it was ordained by the divine power to prove to the world her perpetual purity. Youth was not necessary in the Son; but rather the contrary; as it was intended to show that the Son of God took upon Himself a true human body subject to all the ills of man, excepting only sin; He did not allow the divine in Him to hold back the human — He let it run its course and obeyed its laws, as was proved in its appointed time. "Do not wonder, therefore, that I have made the Holy Virgin a great deal younger in comparison with her Son than she is usually represented. To the Son I have allotted His full age." Condivi makes the remark that "These are considerations worthy of any theologian; wonderful perhaps in any one else, but not in Michael Angelo. He may have been twenty-four or twenty-five years old when he finished this work; he gained great fame and reputation by it, so that already in the opinion of the world not only did he greatly surpass all others of the time, and of the times before, but also he challenged the ancients themselves." That is the young man's work, full of hope and beautiful vision, and deeply pursued for the pleasure of it. The commission for this work, given by the Cardinal Abbot of Saint Denis (called in Italy Cardinal di San Dionigi), is dated August 26, 1498, and was drawn up by a friend of Michael's, Jacopo Gallo. "Be it known and manifest to whoso shall read the ensuing document, that the Most Reverend Cardinal Saint Denis has agreed with the Master Michael Angelo, sculptor of Florence, that the said Master shall make a Pietà of marble at his own cost; that is, a Virgin Mary clothed, with the dead Christ in her arms, of the size of a proper man, for the price of 450 golden papal ducats, within the term of one year from the day of beginning of the work." The Cardinal agrees to pay certain sums in advance, and the contract concludes : "And I, Jacopo Gallo, promise to His Most Reverend Worthiness that the said Michael Angelo will finish the said work within one year, and that it shall be the most beautiful work in marble which Rome to-day can show, and that no master of our days shall be able to produce a better."

We know how Michael's last years turned more and more toward religion, and how much the constant relation with his beloved Marchioness of Pescara influenced him. Encouraged or advised by her, he made many drawings. We have some which are evidently meant for a Descent from the Cross or some form of Deposition. He was then no longer a young man to whom extraordinary efforts of work were natural, easy, daily occupation, and yet we have the record of the French student Vignère that he saw Michael, even at a late period, approaching his end, drive furiously with chisel and hammer into the marble, with a certainty and power such as very few young men could hope to exercise. He describes the chips of marble flying right and left under the passionate touch of the great old man. And we may well consider the degenerate art of to-day, which models in some soft substance, easy to work, to be cast in ugly places and then confided to other and other and yet other hands, while in the work of our great man we feel the chisel play on the hard substance, like the brush of the painter — sometimes light, sometimes rough and hard — polished or not by the mere movement of the hand, and like the touch of the musician on the violin. It is in part this personal touch which makes these statues of Michael so impressive in their reality. The casts, however fine, however interesting, have to be humoured and placed in certain lights to bring out the meaning — the best meaning — of the work. For with him, as with the greatest sculptors, his sculpture is painting and his painting is sculpture. The two arts flow together. About that time he wrote, "Painting nor sculpture now can lull to rest my soul, that turns to His great love on high, whose arms to clasp us on the Cross were spread."

The old sculptor intended his last Deposition for his

THE DEPOSITION. (Michael Angelo)

monument. The head of Nicodemus, clothed and wrapped in a hood, who sustains the body of his beloved Lord, is Michael's own portrait, and, unfinished as it is, expresses the deep emotion of his meaning. Vasari saw this work in progress and gives us a glimpse into the workshop of the aged sculptor, never content out of it, and spending his sleepless nights working, with the paper cap on his head in which he placed a lighted candle. We can imagine him in his vast studio, feeling his way around the huge half-finished marble — a brave and hard-working old age. Vasari tells another anecdote about the Deposition. Pope Julius III sent him late one evening to Michael's house for a certain drawing. The aged master came down with a lantern, and hearing what was wanted, told his servant Urbino to look for the design. Meanwhile Vasari turned his attention to some alteration in the Christ, when, to prevent his seeing it, Michael let the light fall and they remained in darkness. He then called for another light and slipped forth from the screen of blankets behind which he worked, saying, "I am so old that oftentimes death plucks me by the cape to go with him, and one day this body of mine will fall like the lantern and the light of life be put out." A favourite expression of Michael's was this : "If life gives us pleasure, ought we not to expect this pleasure from death, seeing that it is made by the hand of the same master ?" This Deposition was never completed. Flaws appeared in the marble, and perhaps while working in the imperfect light Michael's chisel may have cut too deep. In his accustomed manner he began to break up the work, but very likely his servant Antonio — the successor of Urbino — begged what remained. With Michael Angelo's con-

sent a Florentine exile settled in Rome bought it from
Antonio for two hundred pounds.   It was patched up but
not worked upon, and remained in the garden of his heir.
In 1722 it was taken to Florence and finally placed in
the Duomo by the grand duke.   There it appears all
important, — as described by Trine the main figure of
the entire place, — more important than even the mass of
people in the crowded Duomo.   The great cross of the
altar looks like the Tree from which the body has just
been lowered.   So well does the line of the cross cut the
group that we cannot help imagining that the artist
may have wished some such arrangement.[1]

The most unfinished figure is that of the Mother,
who partly supports and partly embraces her Son.   One
of His arms hangs across her knee; the other over that
of the other Mary, who also helps in holding up the body,
along with Nicodemus.   Nothing need be said about
the beautiful lines which express the abandonment, the
giving way of all; Christ himself, the gentle and kind;
the feebleness of the old man and the half helplessness
of the two women.

There is another subject (or rather the same one
on a smaller scale), which is now in the courtyard of the
Palazzo Rondanini at Rome.   One drives through the
double gate or door towards the steps of the entrance,
and between, in a bare and empty space, stands the

---

[1] It is worth noting that the indifference of the Italians to works of art is as
great as their interest in them; and as we have seen the great paintings in the
Sistine Chapel disfigured by the smoke of candles, so part of this work is polished
because it has been used as a balustrade by the serving-boys, who carelessly run up
and down the steps to light the candles.   On another side, a rough metal handle
has positively been let into the side of Joseph of Arimathea so that a clumsy boy
may climb more easily.

group. It was to have been another version of the group
he gave away, and though apparently less important, it
is also, I believe, more touching — nearer to the great
man, and indicating a still greater emotion at the approach
of death and an acceptance of the fact, with a feeling of
the similar necessity for the Lord Himself. The disciple
of Dante, the friend of Savonarola, the reader of Plato,
the patriot, the stoic, who yet bore in his heart the sadness
of the end of liberty in Italy, is all here. One feels him
alone surviving, and every day more severe towards himself and perhaps towards others, waiting for the call of
the Supreme Judge.

With the end of the thirteenth century the representations have turned from a certain joy in the contemplation
of life (that is to say, a knowledge of its main meaning)
to a rendering of suffering. Herein the Passion addresses
the heart of future men. For the simplicity of the story
the thirteenth century is the proper moment, and the
appearance of accepting an orderly arrangement gives it a
sense of contentment in a world steady in religion. But
however superior that world's position may have been,
the world does not wait, and, right or wrong, we know
that through innumerable generations everything must
go on for better or for worse. If we are astonished at
the suddenness of the appearance of Saint Francis,
we must remember what the world was wherein he
moved, and wherein he invoked the idea of pity and love,
which was that of the thirteenth century, but which
he further inspired by a passion which for ever raised
Christianity to another plane. The phrase of Machia-
velli comes to us: "Christianity was dying; Saint
Francis has called it back to life."

For the ordinary public of the century and those anterior there were representations by many masters, but with the next movement the drama of the Passion becomes more and more sensitive to pain and tenderness, so that an external appeal was all ready to be made through other forms of art, and indeed it was a painting of a Christ on the Cross which gave to Saint Francis the revelation of the passion from which he suffered so deeply that he ended by bearing on his body the marks of the nails which had fastened his Master. His pupils, his followers, the monks of his order, spread his sensitiveness over the world. No one within reach of their voice resists entirely this general feeling. Hence Saint Gertrude tells us how in her meditations the Lord appeared and caught up her tears. Throughout the Western world every detail of Christ's suffering and His death is followed either in verse or in external art. At first the descriptions and the works of art are gentle; by and by the revelation of Saint Bridget tells us how, as we see in the pictures, the Virgin saw her Son raised upon the Cross and then fainted. When she came to herself she saw Him crowned with thorns, His eyes, His ears, and beard running with blood, and so in vision the dreamer saw the Christ walk in His own blood. Then we have the subject of the Descent from the Cross, wherein, all bloody, the dead body is placed on the knees of the Mother. Saint Bridget tells us how Mary tried to loosen this poor body, tried to cross the hands upon the breast, to arrange her Son in the usual manner of the dead, but the limbs were stiff and could not bend; then she threw herself upon the face of her Son and covered it with kisses. When she lifted her head her face was full of blood. Long time she held Him, and begged to be buried

THE ENTOMBMENT. (Ferrari)

with Him.   She wept, so that her soul and her body seemed
about to pass away in tears.

The very sweet mind of Gaudenzio Ferrari has given
us also an Entombment which I put down because it gives
a special feeling of the North Italian, which appeals to
us more and more as we are freed from the tyranny of
Florence and recognize perhaps something of our own
convictions in the Lombards or Piedmontese.   The Christ
lies on his Mother's knees as it were asleep, a smile still on
His lips, a handsome body of the Umbrian school crowned
with a very Germanic head, and about Him a number of
women, all very much interested but in no way weeping,
even if a tear roll down the face of the loving Madonna.
The figure which I take to be that of the Beloved Disciple
spreading out his arms has a feeling of joy and interest
and is a curious success.   A variation of that is given in
his altar-piece at Varallo, where the Christ again has the
same position, but leans somewhat against the Cross, and
is embraced by a beautiful figure, the Virgin, and gently
touched and perhaps supported by another so feminine
that it is difficult to recognize Saint John.   But then we
know the line of sequence, we know Luini, we know
Leonardo and that confusion of the sexes, and that at
times there is an extraordinarily accentuated sense of
feminine sweetness especially connected with the history
of what we call a "school," which is in reality a series of
influences.   The painter is too charming to pass over,
even if the actual painting be not so important.

Twice or three times the subject of the Descent
from the Cross has been given us by Rembrandt.   In
the paintings, and in the etching, the impression of an
actual fact is the same as with Rembrandt always.

The number of collated incidents brought together
in one great unity of appearance becomes more and
more extraordinary as the paintings are studied bit by
bit, and yet they are but fragments in his enormous pro-
duction, so that one can hardly grasp the possibility of
one life having observed all the numbers of points, the
quantities of decisions and their relative play one upon
another.   In the "Descent from the Cross" at St. Petersburg, painted in 1634, photography alone can equal the
reality of the scene.   The Cross passes into the shadow of
the night; at its top one distinguishes the forms of two
men helping to support the body as it slips gently down
the winding sheet into the arms of the beholders below.
Hardly visible as the upper figures are, we can feel their
every action.   Every precaution has been taken by
them, and a third ladder helps to steady the descent.
A figure hardly seen takes the body of the Christ from the
Cross around the breast, so that one of His arms hangs
loose.   The other arm is strained from the necessary
tension of being still held by the upper helper.   A
strong man takes hold of Him below (on some support
not easily noticed), grasps Him around the thighs, and
bends the helpless legs across his own strong ones.   Some
one holds a light, which throws strong shadows.   An
elderly man, with a rope around his white hair, helps to
brace the strong lifter.   A circle of others are ready to
help further.   We see an anxious face and then the backs
of other figures.   Below, in the half light, the shroud is
being spread ready, and two women draw its folds apart.
Further back against the ladder one of the Maries prays.
Then suddenly, at a distance, the light falls on the Mother
— an elderly woman dressed in a garment of the place

THE DEPOSITION. (Rembrandt)

and period of the painter — who, standing, faints suddenly. A man holds her by the waist; another has caught her arm, and her fingers are spread in hysterical failure of control.

A lame description this of a scene whose unity and look of art is the one thing visible at first. The other Descent of the year previous (1633) has a similar placing, a similar careful dropping of the poor body down the great sheet. Carefully the bearers receive it. Ancient figures look at it out of the gloom. A turbaned figure before us watches — perhaps Nicodemus. The shadow falls upon all the lower part of the picture. Above, a light, which may be moonlight, makes all distinct, but in the gloom one sees, as in Rembrandt's pictures, more and more detail, more and more effects, just as in nature our eye follows more and more the point of interest, even if we began by seeing almost nothing. In shadow, quite near us, the Virgin is standing, fainting, partly supported by two of the women, and stretched out rigidly. Her head and chest and a hand are seen; the rest is felt. Again, in 1642, Rembrandt sketched the meaning of the entire scene, with the Christ lying on the lap of the Virgin seated on the ground, herself supported by the figures all about her — men and women. At their feet, the curved, crumpled Mary Magdalen, her head buried in her hands, weeps. Behind, other figures and the Cross, with ladders; and upon another cross one of the thieves, and again the distant city. If finished, it would have been another marvel of perception, and as different from the other two as if invented by another artist.

Rembrandt's so-called "Great Descent from the

Cross " gives us in an etching a reversal of the painting. We see the same picture, as it were, from another side. Here, however, the rays of the moonlight fall distinctly, as needed by the graver. The actions are more violent, perhaps. Below the women wait with a shroud, but one can only distinguish the weeping Mother by her bent form covered with a hooded drapery. All these interpretations, and that of the carrying of the Christ to His tomb, make the subject part of the inheritance of Rembrandt, part of what we owe him in the history of art and in the special illustration of the Gospel.

THE DESCENT INTO LIMBUS. (Sodoma)

CHAPTER XVIII

THE DESCENT INTO LIMBUS. THE RESURRECTION. THE APPEARANCE OF CHRIST TO THE MAGDALEN

THE Apostles' Creed says that "He descended into Hell." Up to the sixth century the reason among Christian writers was that the Lord's visit was for the purpose of liberating souls, and that the souls He there set free were those of the righteous. The false gospels, of course, have given much detail, and Dante has illustrated the idea and fixed it for ever. With him the subject is terrible, but there is a sweet side to it which is told in the fresco of the Sodoma in Siena.[1]

The Christ has the elegance which we must expect from the lessons of Leonardo, the studies and following of Florence, long practice in Rome, and the painter's Northern blood and habit of life. We never wonder at Raphael's liking him and refusing to destroy his work in the great Camera della Segnatura, and moreover introducing his portrait into the School of Athens side by side with his own. Is it the grace of Raphael or the grace of Leonardo which tells through the work of Sodoma? Certainly the Eve in the painting, as well as the Christ, points to these origins; the lovely being looks tenderly towards the Christ, who has come to relieve not only her but so many others, and she presses against Adam, who

[1] This has been cut out from the wall and is now in the gallery.

folds his arms in astonishment as he looks at the bended
form of the Redeemer. The injury to the fresco allows
it to tell us but little of many figures once there; we see
part of a young man just lifted by the Lord from a sort of
tomb, — Abel, perhaps, or some hero of the Old Testament whom we remember as a youth, — and behind them
the landscape of a beautiful world. The Christ holds the
arbitrary and traditional flag, generally useless, but here
helping him to lean as he bends over. A winged figure
behind embraces some long-lost friend.

The Resurrection of the Lord had been represented
on ancient Christian sarcophagi whereon the women and
the watchers sat at the grave. Then, long afterward
(as late as the thirteenth century), the subject came forward again. Giotto paints it, and Fra Angelico. The
form of the story is as simple as it could be made. The
women have come to the tomb, which is a Roman sarcophagus. One looks in, and an angel seated on the edge
tells them: "He is not here; He has risen," and in a
glory above appears the image of Christ, holding a palm
in one hand and a flag of triumph in the other. He looks
up; and is passing away from all below. In the corner
of the painting Fra Angelico has put a Dominican saint.
Of course it is an abstract representation such as might
have occurred in older work.

Dürer has engraved it in the "Great Passion." The
Lord is moving up in a cloud with a flag of triumph.
The tomb is sealed with a stamp or signature, and some
of the soldiers on watch see Him. The others are sound
asleep, and an older one wakes the sleepers.

The Resurrection has been told by Titian, strangely

THE RESURRECTION. (Titian)

and abstractly, notwithstanding the realism of each part. Christ stands, rising as we feel; His shroud flows about Him like a cloak; He holds a great banner in the left hand, and He looks up, half pointing to clouds above. The cover of what must be a tomb has been moved. A man in armour looks up; another is waking, and one sleeps in the foreground, his arms and head sunk within his shield.

Apart from what we must recognize as the business demand, the subject was one to tempt the habit of mind of Tintoretto, so that we have first a strange composition where Christ has risen, and floats in the air freed from His shroud, which is held up by many angels; and He looks down upon the earth where angels are seated at the corner of the tomb and guard it gently. Behind them, and under the roll of clouds, a beautiful corner of landscape appears. Then suddenly, at the side, the donors of the picture — the Morosini family — appear. They are not part of the meaning; only one of them seems in any way to notice or attend, but they are watched by their patron saint, who holds a great cross to indicate his personality. The Christ looks down to see him, almost as if bending over to bless the family who have dedicated the painting.

Very different in intensity of emotion is the "Resurrection" in the Scuola di San Rocco in Venice. Christ has risen, and is swung off by some mighty power, floating upward out of the rocky tomb into which we are partly allowed to see. Angels flying down with violent sweep pull at the edge of the cover of the tomb, and others kneeling help to hold it. All this is in mysterious light, wherein some figure reclines — perhaps a watcher. There is another who lies on the hard ground, with yet another below him.   Through the opening of the cavernous space we look out into light and air and see the women approach.

Different, again, the "Resurrection" by the Sodoma in the public palace of Siena.   It has not the special Northern feeling, although he was born in Piedmont and therefore is frankly from the North, but he belongs to that wide circle which touched Rome at one spot and Milan at another, and took in the teaching of Florence, almost all under the general patronage and name of the great Leonardo.   So in this painting we have, stepping out from a square-edged tomb, a Christ of great elegance, draped in a flowing mantle, holding the traditional banner in one hand and raising the other in some uncertain gesture.   He steps out upon a rock.   Two little child-angels lean upon the edge of the tomb and look about. In front a soldier lies, all rolled up from his sudden abandonment to sleep.   Others also lie about, but one has waked and looks up, with outstretched hand.   These fill the foreground.   In the distance spreads a beautiful landscape of many details, such as would have pleased the master Leonardo, and along the edge of the road are seen the three women coming.   Naturally it is a creation of artifice only, but a work of beauty.

These representations are artificial in the sense that we have no narrative of the actual scene of the Resurrection.   Paintings have often asserted traditions as established facts, and have testified concerning interesting persons, such as martyrs or saints, the statements being incorrect or purely inventive, or else a commonplace repetition of other honorary statements.

THE RESURRECTION. (Tintoretto)

"They have taken away my Lord," she said, "and I know not where they have laid him." And when she had thus spoken she turned back and saw Jesus standing and knew not that it was Jesus. Jesus said unto her, "Woman, why weepest thou? Whom seekest thou?" She, supposing him to be the gardener, said unto him, "Sir, if thou hast borne him hence, tell me where thou hast laid him, and I will take him away." Jesus saith unto her "Mary." She turneth herself, and saith unto Him "Rabboni"; which is to say, "Master." Jesus saith unto her, "Touch me not."

The subject is so beautiful, so simple in meaning, that one would think that there could be no misunderstanding or misreading of the text. Although Giotto has kept the two angels at the head and foot of the tomb within a few feet of the Magdalen (perhaps because of the temptation of composition in his long panels), her expression is that of the most sudden surprise and abandonment. She has dashed herself on her knees as if ready to clasp the beloved feet of the Master.

Later the gardener is brought in. Fra Angelico makes the Christ shoulder a spade, without any real excuse for it, and Albert Dürer has the spade and the standard of victory both together, but we must continuously remember that the prints of Dürer are business matters, and that it is only their immeasurable superiority which hides the fact from us. Dürer is getting up church art for a growing public anxious to profit by the new inventions of printing and of paper.

Raphael is more deficient than the men who were working about him, and his man with the hoe and the gardener's hat has no meaning, nor has the Magdalen, expostulating with Italian verbosity. But Raphael, too, is not over-responsible; he feels the necessity for a tremendous amount of work and the little fragments have to be taken up as best they may be.

One is astonished that the slow-working Poussin should have carried out the notion of a gardener and given us our Lord actually digging. The subject, however, is too beautiful in its actual fact and in its implied meaning to have often failed.

The Titian of the National Gallery has all that we could wish in the suddenness of action and the beauty of the woman. The Magdalen of Correggio in Madrid has again the beauty of woman. But Rembrandt, in another painting which has no reference to a gardener, has something more important than the mere story, that is, the consolation given to the Magdalen by the Christ; an indescribable turn in both figures tells us that the Lord is full of pity and is taking care of her distress and that she will rise another woman.

In looking at an early bronze supposed to have been made about 1150 for the door of the Basilica of Saint Bartholomew we must remember the perpetual connection of the East and West at an early period, which varied, of course, according to places, according to wars, and so on; for instance, we have the strange anomaly that far up in Sweden the system of weights and measures is derived from Mohammedan example. So these early gates come from Constantinople. A certain Byzantine taste is associated with the Mohammedan; then comes more freedom, as in the case we speak of.

The angel sits upon a tomb and lifts his hand to explain to the holy women; above them is a little build-

THE APPEARANCE OF CHRIST TO MARY MAGDALEN. (Le Sueur)

ing with rounded roof and arches, to which the women come. Already one distinguishes the beginning of handsome gesture and a certain beauty of grouping; perhaps this may not be so much a new movement, but rather some reminiscence or old tradition, such as this:

"Mary Magdalen arrived first at the sepulchre while yet it was dark, found the stone rolled away, and returned back to tell Peter and John. Meanwhile her companions, bearing sweet spices, came to the tomb at the rising of the sun and found that the stone was rolled away from the door of the tomb, and they entered and saw a young man sitting on the right side in a white garment, and they were afraid. The angel spoke to them, telling them that the Lord had risen from the dead; and they fled and trembled and were amazed. Mary Magdalen was left weeping beside the tomb, and she saw two angels in white sitting, one at the head and one at the feet where the body of Christ had lain, and they asked her why she wept, and she turned back and saw Jesus."

In the story three women have usually been taken as the traditional number. In the earlier representations there comes again the apparent necessity of the guards being represented as there while the Maries come in and the angel in white addresses them. In the apocryphal gospel of Nicodemus, one of the soldiers who reports the scene says that they became like persons dead, yet they heard the words which the angel spake to the women. When it was asked of them, "Who were these women? Why did you not seize them?" "We know not who the women were," was the answer. "Besides, we became as dead men through fear."

Already Duccio leaves out the guards. There are few representations, and it is a pity, for the subject has all the dignity in form and implied meaning that is needed for the continuance of the Story.

Le Sueur was sometimes able to rise above the academic limitations of later French art, and his "Appearance of Christ to the Magdalen" is a noble composition, full of feeling, although the grouping of the figures is somewhat formal and orderly. Christ stands, pointing to Heaven with one hand, and with the other forbidding any closer approach on the part of the Magdalen, who kneels with suppliant hands and lovely streaming hair. There are no guards, and the spade merely lies at the Lord's feet as an indication of the text.

At the end of the images of the Appearance of Christ to the Women we may place the painting of Rembrandt at Brunswick. The Christ is in His own light, if one may so say, or else some special rays light Him and the face of the Magdalen, a face of surprise. The Christ is but just out of the tomb; He stands dubiously, half covering Himself with the shroud, and He lifts a hand—not repellent, but as of warning — in answer to the Magdalen's anxious appeal. The right hand is wrapped in the cloth brought by her, and the vase of ointment is by her knee. All about them is the gentle gloom of evening; the great door of the tomb is open; we look down behind them into some passage or landscape seen through a natural arch, and above there is again the faint light of the sky where night is beginning.

The effect of the picture is not to be described in words; this is again one of the cases where one understands how there is such an absolute division of the arts, — a little

THE APPEARANCE OF CHRIST TO MARY MAGDALEN. (REMBRANDT)

more and the figures would be of no importance, or common-place; instead of which a thrill of meaning beats through each part of each figure, and we feel that each separate detail helps to make the impression that we receive.

CHAPTER XIX

THE JOURNEY TO EMMAUS. THE SUPPER AT EMMAUS.
THE ASCENSION. THE PENTECOST

Saint Luke tells of the two who went that same day
to a village called Emmaus, which was from Jerusalem
about threescore furlongs. A stranger drew near, with
whom one of the disciples, Cleopas (here appearing for
the first and only time), conversed about the happenings
of these days, and asked if He were only a stranger in
Jerusalem. He made as if He would go further, but they
constrained Him, saying, "Abide with us, for it is toward
evening, and the day is far spent." (Peter may have
been the other disciple, according to Origen, and art has
inclined that way.)

In many cases our Lord is represented in the dress of
a pilgrim, and the Latin text says "stranger." Hence
also the beholder is reminded of hospitality to pilgrims;
and that angels might be entertained unawares. Therefore over the door open to strangers in the Convent of
San Marco, Fra Angelico painted the idea. We all know
the beautiful thing; the Dominican monks welcome the
Pilgrim whom the disciples have yet to discover. "Inasmuch as ye have done it unto one of the least of these
my brethren, ye have done it unto me."

Sometimes, finally, all three of those who went to
Emmaus are represented in pilgrim habit, and the French
title for the subject is, "Les Pèlerins d'Emmaüs."

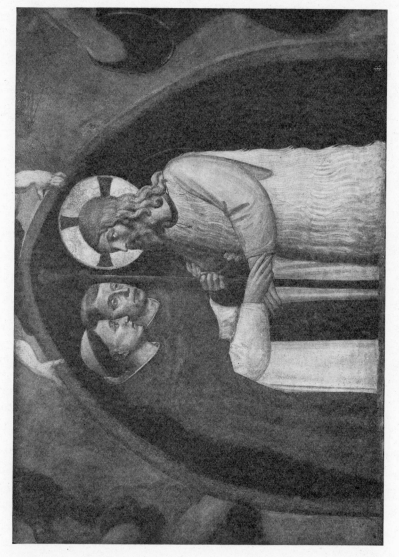

CHRIST AS A PILGRIM. (FRA ANGELICO)

Our Lord appears thus in Saint Luke : "And it came to pass, as he sat at meat with them he took bread, and blessed it, and brake and gave to them. And their eyes were opened, and they knew him ; and he vanished out of their sight."

The supper was a reminder of the sacrament of the Last Supper, shown in the Breaking of Bread, the first painting in the Catacombs, which may have been, as we have said, a memorial of what had happened to men still living.

And suddenly their eyes were opened, and in spite of the altered form they recognized the truth, that He who was with them was the Lord. But even as they recognized Him, He was with them no longer. "Did not our heart burn within us while he was speaking with us in the way ; while he was opening to us the Scriptures ? "

For the Stranger had shown them on their walk, with reproval for their dulness, how all through the Old Testament, from Moses onwards, there was one long prophecy of the sufferings no less than the glory of Christ. "And beginning at Moses and all the prophets he expounded to them in all the Scriptures the things concerning himself."

The Supper was a most evident subject for art, and the natural tendency to bring in an allusion made the paintings fit anywhere from a church to a refectory.

The moment chosen is always the Breaking of Bread, and among the Venetians we have the glorious but unreal painting (so far as recalling the text) of the great Bellini, in the Chapel of the Sacrament in San Salvatore, who gives, we remember, the turbaned head of his brother Gentile.

By and by, as all this became allegory or polite allusion, there came up the reflection of the generous fare which the painter knew. To take only one instance, think of Titian's dinner with Aretino:

"The first of last August," writes a Venetian scholar,[1] "I was invited to a festival in a lovely garden belonging to Master Titian, an excellent and famous painter. As like draws like, some of the foremost men of our city were there; namely, Peter Aretino; Jacopo Tatti, called Sansovino; Jacopo Nardi, and I, the fourth, happy to be admitted into this illustrious company. The heat of the sun was still great, although the place itself is shady; so that we passed our time, before the tables were carried outside, in looking at the paintings, almost living, which filled the house; after which we enjoyed the beauty and charm of the garden, which stretches along the sea, to the first port limit of Venice. Thence one can see the pretty island of Murano, and other places. Hardly had the sun gone down when innumerable gondolas appeared on the water, filled with gracious young women. Songs and music came floating towards us, and accompanied our joyous supper until midnight, in that magnificent garden so much admired.

The supper was very good, rich in delicate dishes and in costly wines, and the pleasure exquisite because of the season, the guests, and the feast itself. We were just on the point of beginning the fruit when your letter came to me, and when I told the company how you therein sang the praises of the Latin language, at the expense of the Italian, Aretino was quite angry, so that we had difficulty in preventing his making the most cruel speeches. He asked for ink and paper, although he had sufficiently expended himself in words; and after that the supper ended as gaily as it had begun."

All this gives us the manner of life led by the friends of the old painter, and they passed easily into representations of it. If anything, our painters have refrained a little on the side of sobriety, but the supper and dinner

---

[1] Francesco Pricianese.

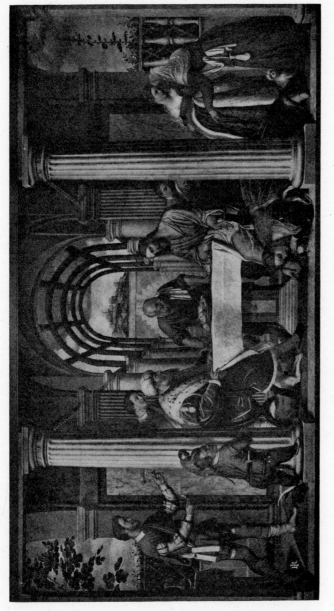

THE FEAST OF THE PHARISEE. (MORETTO)

analogy remained, so much that Baldassare Peruzzi gave us what is known as the Four Banquets; The Marriage of Cana; The Pharisee's Feast; The Last Supper, and the Supper at Emmaus. We can also understand the natural introduction of friends and distinguished people among the architecture and accompaniments which the artist saw and copied.

Sometimes the personages are surrounded by a court of animals, fed from the table then and there, or favourite pets are introduced, as in a charming picture by Moretto, then pages are necessary, but are a note of still further impossibility.

We are not the same to-day; some grayness and good sense, due to hard pressure, has passed over us, and even the kindness of churchmen to Rubens and his followers has not allowed the irrational and buoyant mood to last.

It was reserved for Rembrandt to give us both the fact and the mystery. The little painting in the Louvre, which I remember as shabby, is notwithstanding one of the few greatest pictures of the world, and we feel, as I say, that his Bible is *the* Bible. The story shows us the recognition, as if we were there. There is the disciple who, recognizing, joins his hands in prayer; the other stops in astonishment, placing his napkin before him, and gazes at the Christ; the boy sees nothing as he brings a plate.

They are of earth, and properly and rightly, — but the central figure has passed through Death. He is alive, and yet — a little breath, a slight look, make all the difference.

Then, once again, an etching of Rembrandt's is a marvel of imagination, and yet I am not sure that it is as sincere as the other. There is a little theatrical touch, if I dare so blaspheme : the Lord is gone — the disciples and we ourselves are astounded. The bread He broke we see, and the empty chair. And yet so it must have been.

The doubting Thomas is enshrined in all the languages which have known the Gospel, and his importance as bringing together the whole point of the actual Resurrection made him an early subject for art. We need not recall the Byzantine; Giotto has enforced the rude fact; Thomas actually places his finger in the wounds, although long ago there was doubt as to whether he did so. But the meaning of the story might require anything, especially if, as later, the subject was taken as an appeal to the doubter. In the early sculpture of Paris, says Diderot in "The City of Skepticism," it was used as a reinforcement of the truth of the Resurrection. The grouping of the Apostles made appeal to the artist later, but the difficulties of the many variations of expression or attitude are evident to the trained mind.

There is a painting by Delacroix which is apparently little known. It is wanting both in colour and effect, a strange case for that artist, but the composition is fine and remarkable as showing his happiness in the naturalness of gesture and the grandness of moral expression. The indulgent resignation of the Lord, tender, but with a little indignation against Thomas, and the pitying gestures of the apostles, make a noble and adequate work.

The other part of the text, the gift of the Holy Ghost and remission of sin, is not represented in art in any important or interesting way to my knowledge.

THE SUPPER AT EMMAUS. (Rembrandt)

Breathing on them, He said "Receive ye the Holy Ghost. Whosesoever sins ye remit, they are remitted to them; and whosesoever sins ye retain, they are retained."

"When he had spoken these things, while they beheld, he was taken up and a cloud received him out of their sight, and while they looked steadfastly toward heaven, behold, two men stood by them in white apparel, which also said, "Ye men of Galilee, why stand ye gazing up into heaven? This same Jesus which is taken up from you into heaven, shall so come in like manner as ye have seen him go into heaven."

Always, and very early, Christ appears in glory. In the fifth century, He is represented on the door of Santa Sabina in Rome. As giver of the new law, in gracious, antique reminiscence of the beauty of the pagan gods, He stands clothed in the philosopher's pallium, above the world, in a circle — a frame edged with laurel. Also like a philosopher He holds in His left hand a scroll in which His name is written in Greek. He extends an open, kingly hand, offering the protection of the divine power. Alpha and Omega, carved in the background, mark Him as the first and the last, the beginning and the end. In corners, on the background, we see figures which are meant for the evangelical symbols — the eagle, the angel, the lion, and the ox. Below, in a separate division, Peter and Paul lift a garland with a cross inscribed. A ray falls from a star above. On the left and right of the arched representation of the vault of heaven, we see the images of the sun and the moon. The crown that Peter and Paul, draped as Greek philosophers, hold up, hangs above the head of a woman with hands lifted and face turned upward with inquiry. That is the image of the Church left desolate on earth, and also perhaps the image of the Virgin comforted by the knowledge of her Son's glorified existence.

Later, the beautiful confusion of the Church and Mary, each one the symbol of the other, melts away into a distinct representation of the Virgin. The Syriac manuscript of the monk Rabula, often quoted, tells the story between the sixth and seventh centuries. There, angels point out the Christ to the apostles gathered together. He is above in the conventional aureola, a philosopher again, with some gesture similar to the beautiful one of an earlier date, also with a scroll, also long-haired, but now bearded and heavy, instead of a youth and beardless as in the earlier work. A curious winged device, spotted with peacock's eyes, combines with strange images of the evangelical beasts and helping angels to support the artificial frame. Angels come forward, with the veiled hands of the Eastern receptive habit, offering crowns of glory. Below, in the middle, a Virgin stands with the spread-out arms and hands familiar to us in the representations of earliest art, a gesture still preserved in the manner of prayer of the Catholic priest of to-day at the altar, in those parts of the mass which retain the ancient form of words. The barbarous representation has new elements, and a certain beauty of imagination.

The Middle Ages bring on another form of image, no longer of convention. Once, in some little corner of a manuscript, the Christ rushes up the mountain and His extended hand meets the Hand from above, and even in

THE ASCENSION. (Giotto)

the little sketch one feels His joy and His freedom from earth. Angels flit about, and the little faithful company gaze upward. The Mother now folds her hands and prays.

Giotto takes the same movement and arrangement, and we see again the Christ passing away, freed from the entire world that He leaves. A chorus of angels in a mass, as if of clouds, praise and glorify Him. Below all kneel, and two angels in official garments point upward. They are those who said: "Ye men of Galilee, why stand ye gazing up into heaven?" The image of Giotto, as usual, carries more of the sense of reality than even the very beautiful later attempts. Most of them, even with such a master as Mantegna, have given a Christ who has to be treated as if not really within the simple story, but placed as a sort of image of Himself. The blessed Angelico has avoided the great difficulty of the figure of the Saviour while keeping all the more to the text. The Lord has disappeared; some mark of cloud and shine (above the beautiful line of hills) tells us the meaning. Below, in a circle, the apostles kneel, and Mary among them. Some look up, all evidently unprepared; Mary apparently is not surprised, and merely folds her hands. On either side, two angels address the apostles, one of whom turns around to listen. It is a simple composition of extreme peace and acceptance of what has happened; a wonderful expression of something which is implied and not told.

Of course, many magnificent representations have followed the two great, early men. We should consider, I suppose, the Ascension painted by Perugino, which was given by Pope Pius the Seventh to the city of Lyons.

It is an official representation, and has the necessary beauty of the figures of Perugino, with each character of the apostles carefully made out as they pose for the spectator; Raphael is there, with his charm and sentiment; our Lord is posing like all the other figures, and is encompassed by the almond-shaped glory.

The great Raphael designed an Ascension for a series of tapestries, with the same Peruginistic view as to our Lord's posing, but the group of the apostles is more lifelike.

In the East the subject generally occupies the principal cupola of a Greek Church. Our Lord is represented seated upon clouds and welcomed by the angels. The Virgin stands below, with angels in white on either side.

There is a bas-relief by Donatello in London, in the Victoria and Albert Museum, which in its general arrangement has that masterly sense of the proper place which the sculptor has rarely a chance to express, as he is usually confined to an image which is placed for him, or which he places as he is forced to do. Nothing tells us how much he has seen around it, and yet he may be a great landscape designer, as Donatello was. Two or three of his bas-reliefs, of no apparent importance, have all the space and interest that any of the fullest masters of light and space have attempted to give. The bas-relief allows the sculptor to be also a painter, and in this one we see the back of the mountain, where Christ passes away. The apostles and the Virgin are on the edge, and help by their attitudes to give the impression of the suddenness of His disappearance.

The Acts of the Apostles give the story of the passage from the Ascension to Pentecost. Our good monk

THE PENTECOST. (GIOTTO)

THE PENTECOST. (BORDONE)

Rabula is again to be quoted. The Virgin stands among the apostles, who are absorbed in thought, while above them burns the flame of the Holy Spirit. The Dove, pouring down a flame of light, descends over the head of Mary. Giotto has seen the miracle as happening in a closed room, which is called in one place in the text an "upper room." There the apostles all sit in a circle, while rays of light come down upon them, at which they show a certain gentle surprise. Later Fra Angelico and others represent a house wherein are gathered the apostles, while below, out of doors, devout men of every nation under heaven move about — in Fra Angelico gently, with some appearance of discussion; in other paintings, such as those of Gaddi, with much conversation and curiosity. Donatello, with his usual ferocity, gives us a turbid scene of astonishment and joy and fear, wherein even the Mother trembles. At first the sense of Italian exaggeration comes upon us, but slowly one recognizes the certainty of the portrayal. This is a message from heaven, taking each individual in some sudden way, without preparation. There is also in the manner of some of them a reaching up as if in thanks for receiving the gift, which they realize. Their hands are spread out almost to catch it.

Then, by and by, Titian in Venice and Paris, and Bordone in Milan, give, in late and perhaps over-artistic rendering, the apostles in beautiful poses, and the Virgin, more natural, because more like a woman, gracefully yields to the feeling of the moment, but she is no longer Our Lady of Sorrows or the Queen of Heaven; the simple faith of the earlier day is gone.

2 E